Love, Lies, *and* Consequences

Love, Lies,
and
Consequences

*Blake Karrington
and
Genesis Woods*

www.urbanbooks.net

Urban Books, LLC
300 Farmingdale Road, NY-Route 109
Farmingdale, NY 11735

ISBN 13: 978-1-945855-75-7
ISBN 10: 1-945855-75-4

First Mass Market Printing December 2018
First Trade Paperback Printing February 2018
Printed in the United States of America

10 9 8 7 6 5 4 3 2 1

Distributed by Kensington Publishing Corp.
Submit orders to:
Customer Service
400 Hahn Road
Westminster, MD 21157-4627
Phone: 1-800-733-3000
Fax: 1-800-659-243

Love, Lies, and Consequences

A Novel by

Blake Karrington
and
Genesis Woods

Savannah

"So are you excited about tonight?" Reign, my best friend since childhood asked as she plopped her small frame onto my bed and crossed her legs.

I looked in the full-length mirror at my reflection and smiled at the way my body filled out the black leatherette cutout strapless pencil dress I had on from the House of CB.

"I'm a little excited."

"A *little* excited?" she asked with a hint of sarcasm. "Girl, you know damn well you're about to bust through the seams of that tight-ass dress you have on. I mean, at least I would. The whole city will be out tonight just for you." She smacked her lips. "That brother of yours spared no expense to make sure his baby sister got the biggest welcome home party Charlotte's ever seen."

I looked at Reign through the mirror. "He did get a little carried away, didn't he?" We both laughed. "But it's cool, though. Naheim and I are all we got since our parents died, and after paying all that money for me to go to school the last eight years, it's only right that he dishes out a little more to celebrate me passing the bar as well as coming back home."

"That brother of yours is something else," she said as a blush crossed her face.

I didn't know what that look was all about, but I bet it had something to do with the little secret crush Reign had on my brother ever since we were little. I could tell that while I was away, the two had become closer in some kind of way, but whenever I asked her if she and Heim had crossed the line, she always pled the fifth.

For the last ten years, I'd been in California enjoying the nice sunny weather and crazy nightlife atmosphere as I went to school full time to become a lawyer. I worked my ass off night and day studying for exams and interning at a few law firms just to get the feel of my career of choice. After I graduated from USC Law School, I took the California Bar exam and passed with flying colors. I ended up getting a job at a prestigious law firm and really enjoyed it at the time, but for some strange reason, I always felt like something was missing. My plan was to stay out there in the Golden State and open up a small practice of my own with one of my sorority sisters who also studied law and would join me as partner, but after going over a few numbers and becoming more and more homesick, I decided to pack my things up, move back to Charlotte, and open up my first firm here. It would take a few years for me to more than likely make a name for myself, but once that happened, I'd return to California to open up a second practice out there.

I picked up my phone and scrolled through my e-mail, stopping on a notification that I received a few days ago but hadn't opened. Unbeknownst to my family and friends, before I made the announcement of moving back home, I flew in for a few days and took the bar exam for North Carolina almost four months ago. I wasn't sure on what side of the U.S. I really wanted to reside at the time and figured having my law license in both states would be a great way to help me decide. The funny thing is, California never really had a chance. It took me about two seconds of seeing one of the most beautiful skylines I'd seen so many times to help me finally make up my mind. The minute the sun set and the dark sky and bright lights illuminated my beloved Queen City, I knew I had to come back home. I was so sure on where I would be that I put down a deposit on a small office space in downtown Charlotte the day before I left. My results were e-mailed to me a week ago, and even though I hadn't opened them yet, I already knew that I passed.

Pushing the thoughts of my bicoastal dilemma and that Reign and Heim thing to the back of my mind, I sat down at my makeup vanity and applied another layer of lip gloss to my lips. After spraying a few splashes of perfume on my neck, wrists, and chest, I slid my freshly manicured toes into my six-inch peeptoe leather booties and grabbed the matching clutch from off of my dresser.

"You ready to go?" I asked Reign, who was still sitting on my bed with her face buried in her phone. Her fingers were moving a mile a minute as she responded to the text message someone just sent her.

"Yeah, I'm ready." After sending one more text, she slid her phone into her purse, then looked up at me. "Damn, bitch, I know this is your party and all and you have to stand out, but how do I look?"

I took in the little white cocktail dress she had on that barely left anything to the imagination. The thing was so short and low cut that she'd be flashing and mooning everybody if she bent over a little bit. If she and my brother really had something going on between them, I knew for a fact that he was going to blow a lid as soon as she walked into the club dressed like that. One thing Heim didn't play with was his girl showing off his goods, and although Reign wasn't technically his girl, I knew he'd still feel some type of way. There were plenty of times that I witnessed him going off on one of his little girlfriends about the way she dressed when we were younger. I don't think it was so much of an insecure thing, but more like a respecting yourself thing. If you dressed like a ho, you get treated like a ho, and Naheim prided himself on dating the wholesome good-girl type. He used to get on me sometimes about the way I dressed back then too. Heim was on my head so tough about the way I dressed that I didn't attempt to wear a bikini until after I turned twenty-one and was on the other side of the world.

I laughed at the memory and the way my brother was always being so overly protective of me and anything else that he loved. Looking over Reign again and remembering the silly smile Heim would have on his face whenever I mentioned her name, yeah, he was going to be tripping hard tonight. The tiny dress looked good on her small frame, and the messy bun on the top of her head and light makeup on her face let you see how beautiful my best friend really was.

"You look good, girl, but I hope you have something else to put on after Heim shows his ass. You already know he's going to curse you out six ways to tomorrow."

She rolled her hazel eyes, then headed for the door. "Girl, I ain't worried about your brother or how he feels about anything I have on tonight. I'm pretty sure that little Blac Chyna-looking bitch he's been kicking it with lately will be there hanging on his arm, so his mind is going to be far from on me."

Reign spun around on her heel and looked at me with a smirk on her face. "Now what you *should* be worried about is this little reunion between you and Lyfe. The nigga ain't seen his *little cutie* in what . . . ten years? When you left you were that fresh eighteen-year-old that he claimed was like a little sister to him. Now you're back and on your grown woman shit." Reign walked around me in a circle and looked me up and down. "And I must say, sista, girl, twenty-eight does look good on you. That California sunshine got a bitch glowing and shit."

I laughed. "Girl, shut up."

"Naw, I'm not about to shut up. You know I'm telling the truth." She smacked my ass. "Then look at this thang back here. Before you left, I don't think your body knew what it meant to have hips, ass, and titties. Whatever you were eating and drinking out there did your body good, honey. Thighs thick, ass fat, waist slim, and your titties are sitting up like they got some silicone in them."

I rolled my eyes and pushed past her crazy ass heading to the door. Just hearing his name always did something to me, even on my birthday sixteen years ago. I had just turned twelve and was waiting on Naheim to come back from the store with my gift. When he walked through the door, not only did he have an armful of bags just for me, but his friend, who I'd never seen before, did too.

"Happy Birthday, baby girl," Heim said as he dropped all the bags in front of me and kissed me on my cheek. He raised up back to his full height, then turned to the boy standing behind him. "Yo, sis, this is my boy Lyfe. Lyfe, this is my little sister Savannah. I told the nigga he didn't have to get your little spoiled ass anything, but he insisted that he did."

I looked into the cognac-colored eyes of the boy standing in front of me and fell head over heels in love. The breath I was just breathing got caught in my throat, and I just sat there speechless. I could see his mouth moving, but I couldn't hear a damn thing he was saying. It wasn't until Naheim started to frantically wave his big hand in front of my face that I finally broke out of whatever spell this gorgeous man in front of me just had me in.

"What the hell is wrong with your little ass?" Heim asked with a frown on his face. He looked at me, then to his friend, and cleared his throat. "Aye, man, just drop the gifts you bought next to mine and let's be out. We have to go handle that business we talked about earlier so I can be back in time to take little sis out to her favorite restaurant."

Feeling a little bold at my preteen age, I jumped up off of the couch, damn near tripping over the bags at my feet, and stood in front of Lyfe's face. "Would you like to join us? It would really make my day."

Lyfe looked down at me with a warm smile on his face, then back up to my brother who had this weird look on his.

"Nah, Savvy, I'm pretty sure my boy has other things to get into tonight. Besides, we always celebrate your birthday together, just me and you."

I could see in his eyes that he didn't want to share my day with anyone else, but shit, I wasn't about to let this opportunity to be in Lyfe's face all night pass me by.

"How about we change it up this year, Heim? I mean, it is my day and my choice, right?" I blushed when I noticed a smile slowly start to display across Lyfe's face. "I can call Reign and see if her parents will let her go, then it can be the four of us."

Naheim wiped his hand down his face and sighed. "I don't think that would be such a good idea, Savvy. Plus, I don't feel like driving all the way across town to pick up Reign's annoying ass."

"We have to go out that way to handle this business anyway, so we can just pick little cutie's friend up on our way back." Lyfe finally spoke. He smirked at me, then put on a straight face when he looked at Heim. The sexy little fucker knew I was crushing on him. I sat my hot ass down on the couch and let out the breath I was holding yet again. I don't know what it was, but his voice did something to my little body that had me feeling faint and all gushy on the inside.

"Uh . . . Hello . . . Earth to Savannah. What the hell is wrong with you?" Reign said, breaking me from my trip down memory lane. "Your ass zoned out for a few minutes. Are you OK?"

"Yeah, I'm good," I replied, walking through my living room and heading to my front door. "Just was thinking about something."

"Or *someone?*" I could feel the big-ass smile on her face without even turning around. "I don't know why the two of you act like there's nothing between y'all. I've never seen two people so right for each other, yet they get into these wrong-ass relationships with other people."

I opened the door to let Reign walk through, then set the alarm and followed behind her, not forgetting to lock up.

"I'm not in a relationship with anyone right now, and as for Lyfe, he's happily married with kids and the whole nine," I said with a happiness I wasn't feeling in my heart. "Besides, we tried to have something for a couple months before I went away to college, but he couldn't leave that crazy bitch alone."

I unlocked the doors of my new ride, courtesy of my big brother, and slid into the sexy interior. Reign followed suit and melted into the soft leather seat herself.

"That crazy bitch is his crazy wife now. I know you, and I know how you feel about Lyfe. Just promise me you'll be careful if anything does pop off between y'all."

I nodded my head and pulled off, heading in the direction of the club my party was going to be held at. Reign's warning went in one ear and flew out the other. Lyfe and I had our time years ago, and he couldn't decide on who he wanted to be with then, so I made the choice for him. It had been ten years since the last time I'd seen him, and I knew the minute I did lay eyes on him that some of those old feelings would try to come back, but with him being a married man now, he and I would never get to explore what should've, could've, and would've been. I may be a lot of things, but one thing I ain't is a home wrecker.

Lyfe

Checking the rearview mirror from the passenger's side of the SUV, I reached down and turned the radio up. Yo Gotti's voice flowed through the speakers and surrounded every part of my body. Trap music touched a part of my soul and allowed my mind to travel to a place where I could handle the business at hand. Gazing down at my watch, I figured it had been at least fifteen minutes since I'd seen another car or another person on the road. Isolation was always a good partner to have in this line of work.

I gave the signal to my driver and top enforcer Kiko to pull into the dimly lit and partially constructed neighborhood, then glanced back at Lenny, who lay in the backseat whimpering like a wounded animal. I had stopped listening to Lenny's pleas miles back. These little niggas didn't understand the word *loyalty,* and what it meant to take an oath—an oath that was like blood, something that stains your very essence, and you carry inside of you for life once taken.

I continued looking at Lenny with disgust and shook my head. This punk-ass nigga didn't have the heart or dignity it took to be down with my crew. Shit, I'd been in far worse situations than the one Lenny was currently in, but never let a motherfucker see my fear. I shook my head again, wondering how I let this fuck pussy nigga become one of my soldiers in the first place.

"How we doin', Lenny?" I taunted.

"Lyfe, listen to me, bruh, you know I would never betray you like that, my nigga. I know where my heart and loyalty lies. Why would I set up the man who helps me eat generously?" Lenny groaned in pain and coughed up a little blood. Lining the car seats with black garbage bags was an unnecessary precaution, due to the fact that I was going to have the car torched, then crushed later, but being thorough was what had kept me from behind bars and out of the casket thus far.

Lenny moaned when he heard the sounds and felt the vibrations of Kiko turning off the asphalt onto the gravel dirt road.

"Lyfe, man, I think my damn leg broke, bruh. Shit, you fucked up my knee with that bat earlier. Come on, you know me; you know that I honor the brotherhood. I ain't one of them 85 percenters. I know the truth and would never betray you by talking to the feds. Toby was the one that was never all the way in with his oath; he the one, not me, bruh. Come on, Lyfe, you know me. You know me," he pleaded.

"Yeah, Lenny, I know you, and we 'bout to find out what is the real in a few minutes," I barked back, tossing my Black & Mild out the window.

Kiko stopped in front of a partially framed out home. The wood planks were up and the ground had been even, awaiting the pouring of the concrete foundations. It was times like these that my connection to the Irish Mafia really paid off. One thing I'd learned some time ago was that the last thing that would get dug up was the foundation of a freshly built half-a-million-dollar home. No way were them crackers going to go through that much trouble for some dead nigga.

"A'ight, Lenny, get your ass out," I calmly spoke as I opened the back door.

"Man, I'm telling you my damn leg is broke," Lenny moaned, with tears streaming down his face and dried mucus under his nose. My stomach was starting to turn just by looking at this nigga more and more. I pulled my gun out and placed it between his eyes.

"I said get your ass out of the fucking car now!" Lenny sat up, his hands were handcuffed, but he managed to push himself up onto the seat. Sweat was pouring down his forehead. He panted as he slid his injured leg outside the car.

"Fuck!" Lenny screeched in pain as he fell to the ground. I threw him the handcuff key.

"Take them shits off!"

Lenny leaned back against the back door. He only had on his boxers and a pair of socks. Kiko and his boys grabbed him from some nasty-ass motel that he was laid up in, fucking some hood rat. The girl screamed when they kicked the door in. Kiko put a bullet in her head to silence her cries. Lenny attempted to run out the door, but Man knocked his ass out, then had him delivered to me.

I turned my head and looked to the left at the sound of another truck approaching. A white SUV with a cement mixer hitched to the back of it pulled up alongside the black suburban we just got out of. Naheim and Man stepped out, along with Toby, whose hands were strapped together. Naheim adjusted his belt looking over to Lenny with a screw face. This nigga's arrogance went beyond what could be mistaken as confidence. His beauty routine was that of a female, and the lure of money and status consumed this nigga's whole mind-set. However, he was my right-hand man and best friend. So he was not to be fucked with.

"Damn, why we out here in this fucking dust bowl? Shit is fucking with my sinuses," Naheim joked as he walked toward me. I laughed at his crazy ass. I knew my boy was a piece of work, but I loved him like a brother.

He took in the scene before him. "Shit, what's wrong with Lenny's ass?" Naheim continued to joke. "That nigga look like he seen a ghost and shitted on himself."

"His ass is all right. At least he will be once I get through with him." I threw a shovel to Toby, and another to Lenny. "The two of you are going to start digging until I'm satisfied. One of you betrayed me. Your betrayal could cost our family its fucking freedom, and more importantly, our empire. I gave both of you love and money, and one of you spit in my fucking face like I wasn't shit to you," I spat.

"Lyfe, look, man, I don't know what you're talking about. I ain't said shit to nobody," Toby spoke, realizing the ride out here to *handle a nigga,* as Man put it, was to possibly handle him. His mouth became dry, and his palms began to sweat. He contemplated on having a shoot-out, but he was outnumbered.

"Man, I don't want to hear shit else you have to say," I spoke back, raising my gun. "Don't make me say it again."

Naheim pushed Toby and grabbed his strap. Lenny glared at Toby as he began to dig the hole. Tears ran down Lenny's face as he dug silently. I could tell thoughts of his grandmother and how she would be expecting him to stop by later with her dinner was on his mind. He knew he wasn't gonna make it out of the rural area alive.

"Lyfe, man, I ain't digging no fuckin' hole," Toby spoke with confidence.

Pow the bullet sounded as it left the chamber.

"What the hell!" Toby screamed as his foot began to burn. He looked down at the Italian leather shoe. "Fuck, you shot me! You fucking shot me! *Ahh*."

I glared at Toby biting down on my lip. He cursed to himself and began moving the soil into a pile. He had been turning over evidence about my organization since I skipped over him as general for the South Side operations. When the DA approached him with the evidence they had built against him on a separate pills trafficking charge he was doing on the side, turning on me was a no-brainer. He didn't want to go to prison, and he knew if me or any of the family found out about his side business, he was good as dead anyway. Making money outside of the family was against the bylaws, so Toby went the way of snitching, and now he was going to die for it out here in the damn boondocks.

My phone rang. I looked over to Naheim, who pulled out his silver Magnum and pressed it against Toby's temple. Toby continued digging the hole. He looked at the shovel as the cold steel was being pressed against his temple.

"Hey, Bryant," I answered, making sure to step a few feet away so no one would hear this conversation. Bryant was my attorney. There was no way I was going to take the life of two family members without knowing 100 percent if they were snitches.

"Kyle, my contact gained access to the tapes and audio of the boys that turned against you," Bryant explained.

I had been a client of Bryant's for the last fifteen years. He had tried his best to remain blissfully ignorant in regards to what it was that I actually did for a living. All he knew was that money was not an issue, and whatever I asked for, he needed to deliver. As Bryant started to read the names off the list, I dropped my head.

"All right. Thank you for the information," I said, promptly disconnecting the call.

Twenty minutes later, Toby and Lenny were covered in black dirt and sweat from digging the grave.

"Lyfe, please listen to me. I told you I would never turn on you, man," Lenny said weakly.

I didn't utter a word as I walked back over to the hole. It was at least ten feet deep, and four feet wide. Taking one of my soldiers' lives was not something I took pleasure in, but I had to remember how these two set out to destroy me and my foundation. Lenny wasn't a dude that was thirsty. I knew they had to have something on him to scare him into cooperating. I nodded to Man, signaling him to deal with Lenny.

A pop echoed through the air, and then a thud. Lenny fell backward into the grave. He lay motionless, but the shocked expression was frozen on his face. His eyes were open, and blood ran down his nose.

Toby knew he had fucked up, so instead of pleading for his life, he turned to me, swung the shovel at Kiko, hitting him on the chin. Before he could swing it again, he felt a fireball hit his left knee.

"You know, Lenny was just a scared kid, but *you,* nigga? You are just a greedy, grimy mother-fucker," I barked pulling the trigger again. Bone fragments flew from Toby's right knee, causing him to lose his balance, and he fell into the hole on top of Lenny's body.

"Lyfe! Fuck, man, I didn't tell anybody shit. Please, bruh, don't do this," he begged.

"Kill that sorry piece of shit," Kiko yelled, holding his sore jaw from the blow of the shovel.

I looked down at Toby.

"Yeah, nigga, ya bitch ass did talk, and you talked a lot. You talked so much that you got your boy Lenny caught up and made him a rat."

Naheim brought the cement mixer over to the hole. The thick gray sludge flowed down the ramp filling the hole.

"No, no! You can't do this to me. I had no choice. They were going to send me to prison! Lyfe, come on, man. I knew that you could get off. You're untouchable."

I put my Cazal sunglasses on and looked down at Toby screaming as the concrete poured down on him. We'd already been out here a minute too long. I needed to get back to the city and handle some business before the welcome home party Naheim was giving our little sister tonight. Ten years. I can't believe it has been ten years since I last saw Savannah. For some reason, whenever she came out here to visit, she would purposely ignore me. I felt some kind of way about that but couldn't really get too mad. I was a married man now and have been for a few years. I know me getting married is probably what made her start to hate a nigga, but she has to understand, I saw her being above this lifestyle. Savannah was too innocent, precious, and beautiful to be my down-ass bitch. I needed a chick who wasn't scared to bust a gun if need be or carry some weight across state lines if I asked her to. I would've literally died if Savvy ended up in jail, or even worse, dead, on account of me.

Toby continued to scream for his life, hoping that we would feel sorry enough for him to let him out of that hole. After about ten minutes, the pleas for his life stopped. I looked into the grave and spit. After saying a silent prayer for Lenny's soul, and a curse for Toby's, I hopped into the new SUV that just pulled up and left Naheim and Man to finish everything up.

Hopefully, I can finish everything I need to do in the next two hours, then make it down to the club to catch Savannah off guard. She was going to talk to me tonight if that was the last thing she did.

Savannah

By the time we made it to Club Label, the music was bumping, the parking lot was packed, and the line to get in was nearly down the block. I looked over at a cheesing-ass Reign and shook my head. You would've thought this party was hers with the way she was strutting down the walkway toward the club's entrance. It seemed like the whole city was out to welcome me back home, and I didn't have nobody to thank but my big-headed brother. Just from the decor on the outside, I could tell that he spared no expense on his baby sister tonight.

"Damn, it's packed," Reign said as we stepped to the front of the club.

"I know, and I can't wait to get up in there to see who up in this bitch."

"You mean you can't wait to see if *Lyfe* is up in this bitch," Reign corrected with a small smirk. I rolled my eyes and walked up the small flight of steps.

"You better hope I remember you're my best friend once we walk past that big-ass bouncer with the guest list clipboard in his hand. Your name might just magically disappear you keep fucking with me."

"Girl, please. One phone call to Naheim and my shit will be right back on that list," she said with a laugh. "You know his confused ass wanna keep tabs on me, even though he has a girl already."

I just nodded my head and walked up to the "Tiny" Lester-looking bouncer and gave him my ID. I really didn't understand what was going on with Heim and Reign, and quite honestly, I didn't want to be in the middle of it. I was all for my bestie being happy, and if my brother was who made her that way, then cool, but I also didn't want her to be crying on my shoulder about my brother doing her bad, when nine times out of ten, I was going to know what he'd been up to. I never wanted to be put in the position where Heim or Reign came to me for info on the other, whether they were fucking someone else, talking to someone else, or flirting with someone else. In both cases, I would be the one that lost out on something—my brother's trust or my best friend altogether. Whatever they had going on, I hoped Naheim didn't pursue anything until he was 100 percent sure Reign was the woman he wanted.

"Well, if it isn't the lady of the night," the bouncer said, breaking me from my thoughts. I looked up into his one good eye, and a smile instantly crossed my face.

"Patrick!" I screamed, opening my arms up for a hug. He circled my waist with one arm and picked me up off the ground. "How have you been? I haven't seen you since our junior year of high school. How's your mom? How's your sister?"

He put me down, then smiled. "My mom is doing good. My sister is actually inside already. She's been kicking it with your brother for a minute. That's how I got this little gig at the club."

"Really?" That was news to me. Then again, a lot of things have changed since I've been gone. I made a mental note to talk to my brother about messing with Patrick's sister, Peaches. She was a scandalous little bitch when we were growing up, and I doubt she'd changed any since then. She and her little crew were always setting niggas up to get robbed and shit, and I'd be damned if she did that shit to my brother. I'd kill her, her mama, and her cockeyed brother if anything happened to mine.

"Naheim, Lyfe, and the rest of the crew are already up in VIP waiting on your arrival. I'll radio someone to come and escort you guys up there. What's up, Reign?" Reign, who had gotten real quiet, hit him with a head nod, then turned her attention to the people yelling my name in line. When Patrick went to press the button in his ear and speak into his mouthpiece, I stopped him.

"It's OK, Pat. I want to walk around and mingle with a few people before we make it up there if that's OK." I grabbed Reign's hand and started to walk through the door. "It was nice seeing you again, though. Tell your mama I said hello. We need to catch up one day and go have lunch or something."

He nodded his head with a smile and saluted me, then turned back around to the people standing in line with that mean bouncer look on his face. "As you can see, the guest of honor just walked in, so the party is about to start jumping off even more. If your name isn't on the list," he held up the clipboard, "then get your ass out of line now because you won't be getting in here tonight. This is an invite-only event, so please don't waste my time or your time with the fuckery."

I grabbed Reign's hand and continued to make our way through the crowded club. Family I hadn't talked to in months and friends I hadn't seen in years stopped me every few feet to get a hug, say congratulations, or just to tell me how beautiful I had grown up to be. I was starting to get a bit overwhelmed, so I decided it was time for us to head up to VIP.

"You ready to go chill with my big-headed brother and the rest of the crew?"

Reign looked at me with a twisted face and rolled her eyes. "I'm not trying to be up there with your brother and his little bitch right now. You know I'm not one to hold my tongue, so before I ruin your party, let's go to the bar for a few drinks, grab a few of these cuties, and get our asses on this dance floor," she said, now snapping her fingers in the air and swaying her hips from left to right. "I need to find a nigga in here to help take my mind off of your brother tonight, and hopefully, for good."

I'd heard everything Reign said, even over the loud music, but something told me that her feelings for my brother were way deeper than what she was letting on, even if they were more than likely one-sided. Not wanting to leave my bestie hanging, we hit the bar and had a few shots, then found a couple of cuties to get down with on the dance floor.

Even though this welcome home party was for me, I was not about to let Reign feel some type of way and not enjoy the night as well. I made a mental note to talk to Heim and see what was really up with him and Peaches. Although I didn't like the idea of my brother and my best friend potentially being a couple, I'd ride with whatever made her happy.

"Thing for You" by Drake and Bryson Tiller was playing, which had me slow grinding my ass and hips on the light-skinned, six-foot-two Future-looking dude that I was dancing with; however, my attention was focused on the two-way mirrors that were lined up at the top of the club. Although I couldn't see who was behind the glass, I could feel eyes staring a hole right through me. My stomach began to flutter, my hands became clammy, and my mouth all of a sudden went dry. The last time that happened was when I was in the presence of the only man who ever had that effect on me.

He was here. Lyfe was somewhere in the building, and I knew it would only be a matter of time before I came face-to-face with the only man I've ever loved.

"Go, best friend," Reign yelled over the music as she watched me move my hips a little to the beat. She had the biggest grin on her face as she stuck her tongue out and waved her arms high in the air. "Show him what us Carolina girls are working with."

Shaking my head and laughing at her crazy ass, I continued to dance with the brother behind me for the next few songs, but I stopped when some slow jam song started to play.

"Not a fan of this song?" he asked, hands on my hips and mouth close to my ear as we walked toward the bar together. The hairs of his neatly trimmed goatee tickled the side of my face.

"Naw, not really. I like his other stuff, but something about this song doesn't move me to dance," I returned as Tory Lanez "One Day" continued to play.

The bartender walked over to me, wiping the bar counter in her stride. "What can I get you, honey?"

"A double shot of Coconut Cîroc for me, and for him . . ." I turned toward my dancing buddy whose eyes were roaming my entire frame from head to toe. He licked his lips when his eyes stopped on my thighs, and then smirked when his gaze connected with mine. "Did you want something to drink too . . .?" I trailed off, alluding to the fact that I didn't know what to call him. "I would say your name, but we haven't exchanged those yet."

A dimple I hadn't noticed before surfaced when he bit his bottom lip. "My name is Hash. What's yours?"

"Is Hash the name your mama gave you?"

He nodded his head with a smirk, full lips looking like they could do some damage to my clit. "It's not, but it is what you can call me, for now."

I nodded my head and turned back to the bartender, who had already poured my double shot of Cîroc.

"How much do I owe you?" I asked, opening my clutch.

Hash grabbed my hand. "Now what kind of gentleman would I be if I didn't pay for your drink?" He dug into his pocket and pulled out a hundred-dollar bill. "Get her another round of whatever she just had." His eyes went to Reign, who had just walked up with his friend behind her. "Get them whatever they want. And for me, I want a triple shot of that top-shelf Hennessy I know you have behind there. Not that watered-down corner bodega or grocery store shit either."

"Got it. And, sir, there's no need for your—" the bartender started to say, but Hash cut her off, eyes still on me.

"Just get the drinks, sweetheart. I promise to leave you a nice tip once you bring me back my change."

I laughed at the way the bartender rolled her eyes and walked away, but not before low key snatching the bill out of his big hand. What she was probably trying to let him know was that there was no need for his money due to the bar being open, but I guess Hash wanted to impress me some kind of way.

Downing my second round of shots, my eyes scanned the crowd trying to see if I could spot Lyfe, my brother, or anyone from their crew. I knew I felt his presence a few minutes ago, and that he was still around here somewhere, but I had yet to lay eyes on him.

"You expecting someone or something?" Hash asked, his glass of dark liquor in midlift to his mouth.

"What makes you say that?"

"You." I looked at him like he was crazy, and he laughed. "I noticed how you haven't stopped looking around the club since we got to the bar. You've been so distracted with trying to find whoever you're looking for that you never told me your name."

I turned my attention from the crowd back to him. Sticking my hand out, I gripped his when he placed it in mine and shook it. "My bad, Hash, how rude of me. My name is Savvy."

"Is Savvy the name your mother gave you?" he asked, mocking me, trying to be funny.

"It is. For now," I returned, biting my bottom lip and batting my long lashes. With a flirty smirk on my face, I turned away from him, making sure he had the perfect view of my ass, and began to search the crowd for that familiar face again. After five minutes of searching the floor with no such luck, my gaze went to Reign, who was back on the dance floor with her new friend and in a world of her own as she grinded her ass farther into his lap. Matter of fact, everyone in Club Label was getting real live with their dance moves after the DJ dropped the beat to Young Thug and Travis Scott's "Pick Up the Phone." Not one to let a good song pass me by, I grabbed Hash's hand and made my way back to the dance floor while bouncing my hips to the beat. Right when I turned around to dip it low and show Hash a few more of my tricks, something, or rather someone, walking toward me in a hurry caught my eye. With a tight scowl on his face and from what I could see, thoughts of murder on his mind, I knew shit was about to hit the fan.

"Shit," I hissed, already knowing that by the way Heim had his eyes focused on Reign and the dude dancing behind her that this was not going to end well. I tried to step away from

Hash and get Reign's attention but stopped when he grabbed my elbow and gently pulled me back to him.

"Where you runnin' off to?" he asked, circling my waist with his strong arms and pulling me closer to his chest. "I wanted to get a few more dances with you before you decided to leave."

"I'm sorry, but I can't right now, Hash. I need to go handle something real quick."

"Something like what?"

When I looked back over my shoulder, Naheim had already reached Reign and had the back of her dress balled up in his hand, while he went off on the dude she was dancing with.

"Look, if I run into you before I leave, maybe you can get a few more dances. But right now, I really need to go," I said, pulling away from him.

"Okay, but before you go, let me get your—"

Pop, pop, pop!

Snatching my arm from his grip, I started to panic when I heard the gunshots go off and noticed that neither Heim nor Reign were standing in the same spot that they were just in. I frantically searched the crowd for a glimpse of them, but couldn't really see shit. With so many people screaming, running, and falling to the ground, trying to find a safe spot to get to, it was total chaos. Hash tried to pull me toward the exit with him and everyone else, but the nigga had another think coming if he thought I was going to leave my brother and best friend behind.

"Let me go." I flung my arm from his grasp again. "Heim!" I yelled out, my lungs feeling like all of the air was gone from my body. "Reign!" I screamed out the second time and could feel the tears building up in my eyes. I started for the middle of the dance floor, pushing and shoving my way through the bodies still trying to get out of the way when my body started to get that funny feeling again. Turning my head to my left, my heart started to beat rapidly just at the sight of him. Lyfe was about ten feet from me and was looking good as hell. Ten years had done his ass good. I mean, he was fine as hell when I first met him at twelve years old, but right now, in this moment . . . my God.

"Savvy," Heim called out, pulling me from my thoughts of Lyfe. "Savvy." He turned me toward him with both hands on my shoulders and shook me a bit. "Baby sis, I need you to get the fuck up out of here now. Take Reign with you, and I'll be by your spot in about an hour."

I stuttered. "Heim . . . wh . . . What the hell? Who was that shooting?"

He shook his head and started to push me toward the back of the club. "Not now, Savannah, please. I'm already hot as fuck about someone shooting up your party. Let me handle this, and I'll get up with you in a minute, okay?"

Slowly nodding my head, I turned toward Reign who was at my side, a little shaken, but ready to get the hell out of there.

"Call me when you make it home. Man and Brutus will walk you to your car," Heim hollered at me and then turned his attention to the two big-ass bodybuilding niggas dressed in all black. "If anything happens to my sister or my girl between now and on the way to the car, I'm killing both of y'all niggas before y'all even blink an eye, straight up."

After agreeing to his threat with a simple nod of their heads, Man and Brutus surrounded Reign and I and walked us out of the club just as quickly as we walked in. Patrick, who must've been summoned through his earpiece by the dude Heim addressed as Brutus met us at the back door and pulled up the rear of our security detail. Once we reached my car, the three men stood guard until Reign and I were backing out of the parking space and heading toward the highway. Looking through the rearview mirror, I watched as the club and the people who were still outside trying to get in became farther and farther away, until I couldn't see them.

"Some kind of welcome home that was, huh?" I asked Reign but didn't get a response. Looking over at my best friend, I noticed that she was so into the text messages that she was receiving that what I just said totally flew over her head.

Turning the radio up, I decided to focus back on the road and do the same. No further words were exchanged between Reign and me for the duration of our ride, both with a lot of shit on our minds and obviously lost in our own thoughts. Hers were no doubt about my brother, who I knew she was texting by the frown on her face, while my mind was consumed with thoughts of Lyfe and how, after seeing him after all these years, he can still make me feel all gushy and shit on the inside even in the middle of a shoot-out.

Lyfe

The minute we walked into the VIP section of the club and I looked out over the crowd from behind the two-way mirror, my eyes connected with hers. Savannah was here and looking as beautiful as ever. It had been almost ten years since the last time I saw her, and there she was. Flawless, dark brown skin, makeup light but just right. Her hair was up in this sleek pony-tail that showed off her long neck and beautiful facial structure. The way that little black dress hugged every dip and curve of her body had me adjusting my dick and trying to keep it at bay. The smile on her face made my heart swell a lit-tle. Just to see her after all these years, having a great time at the welcome home party Heim and I were paying for had me feeling some type of way. I watched as she and Reign laughed at something they were looking at, then got pissed as hell when I saw her walk to the dance floor hand in hand with that lame-ass nigga Hash.

"Yo, man, what's gotten into you?" Kiko asked, standing next to me, dressed in all black, looking out at the crowd. "It's packed as hell tonight. You should be happy, but you got a frown on your face. Shit, a lot of bodies mean a lot of money."

I took a sip of my drink. "Normally that would be correct, but, unfortunately, tonight, the only people that will be making money are the party planners who put this shit together and the vendors who supplied all of that extra alcohol for the open bar."

"Open bar? I see you and Heim didn't spare any expense for little sis. Is she here yet?"

I nodded my head toward the middle of the dance floor where Savannah was damn near fucking this nigga with her clothes on.

Kiko covered his mouth with his fist and laughed. "No wonder your attitude changed. Li'l sis down there with the corniest nigga in the club and probably got him hard as fuck with the way she shaking that ass on him." He squinted his eyes. "Damn. Savvy done grew up on niggas too. Look at those titties sitting up all nice and shit. Then you can tell by how wide her hips are that she got some ass behind her."

I cut my eyes at his overgrown Chico DeBarge-looking ass. "Nigga!"

"What?" He held his hands up in surrender, laughing. "I'm just looking, bro, like everyone else is and will be. I know you already got claims on her and shit, so you don't have to worry about me. But *him*," he pointed toward Hash and Savannah, "you might have to keep your eye on. Do you want me to go down there and throw that nigga out?"

My eyes traveled back over to Savannah, and I licked my lips. Watching her thick body twist and roll to the beat had me wanting to say yes, but the smile on her face and in her eyes had me going the other way. "Nah, let him live and get a few more dances. I'll go down there in a minute and make the sucker fall back."

Kiko nodded his head and continued to look out into the crowd. "Is that Reign out there on the dance floor too? Her little ass knows Naheim is on his way up here, and it doesn't matter if he has Peaches with him or not. If he sees her all up on that nigga, you already know he's going to snatch her up."

I nodded my head in agreement, while my eyes stayed trained on Savannah. I didn't really understand the relationship between Heim and Reign, nor did I really care about it. I just wanted my boy to find him a girl who would have his back to the very end, and Peaches wasn't the one to do that. Yeah, she was a down-for-whatever, you-bust-I-bust type of chick, but that shit all came with a price. Peaches was the kind of girl who was about the almighty dollar. As long as the money was flowing in, she was riding; once the money slowed down or stopped, her ass was on to the next.

A few times Heim tried to get her on with the team. We did need someone to be over the new setup we had with shipments, storage, and transportation, but I didn't trust her ho ass for some reason. I don't know if it was because she tried to love on all of the homies before Heim finally bit or what, but there was something about her that I didn't trust. Plus, I remember when we were younger, she and Savannah didn't really get along, and if Savvy wasn't fucking with her, neither was I.

"Look at this muthafucka, Lyfe. He must not know that the bar is open tonight."

I shook my head watching this clown Hash front like he was the man to Savannah. I let him rock with his little game for right now, but if he started to get a little too touchy-feely, I was going to let my presence be known—and not in a good way.

"Yoooooooooooo, what's going on up here? Where the bitches at?" Naheim asked, walking

up into the VIP section, an open bottle of Ace of
Spades in his hand. He took a few shots to the
head before dapping up me, Kiko, Man, Brutus,
and the rest of the crew. Taking his jacket off, he
laid it over an empty chair and started dancing
with one of the waitresses, who was collecting
the empty glasses on the table. I could tell by his
eyes that he was pretty turned up already and
silently hoped that he somehow missed seeing
Reign on the dance floor with that other nigga.
Don't get me wrong, though; if Heim did go
down there to beat ole boy's ass, I would most
definitely be right behind him, but I didn't want
Savannah's welcome home party to be ruined
behind some relationship shit he wasn't even
sure he wanted.

"Heeey, Lyfe." Peaches purred as she swayed
her thick hips over to me, reaching out for a hug.
"Damn, you always smell so good," she whispered in my ear, pulling back from our embrace.
"What's the name of the cologne you have on? I
might cop some of that for Naheim. You always
smelling like money and shit." She licked her
lips and eyed me up and down. I'm not gonna lie,
even though I didn't like Peaches on a personal
level or rock with her like that, the girl was still a
bad one, and I could see how Heim got wrapped
up in her clutches. Standing at about five foot six

with a nice tight frame and some ample assets to match, her big doe eyes, full lips, sandy brown complexion, and hustle mentality was probably what drew my boy in.

"What the fuck y'all over here talking about?"

"Your boy's cologne and how I might wanna cop you some if he tells me the name of it."

"What you talking about? I smell just like this nigga, baby," Naheim said, walking up behind Peaches, wrapping his arms around her waist and kissing her on her cheek. "Or should I say the nigga smell just like me. *I'm* the one who put him on to this grown-man scent."

I laughed. "Nigga, you ain't put me on to shit. We was both in the Hermès store when the salesgirl gave me the sample first. You was too busy looking at bags—"

Peaches cut me off. "Bags? Hermès? Nigga, who the fuck were you buying a bag for? It better not have been that bitch Muddy Waters."

Naheim rolled his eyes. "Don't start that shit tonight, Peaches. I could've left your ass right on your couch if you gonna start tripping." Peaches opened her mouth to go off again, but Heim cut her off. "What I was doing in the Hermès store isn't really none of your business, and you know I don't answer to no bitch. But to keep the peace and not fuck up my little sister's party I'll tell you."

"Okay, I'm waiting, nigga."

Raising the bottle up to his mouth, Heim was about to take another swig of his drink but stopped when something on the dance floor caught his eye. "What the fuck!"

"Um, Naheim, nigga, why the fuck was you in the Hermès store if it wasn't for me?" Peaches retorted. "I know you hear me talking to you, Heim. Why the fuck you ignoring me?"

"Shut the fuck up," Heim snapped, all of sudden sobering up. "Is that that nigga Hash dancing with my baby sister?" He stepped closer to the two-way mirror with squinted eyes. "Yeah, that's his lame ass. And why the fuck is he holding her like?"

All eyes turned to the dance floor as Heim's words trailed off.

"Is that? Nigga, I'm about to kill this bitch," he mumbled, pulling his pants up and setting the bottle of champagne on a nearby table. "Down there showing all of my shit with that little-ass dress on." He pulled his .357 from behind his back and cocked it. "Always crying about me tripping, but steady doing stupid shit."

I grabbed his shoulder. "Heim, man, put that shit away. We don't need nothing happening at the club or any bodies lying around this mutha-fucka, for that matter. You know we got eyes on us because of Lenny and Toby's bitch asses. Ain't no telling who's in the crowd right now. Man, think about that shit. Plus, you don't wanna ruin Savvy's welcome home party. I'll have Kiko go down there and kick Hash's ass out, then everything will be cool."

"Hash?" He turned to me with confusion on his face. "I'm not worried about that lame-ass muthafucka. I taught my sister what to watch for in a nigga, so I'm pretty sure she ain't falling for none of his weak-ass game."

"Then what the fuck are you getting all mad about?" Peaches asked, walking over to where we were standing, attitude still on twenty. "And you *still* haven't told me why you were in the fucking Hermès store."

"I was in the store copping a new suitcase for my sister. Some calfskin shit she wouldn't stop talking about last year that she wanted me to get her for her birthday, but I gave her cash instead."

Plus that octagon-looking clutch thing you bought for Reign that cost you five stacks I wanted to add to see Peaches's face drop, but I wasn't going to dime my boy out like that.

"Put your gun away, Heim. Like Lyfe said, you don't know who's down there in the crowd watching. I got this. I'll take a few fellas with me down there, go get little sis, and bring her back up here," Kiko offered.

"Who said anything about going to get Savannah? I'm about to go kick Reign and that nigga she's dancing with ass."

"Reign?" Peaches yelled. "So you *still* going crazy over that bitch and whatever nigga she's fucking now?"

Heim walked up to Peaches and hemmed her up against the wall so fast, we didn't have enough time to react. "What I tell you about questioning me, Peaches? You already know what the deal is. Now either stay in your lane and play your position or get the fuck on. It's your choice. You don't have to be here."

"I don't have to be here? Muthafucka!" she screamed and started punching Heim all over his face and chest. Her legs were kicking so high that the short red sequin dress she had on started to rise up and give everyone in the room a glimpse of her ass and the white thong she had on. "You always running behind that bitch, when *I'm* the one that's been holding you down for the last year. What the fuck does she give you besides pussy whenever you decide to jump out of mine for a few minutes?" Tears were now streaming down her face, and her hair was all over the place.

Releasing his grip from her neck, Heim stepped back and pulled up his dark jeans, before thumbing his nose and pulling at the front of his white shirt. "Like I just said, you already know what the deal is *LeNora*. I don't have to explain my relationship with Reign to you or anyone else." He turned to me. "Yo, check to see if they still on the dance floor."

Looking out in the crowd, I easily found Savannah back by the bar again, still talking to Hash, while Reign was with the same dude twerking her ass all over him.

"What you wanna do?" I asked, giving him the head nod, letting him know that they were still down there.

"I don't wanna mess my sister's party up, so I'ma go down there and pull Reign to the side and have a couple of words with her." Heim turned around and headed toward the stairs.

"Keep an eye out just in case I need you to come down here and get this nigga. You already know he 'bout to beat ole boy ass," I told Kiko who just nodded his head.

Peaches started calling after Heim, who continued to ignore her as we walked out of the VIP section and down the flight of stairs. Walking into the crowd, the majority of the people already knew what time it was by the look on Heim's face. Moving out of his wrath and parting like the Red Sea, we were in direct line to Reign who hadn't noticed the crowd moving from around her. Just as we got close enough for Heim to call her name over the loud music and grab her by the back of her dress, pulling her out of ole boy's face, shots rang out.

Pop, pop, pop!

Jumping into action, I pulled the gun from behind my back and pointed it in the direction of where I heard the shots coming from. So many people were screaming and running around after the shots went off that I didn't have a clear view of who the shooter was. My mind went to Savannah, and I immediately ran toward the bar. Looking around, she was nowhere in sight, and neither was Hash's ass.

"What the fuck?" I heard Kiko yell behind me, guns in both hands looking around the club. "Who the fuck would be stupid enough to shoot your spot up?"

"I don't know, but make sure you find out and have that dead muthafucka's name to me by the time I wake up in the morning."

Kiko nodded. "You good? Where's Heim and li'l sis?"

I scanned the crowd trying to find Savannah but didn't come up with nothing. "Heim," I called out, as he swung the dude Reign was dancing with around and punched him in his face, teeth and blood flying everywhere. "Heim, let that nigga go. I can't find Savvy. Where's Reign?"

He punched the dude one more time in his face, and then let him fall to the ground like a rag doll before he turned to me and walked my way, murder in his eyes and obviously on his mind.

"Nigga, you trying to beat his ass, and we don't know if Savannah got out of here safe," I snapped, still searching the thinned out crowd trying to find her.

"They good. Savannah grabbed Reign after the shots went off, and I pointed them to the back exit since everyone was running toward the front."

"You sent them back there by themselves? What if the nigga who shot up the place went the same way?" I yelled, already heading to the back of the club.

"I sent Man and Brutus with them. Reign already texted me and let me know that they were in Savannah's car and headed back to her house."

A sense of relief flooded over my body. I don't know what I would've done if something would've happened to Savannah. Shit, I just got her back after ten years, and I wasn't going to lose her already. Not before I got a chance to catch up with her and see how she's been. Who the fuck was I kidding? There was so much more I wanted to do with Savannah and her being back in Charlotte for good was only the beginning. After I handled the little situation that happened here tonight, I was going to find my girl and see where her head was at when it came to me . . . her . . . and whatever the future held.

Walking back up to my office with Heim close behind me, I pulled my phone out of my pocket to see who was calling me back-to-back. Fifteen missed calls and seven voice messages. I didn't even have to open my phone to know who the calls and messages were coming from. Letting out a frustrated breath, I opened my office and pulled up the security camera footage on my computer to see if I could get a good look at the shooter.

"Nigga, I know you hear your phone vibrating on the table," Heim said as he pulled two beers from my fridge, handing me one. "Sarai gonna kick your ass if you don't answer," he laughed.

"Sarai needs to watch my kids and do whatever it is that she's been doing."

"Ahhhhh, trouble in paradise for the happy couple?" Heim joked, sitting on the chair across from me.

Ignoring him, I clicked through the footage on the screen until I got to the time just before the shots went off. Zooming in on the angle from the camera above the bar, I watched as Hash grabbed a nice amount of Savannah's ass and instantly became heated.

Heim sat up in his seat. "What's going on? You see the dumb asshole that just signed his own death certificate?"

I zoomed out of the screen and rewound the footage a few seconds back. Looking at the entrance area, I watched as a dude with a black hoodie on walked into the club and headed straight for the direction Heim and I were in.

"Yo, this nigga was aiming for us," I said as I watched the shooter pull his gun out and aim it in our direction. "But he can't shoot worth shit. Bullets hitting everything but me and you."

Heim rounded the desk, and I showed him the footage I just saw. Peeling a banana, he leaned against the wall and took a bite.

"Sure was. Did you put Kiko on it already?"

"Yeah. He should have something for us by morning."

"He better. Whoever that muthafucka is on that video needs to die before tomorrow night. He could've shot my little sister or Reign, and I'm not with that at all." Heim threw his banana peel in the trash and headed for the door.

"Where you goin'?" I asked, looking at the time.

"Shit . . . to drop Peaches off, then to check on my sister and Reign."

"Why you gotta drop Peaches off to do that? You must plan on staying with Reign for the rest of the night."

He laughed. "Her little ass needs to be taught a lesson again."

I picked up my ringing phone and ignored the call from Sarai again. "And what lesson is that?"

"That she belongs to me, and I will dead any muthafucka that tries to get in the way of that."

"Nigga, you crazy. Why don't you just let that girl do her? You and Peaches been rocking pretty hard anyway, right?"

He scrunched up his face. "Man, Peaches already know what it is. We Bonnie and Clyde'n when it comes to these streets, may even do some fucking in between, but I don't want a girl like that 24/7. Peaches don't know when to turn that hood shit off, and it's irritating as fuck."

"So why not just be with Reign and leave Peaches alone?"

He shook his head. "Man, I've tried to, but Peaches got that fiyah head, and her pussy is good. And as much as I hate her hood rat ways, that shit is a turn-on sometimes. If I could put her and Reign together, bro, I would have the perfect girl."

I got up from my desk, put my suit jacket on, and gathered up my things. "What you need to do is leave crazy-ass Peaches alone. Fuck around and lose Reign behind her looney ass. You know that girl's been in love with you ever since we were young. Keep putting her off for Peaches and she gon' find her a nigga that will wife her up real quick."

"Reign knows better," was his answer as we walked out the door. "And while you giving out advice, my nigga, you need to take some of your own and leave that crazy bitch Sarai *all* the fuck away alone too."

I locked up my office. "True, but for me, that would be easier said than done."

"Why is that? You've never had a problem with dropping females before."

"No question, but Sarai isn't just any female. She is my wife and the mother of my children, bro. A wife I can't stand 85 percent of the time and probably should've never married, but still. Plus, we have a family together, and I don't want to just up and leave my kids like that."

"Well, you better hurry up and figure out what it is you want to do before you even think about stepping to my sister."

I looked at him surprised. "What—" I started to say, but he cut me off.

"Man, we've been boys for damn near twenty years now. You don't think I know when you feeling a girl or not?" I shook my head confused because I didn't think he knew how I felt about his sister. "By the look on your face right now, I already know you're overthinking. Just know that I've peeped the way you used to look at her when we were younger and how you used to always be around her before she left for college. Then when I told her that you got married to Sarai over the phone, it sounded like her heart broke the minute the words left my mouth."

"Heim, man, look—"

He shook his head. "No need to explain shit to me. Savannah is a grown woman now and can make her own decisions. You just make sure you allow her to make her own choices when it comes to you and your situation. You my brother and all, but I will kill you, Sarai, and anyone else who fucks with my baby sis. We good?"

Sticking his open palm out to me, I clasped his hand in mine and brought Heim in for a brotherly hug. "I got you, nigga. We good," I said before hopping in my car and heading to the one place I dread going to most nights.

Reign

I had just lain down in my bed and closed my eyes when a loud bang on my front door woke me back up. It was going on four in the morning, and I had to be at work in a few hours. Normally, I wouldn't have gone out on a night where I had to work the next day, but with my girl being back in town, I couldn't let her go to her welcome home party all by herself. So, being the best friend that I am, I sucked it up, got dressed, and hit the town with Savannah.

Everything was going great until Naheim's dumb butt wanted to show his ass and niggas decided to shoot the club up. So much shit went on that night that I was completely drained and ready to lay it down. I didn't even remember what time Savannah dropped me off at home. All I remembered was giving her a hug, saying good-bye, and falling onto my couch as soon as I walked into my house. I lay there for a few moments trying to gather enough strength to take a shower and make me a little something to eat. After I took care of my hygiene and fed my belly, I went through my phone and ignored all of the text messages Naheim was sending back-to-back. It got so bad that I had to power my cell phone down and turn the ringer to my house phone off just to get a little sleep. Now, here we were an hour later, and someone was banging on my door like they were the feds.

I lay in my bed for a few more minutes, hoping and praying that whoever it was would get the picture that I was asleep and leave. But unfortunately for me, I had no such luck. Throwing my comforter off, I slid my feet into my house shoes and dragged myself from my bedroom to the front of the house. Leaving all of the lights off, I navigated through my small home with ease until I reached the door. Pulling the leg of the light blue boxers I had on up, I scratched my thigh, and then my arm.

"Yeah?" I called out and sighed while leaning against the door.

"Open up, baby."

I rolled my eyes, already knowing his ass was the one on the other side. "What do you want, Naheim? You know I have to go to work in the morning."

"Open the door, Reign. We need to talk."

"Talk?" I looked at the digital clock on my television. "Nigga, it's after four o'clock in the morning. How about you go talk to that bitch you were hanging on in the club? I'm sure her unemployed ass would love to listen to you talk all morning."

"Come on, Reign. Why you always bringing Peaches up whenever I come over to kick it with you? You and I both know where my heart is, so stop playing and let a nigga in."

As mad as I was with Naheim, it was shit like what he just said that always had me going against my word of not fucking with him anymore and letting him right back in. Naheim and I had been doing this same song and dance for the last seven years, and I was so tired of it. The nigga wanted all the perks of being in a relationship but didn't want to have anything to do with the title. If you ask me, that was just his way of being able to justify his reasons for fucking with other bitches. Oh, but don't let another nigga try to talk to me or, let alone, look my way. Naheim was not having that at all. I was like his well-known secret to the niggas and his best friend to these bitches.

"Reign, baby, let me in. Please. Just let me see your face and make sure you're okay. I know all that shit that went down at the club had you a little shook."

Stepping up to the door, I lightly pressed my forehead against it and took a deep breath. I *was* a little shook, but not to the point where I needed him to come over and comfort me. Besides, the shooting happened over six hours ago. Where has his ass been all of *that* time? I shook my head placing my hand on the knob. Something had to give with whatever this thing was between Naheim and me. I wasn't going to spend the rest of my life being his in-home girl-friend, regardless of how much I was in love with him.

Opening the door, I stepped back and allowed him to walk into my home. Familiarity had him stepping to the side and missing the small end table that stood under the window to his right. I remained behind the door and watched as he pulled off his jacket and hung it on the coat rack; again, very familiar with every piece of furniture I had in my house.

Stepping back, he turned around and stood still in the dim hue of the flickering streetlight. Even with the room being pitch black and the little bit of light shining through the crack in the door, I could still see his every sexy feature of his handsome face. His scent, which was thoroughly intoxicating, surrounded my whole body and had my nipples shooting through my white sports bra and rubbing against the coolness of the door. A small gasp escaped my lips when Naheim cradled my face with both hands and pulled me closer to him. Searching my eyes and face for what felt like an hour, he finally kissed me on the forehead and wrapped me in his arms.

"I'm sorry for snatching you by the back of your dress like that. But you just don't know how angry I get when I see you entertaining another nigga."

"Naheim, please don't do this right now. You see that I'm okay and not shook up anymore," I said, pulling away from him and already missing the warmness of his body. "Anything else you want to talk about, we can do that after I get off of work." I opened the door. "Now, if you don't mind, can you please go? I want to at least get a few hours of sleep."

His eyes cut to the open door, and then back to me. "I ain't going anywhere, so you might as well shut that shit and get your ass on the other side of the bed because you know I hate sleeping next to the window."

"Heim . . ." I whined, already knowing that this was going to be a losing battle for me.

"Heim, my ass. Now let's go to bed so that you can get some sleep." Naheim picked me up and threw me over his shoulder while closing the door and locking it in the process. Smacking me on my ass, I yelped as we started to the back of my home and made it to my bedroom.

"Can you put me down now?" I laughed.

"Not until you tell me what I want to hear."

"Come on, Naheim. It's already close to five, and I have to get up at seven."

"How about I drop you off at work instead? You'll be able to get an extra thirty minutes of sleep fucking with my driving skills."

"As good as that sounds, I have to drive my own car. I have something to do after I get off."

He smacked me on my ass again, this time a little harder. "What the fuck you have to do after work that doesn't involve you sitting on this dick?"

"Who said anything about sitting on your dick?"

Naheim threw me down on my bed, and I bounced to the side I normally sleep on when he stays the night.

"The way you showed your ass tonight . . ."

I shook my head. "Maybe we need to chill out for real for a minute, at least until you can decide on where you really wanna be."

He wiped his hands down his face and let out a dramatic sigh. "Don't start this shit again, Reign. You already know what it is,"

I sat up. "That's the thing. I *do* know what it is, and I'm not cool with that shit anymore. It was cute and shit when I was younger, but now that I'm older, got a career going for myself, my own house and shit, I want to settle down. Maybe have kids one day or some shit."

He took off his jeans, and then pulled his shirt over his head. Naheim wasn't the buffest nigga in the streets, but he had a nice body, and you could tell he worked out whenever he got around to doing it. A little over six foot two, he was built like a running back for a pro football team. Smooth dark skin covered his body from head to toe. Thighs thick and full of muscles. Arms cut and held a powerful punch. His chest, stomach, and back could be featured in any fitness ad, and his dick . . . Let's just say the nigga had crazy hang time. I licked my lips the second my eyes zeroed in on the sleeping monster, resting comfortably on the right side of his leg.

"So is this what this conversation is really all about? You mad because I said I wasn't ready for any kids right now?"

"Wait, what?" I asked coming back from my lustful thoughts. "What are you talking about?"

He sat on the bed, and it dipped down. Pulling my comforter back, he slipped underneath the cool sheets and turned to face me. "All that shit you were just talking about your career, your house, and settling down, what was the purpose of you bringing all of that up?"

I thought back to the conversation we were having, trying to remember what we were just talking about. See how fast I can get sidetracked by this man? That's why I didn't want to let his ass in.

"Oh yeah, I was saying—" I started to say, but stopped when his phone started going off again. "Can you answer that or turn the muthafucka off? Every time you come over here, your phone is constantly going off. Like the bitch got radar on your dick or something," I mumbled to myself, but he heard me.

"Maybe. She says the same thing about you when I'm at her house."

I rolled my eyes. "Good night, Naheim." Turning over with my back facing him, I pulled the covers up over my body. "Like I was saying earlier, we need to step back from each other. I'm done being a second thought in your life. Give Peaches the chance she wants. Maybe she might just be the one for you." As much as it hurt for me to admit that, I had to come to some realization about my relationship with Naheim. It's been seven years, and he still hasn't committed to me. Obviously, I wasn't the one for him, or maybe, he just wasn't the one for me.

Scooting closer to me, Naheim wrapped his arms around my body and kissed me on the back of my neck. "Stop talking that crazy shit, Reign. Like I tell you all of the time, you know where my heart is, and so does Peaches. Right now, I'm not ready to be in a committed relationship, and honestly, I don't know when I'll ever be. Especially when I got people like my boy being married to his wife but really being in love with my sister. That love shit is crazy. Can you imagine all of the shit Lyfe is going to be going through once he does finally give Sarai her walking papers, and he gets with Savvy?" His face was so close to the back of my head that I felt him shaking his head. "You and me both know that broad doesn't have it all, and I already told my boy that I will kill that crazy bitch if she steps to my sister in any way."

I didn't comment or anything. Just stayed in my own thoughts. Yeah, that was fucked up for Lyfe to be stringing Sarai along, but you can't keep forcing yourself to stay in a relationship where you aren't happy. I would have thought Lyfe would have left Sarai, especially with all the rumors flying around about the shit she did behind his back, but for some reason, he hadn't left yet. I made a mental note to talk to Savannah about that. There was no denying that she and

Lyfe would eventually get together. I just wanted to make sure she didn't end up like me, stuck and in love with a nigga who couldn't make up his mind on who he really wanted to be with.

For the next ten or fifteen minutes, I continued to listen to Naheim whisper pleas of love in my ear until I finally felt my eyelids getting heavy again and eventually falling back asleep. I don't think I'd even started to dream yet when I woke right back up. Naheim's cell was constantly going off back-to-back on my nightstand and making this loud-ass rumbling noise. Of course, his heavy sleeping ass didn't hear shit and didn't even wake up after I nudged him a few times with my elbow. Fed up and ready to get this last hour and a half of sleep in, I reached over his body and picked up his phone ready to power it off when it started to ring again.

"Hello," I answered with a yawn, not caring who was on the other end.

"Ummm, who is this and why are you answering my man's phone?"

I rolled my eyes and lay my head back on my pillow. Should've known.

"Peaches, you already know who this is, so stop playing. Can you please stop calling Naheim's phone every two minutes? Obviously, this isn't an emergency because you keep calling. Hell, even then, I would hope you'd have enough sense to blow 911's number up instead of Naheim's."

"Ha-ha, bitch. You are soooo funny," she clowned. "Whether it's an emergency or not, that's none of your business. It's Naheim's. Now stay in your lane and put my man on the phone."

See, this was the shit I did not want to deal with. Out of all the women Naheim dealt with over the years during our weird relationship, Peaches had to be the worst one. But I couldn't get mad at her, especially if I was still fucking with him knowing that he deals with her too. Taking a deep breath to calm my nerves, I pinched the bridge of my nose with my fingers while looking up at my ceiling fan.

"Look, Peaches, I'm not about to sit here and argue back and forth with you. Us working people have to get up in the morning and go to work. Unlike you and the rest of your gutter-rat friends who like to stay at home and live off of the next nigga's come up." I knew it was petty, but I couldn't let her smart-ass comment slide without saying something back. "Now, I'll let Naheim know you called him when he wakes up, okay? Until then, give this nigga's phone and my nightstand a little rest, will you?" Before she could say anything else, I released the call and powered off his phone.

Getting up from my bed, I walked to the bathroom to relieve myself and then went to my kitchen to get a glass of water. On my way back to my room, I had to stop in the middle of my hallway and do a double take at the sound of someone knocking on my door again.

"What the fuck," I mumbled to myself, walking back up to the front. "Who is it?" I asked, but got no response. I stood on my tippy-toes to look through the peephole but couldn't see anything due to a finger blocking my view. "Who is it?" I called out again, still with no answer. "Whoever you looking for doesn't live here anymore, now get on before I call the police on your ass."

I heard the most annoying laugh I've ever heard before and started seeing red. Placing my glass of water down on the table, I swung my door open and stepped onto my porch. "Bitch, what the fuck are you doing at my house at this time of the morning? And how the fuck do you know where I fucking live?" I asked a smirking Peaches.

Standing with one hand on her hip and the other one holding a phone that I could hear playing Naheim's voicemail greeting, she stared at me while I stared right back at her. This chick had to really be crazy showing up at my house unannounced, and as if *I* was the one doing her wrong. Looking her up and down, I shook my head. Peaches was as ghetto as they came—and took pride in that shit. Not only did she have on the same red sequin dress I saw her wearing earlier, but she also had on some yoga pants with the matching jacket and some neon orange running shoes. Her hair was wrapped up in a scarf, and the look on her face was like she was ready to fight.

"Bitch, where the fuck is Naheim at? Tell him to bring his ass out here," she screamed in my face.

I bit my lip trying to control my anger because this was a level of disrespect that didn't sit well with me. I wasn't no shit starter or anything like that, but I sure knew how to finish some shit, especially if it was brought to my doorstep. I noticed a few of my neighbors' porch lights start to turn on as well as a few doors start to open—no doubt being nosy and trying to see all of the commotion going on at my house and ready to call the police at any minute. I didn't live in Ballentine like Savannah, but I did live in a middle-class area of Charlotte where hood-like shenanigans were *not* the norm.

"Look, Peaches, right now is not the time nor the place to be on some crazy shit. You need to leave my house right now and deal with Naheim whenever he gets with you."

"Bitch, I ain't going nowhere. Now, go get my man before I *really* act a fool," she said.

"Peaches, I don't—"

She cut me off. "I don't give a fuck about what you 'bout to say. I've been calling Naheim's ass all muthafucking night. Ever since he left my house and out of my bed to come over here. You wanna know how I know where you live? I followed his dumb ass. He was so concerned about you and how you felt after what happened at the club that he wasn't watching his surroundings. I've been out here the whole time calling his phone back-to-back. Had he picked up when I started calling the first time he would've known that." She got in my face. "Now, *like I said,* go get *my man* and tell him to come out here before I beat your prissy little ass."

"Prissy?"

She laughed. "Yes, prissy. Why you think Naheim stay fucking with me and not with you? That man in there," she pointed in my house, "wants a woman who will have his back. Who is down for him in every way. Your scary ass wouldn't bust a damn grape if someone threw it at him." She looked me up and down, disgust all over her face. "Why he keeps running back to you is mind braffling to me. But then again, he does friend zone you all the time, so maybe he's just being the *best friend* he always claims to be when it comes to you."

Mind braffling? This bitch was dumber than I expected, but that really wasn't a surprise. What *did* surprise me was all of the shit she just told me about Naheim. Best friend? Friend zone? So *that* was how Naheim described our relationship to these other women? I mean, I always assumed that was what he did, but it hurt ten times worse getting that assumption confirmed. Hmmm. I could tell Peaches was still talking some slick shit, but I tuned her out and began to replay Naheim's and my relationship over the last seven years in the back of my mind. Why *did* he keep running back to me? Why was it so easy for him to fuck one bitch and then come to your bed a few hours later? Because I fucking let him. At the moment of that realization, anger started to build up inside of me that had me hot as fire. I was trying to keep everything going on inside of me but snapped the minute Peaches decided to take her finger and poke me in the middle of my forehead. Before I knew what was happening, I pounced on her ass and wouldn't let up until a pair of strong arms grabbed me around the waist and pulled me back into my house.

"What the fuck is wrong with you, Reign? What the fuck are you out there fighting like a hood bitch for?"

Gathering myself together, I turned toward him so fast, I gave myself whiplash. "What's wrong with *me*? Nigga, what's wrong with *you*? And when is it all right for your bitches to pop up at *my* house? The bitch shouldn't know where I live anyway," I shouted in return.

Naheim looked out the door to a screaming Peaches, and then back to me. "I know, babe, I know. And I'm going to check her on that."

"Check her on that? That's *all* you have to offer? To *check her on that*?"

"What else do you want me to do? Go out there and beat her ass so someone can call the police on me?" He blew out a breath. "You already know we have people watching us. I don't need any extra atten—"

I cut him off so fast. "Fuck you, Naheim. You don't need no extra attention, huh? You know what?" I asked, walking around my living room and threw any of his shit that I saw into one of my glass bowls. "Take your shit and get the fuck on, Naheim. I can't do this anymore. I *won't* do this anymore." I shook my head as tears began to roll down my cheeks.

He tried to walk closer to me, but I stepped back. "Come on, baby, don't say that. Let me handle her; then I'll be back later on to make everything up to you."

"No." I shook my head and wiped my nose and face with the back of my hand. "No, Naheim. This, this shit right here was the last straw. I was already having doubts about us continuing on with this . . . this . . . sham of a relationship. But I can't—No, I won't do it anymore. I deserve better. Hell, Peaches deserves better, and I hate that bitch. But I can't do this—us—anymore."

Naheim placed the glass bowl down on the top of my suede couch and started walking toward me. "Reign, I know you're a little upset, but, baby, don't let this be the end of us. You know as well as I do that you have my—"

I cut him off again, that same anger from a few seconds ago building back up. "Stop with the lies, Naheim. I don't have your heart. Never have and probably never will. Had I had your heart, you would be able to see how unhappy I've been for the last few years being your in-home girlfriend. You would've felt the tears I've cried night after night wondering what it was about me that you couldn't commit to . . . be with . . . love unconditionally." I handed him back the glass bowl. "I'm sorry, you need to go. And don't come back."

"Reign—"

"I know we will have to see each other because of Savannah, so please just give me my space."

"Reign—"

"Go!" I screamed, my voice going hoarse and tears starting to fall again. "Get the hell out, Heim. Please, just go."

There was a light knock on my door. When I looked up, the neighbor who just moved in peeked his head in. "Is everything okay in here?"

Naheim cut his eyes at him. "Nigga, did anyone call for your help? Get the fuck out of my girl's house."

The neighbor turned his gaze toward me, no fear whatsoever of Naheim in his heart, unlike all of the other dudes in the city. They knew Naheim was certifiably trigga happy and didn't have a problem with any type of gunplay. "You good?" His deep voice vibrated through my home again.

I nodded my head, and then looked at Naheim. "Please just go. I'm sure someone's called the police already with your crazy stalking bitch screaming out there like that."

Taking one last look at me, Naheim grabbed his jacket, the glass bowl, and his shoes from off of the floor. "This isn't over, Reign. I'll be back later tonight like I said." Walking over to me, he kissed me on my forehead and cheek, then turned around and started for the door. The neighbor who was just there a second ago was nowhere in sight and had probably gone back to his own home.

Walking to my door to close it, I could still hear Peaches going off about something and following close behind Naheim who was ignoring the fuck out of her loud rant. After popping his trunk and dropping his things back there, he slipped into the driver's side of his car, started it up, and sped off, leaving a yapping Peaches in the middle of the street screaming his name. When she turned around and looked back at me, I took notice of the silent threat that she was giving me with her eyes, but I didn't give a fuck. Just like I did when we were younger, I'd whip her ass all over again. She knew not to fuck with me on that level, which made me make a mental note to ask Savannah to join me at the shooting range sometime soon. I had a feeling that the next time I ran into Peaches, she wouldn't be fighting with her fists, and I needed to brush up on my aim.

Savannah

"Come on, Savvy, you gotta help me get her back or at least get her to accept some of my calls."

I shook my head. "Nope. You're on your own with this one, playa. You shouldn't have done my girl like that."

"Done your girl like what?" He blew out a frustrated breath. "Maaaan, it wasn't a problem for us to kick it like we've been kicking it all of these years. Why be one now?"

I stopped stacking my law books on the cherry wood bookcase behind my desk in my new office space and turned to look at my brother, who had been begging me to talk some sense into Reign for the last two hours. He was supposed to be helping me unpack, but all he'd been doing was crying over my girl and answering his phone.

"Heim, have you ever put yourself in Reign's shoes? Like really imagined how you would feel if she was the one out here fucking on different niggas and throwing it in your face every chance she got, just to turn around and show up at your house every other night and act like she can't live without you? Not to mention act a plum fool whenever another chick tries to holla at you?"

"Savannah, go on somewhere with that bull-shit. I'm not even trying to hear what you're talking about right now. And I don't know what Reign's been telling you about us, but she and I have never been in an official relationship. I told her the same thing I tell all these other females when we first start fucking around. I'm not ready to be in a relationship, so don't expect any of that lovey-dovey shit, me answering to you, and wondering why I fuck with other females. If you can't deal with anything I just said, then fucking with me may not be what you want."

I shook my head and laughed. "I don't see why Reign ever started messing with you in the first place. I used to tell her all the time when we were younger that she could do so much better."

He held his heart as if he was wounded by my words. "So much better? What the hell does *that* mean? You don't think I'm not good enough for your friend, little sis?"

Placing the last book on the shelf and making sure the bookend was in place, I sat on the edge of my desk in front of my brother and looked him in the eyes. "Naheim, you know Reign's been crushing on you ever since she and I became friends in the fifth grade. Every day, it was Heim this and Heim that. I used to think she became my friend just to get close to you sometimes. One day, I think we were in our freshman year of high school, so I don't know if you will remember this, but you had come home and had that ugly girl with the big nose and big booty with you that used to live up the street. What was her name again?"

"Big nose and big booty?"

"Yeah, her daddy worked as a janitor at Providence, and her mama worked at that grocery store part time on Wilson Grove Road."

"You talking about Food Lion?" I nodded my head. "And her daddy was a janitor at the high school?" I nodded my head yes again. "Big nose and a big boo—Oh, I know who you talking about now. That was Kallie Jones. She graduated a year or two before I did. Hell yeah, I remember her freaky ass." He shook his head. "That girl used to—"

"Uhhh, TMI, nigga. We close and everything, but I don't want to hear anything about your sexual experiences."

He laughed. "I got you, but what was you saying about her? Finish the story."

"As I was saying," I cleared my throat, "before you got all excited and shit, you brought Kallie home with you that day and Reign happened to be there. We were downstairs doing our homework when all of a sudden we hear Kallie's nasty ass moaning and screaming at the top of her lungs. I turned the radio on and tried to drown her out, but she was loud as hell."

He licked his lips and nodded his head. "Yeah, that girl right there was—"

"Hello? Again, TMI."

Pulling out his phone, Heim began responding to a text message that came in, so I continued on with my story. "Anyhoo, after you guys finished doing what it was y'all were doing, you walked her downstairs and out of the house, but not before tonguing her down and telling her you would call her later on that night.

"While you were going back upstairs, I cracked a joke about Kallie's nose that was funny as hell, but Reign didn't laugh. When I looked over to my best friend to see why she was so quiet, she had tears rolling down her face like someone had just broken her heart. I asked her what was wrong that day, but she just brushed it off like it was nothing. A couple of weeks later she finally told me the real reason behind the tears."

"Which was?" Heim asked, still texting on his phone.

I got up from my seat on my desk and began to place my framed degrees on the nails I hammered into the wall. "Welp, that was the day she told me that she had been in love with you ever since we were little and that she thought you were going to save yourself for her just like she was going to save herself for you."

"And she did save herself for me. I'm the only nigga that has ever been with her. That's why I respect and love Reign so much."

"You respect and love her so much, yet you won't give her the one thing that she wants?"

"What Reign wants right now, I'm not ready to give her at this moment."

"Yet, you want her to keep her shit on lockdown while you get whatever it is you got out of your system?"

"That's how it's supposed to be," Naheim responded, still texting on his phone.

"Don't come crying to me when she find her a nigga that is willing to give her what she wants, no extra side bitches included."

He stopped texting and looked up at me. "You know something I don't, Savvy? Is Reign already fucking with another nigga? It's only been a few days since that shit popped off with Peaches. It better not be that nosy-ass neighbor that came over trying to play captain save a ho."

"And if it is? You ain't got shit to say, but I hope he treats her better than you did." I hung the frame on the nails and stood back to make sure it was straight. "Heim, does this look crooked to you?" I asked as he got up from his seat on my plush leather chair and started for the door. "Where you going? I still need your help unpacking all of this stuff."

"I know, that's why I called in an extra pair of hands."

"Nigga, that better not be Peaches you about to let in here. You know I never did like her, and I especially ain't fucking with her now after that stunt she pulled, showing up at Reign's house. How you even messing with a broad like that when you got a girl who is everything you need?"

"First off, no, I'm not about to let Peaches in here. I already know you feel some type of way toward her, and I would dead that bitch if she came foul at you in any type of way. Second, what me and Peaches got going on is strictly business with a little fucking on the side. She knows I'll never wife her ass or try to build a future with her." He turned back around, heading out the door. "I'll be right back, though. I know you hungry and shit. I had some food brought up here for us."

I nodded my head and continued to hang my certificates, degrees, and different personal pictures on the wall. My mind drifted to my best friend and how sad she sounded on the phone when she called me a few days ago to fill me in on everything that happened that morning at her house. I wanted to kick my brother's ass for allowing some shit to go down like that, but I also got on her case too. I knew Reign wasn't going to be completely over my brother anytime soon, but I did tell her that maybe she should go out on a few dates and try to have a little fun. Like the old saying goes, the best way to get over one man is with a new friend.

Speaking of a new friend, I picked up my phone and sent a good afternoon text to Hash. For the last week, he and I had been getting acquainted with each other. I didn't know how he got my number, but the day after my welcome home party, he hit me up to see how I was doing and asked me out for drinks. When I told him that I was going to be busy setting up my new firm, he understood and asked if we could go out this weekend instead. I almost declined then, but changed my mind after I received a special delivery to my office a couple of days ago. The beautiful bouquet of pink and white begonias arrived a little past noon and had my emotions temporarily taking over my soul. How did he even know these were my favorites? After giving the delivery guy a tip, I brought the flowers into my office and read the card that was stuck in the middle of the beautiful arrangement.

Hello, beautiful, I hope you like the flowers. Please forgive my forwardness, but I would really love to have dinner with you this weekend. If you're interested, you have my number now. So send me a text and let me know if everything is cool. In the meantime, here's a bouquet of various flowers for each minute we spent together.

One Love,

Hash

To say that I was impressed would easily be an understatement. I thought Hash was going to be one of these lame niggas that my brother was always warning me about, especially while I was out in California, but so far, he'd been managing to pique my interest more and more, even with the feelings I'd still been feeling for Lyfe. The funny thing was, Lyfe hadn't reached out to me, not once since the incident at his club. Naheim said that he had to go out of town for a couple of days to handle some business and would reach out to me once he got back, but I had yet to receive anything from him. Still, that didn't stop the way my insides continued to get all gushy when I thought of him or how I still longed for his touch. Like right now. That same feeling I always got whenever he was anywhere around came full force and had me stumbling back from the wall a bit.

"Whoa, you all right?" a deep baritone voice asked, damn near causing me to fall all the way to the floor. I turned my gaze to the source of the melodic tone and almost had a heart attack.

"Lyfe?"

He smiled and walked farther into my office, Naheim right behind him, head still down in his phone.

"What's going on, li'l cutie? It's been a minute," he said, setting a few bags from the Cook Out on my desk, the smell of char-grilled hamburgers and hot french fries filling the air.

Grabbing the back of my oversized executive chair, I regained the little bit of stability I lost and stood up straight. Smoothing my hands down the white tank top I had on, and then down the light washed skinny jeans that were hugging my hips and ass like a glove, I returned his smile and then bit my bottom lip to try to keep the satisfied moan of seeing his sexy ass in my throat. Lyfe looked even better than he did the night I caught that quick glimpse of him at the club. His dark caramel skin was smooth and even. His lips full and thick. My eyes roamed over his broad shoulders and the way his shirt hugged the muscles in his arms and chest. The blue slacks he had on were wrinkle free and tailored just right. His six-foot-three frame easily towered over mine, even in my white open toe stiletto booties. I slowly exhaled as my eyes traveled back up his fit stature and back to those cognac irises that were appraising my body in the same way.

He opened his arms. "You gon' show a nigga some love, or what? I know it's been a minute since I last saw you and shit."

Confident that my knees would not give out, I walked around my desk and over to Lyfe, stepping into his embrace and wishing our situation was different from what it currently was. It had been ten years since the last time I felt him hold me like this, and I did not want to let him go. His smell was still the same, a woodsy, masculine scent that had my panties moist and almost soaked. I closed my eyes and hugged him a little tighter as he pulled me into his chest a little more. It wasn't until Naheim cleared his throat that we pulled apart from our embrace, eyes still locked on each other.

"Damn, nigga, let her breath a little. You was about to suffocate her and shit."

Lyfe laughed, and I couldn't stop the butterflies in my belly. His smile was still the same, even sixteen years later, and in that instance, I fell in love all over again. Just like I did on my twelfth birthday when I first met him. He broke the connection between our eyes and looked around my office space.

"So you really 'bout to do this, huh? You're really about to be out here keeping niggas like me from spending the rest of their lives in jail?"

I nodded my head, walking back around my desk and sitting in my chair. "Yep. I told you that I wanted to be a lawyer when I grew up. And now, I am."

He sat in the seat across from me, eyes back on mine. "You did, and I'm proud of you, Savvy. I always knew you were going to make something of yourself."

"I did, and I don't have anyone to thank but you and Heim. You both made it possible for me to attend the school I wanted tuition free, as well as pay for my housing, bills, and car note. Because of that, I was able to focus on school and school alone all eight years, graduating at the top of my class and summa cum laude."

"That's what's up. I've always wanted nothing but the best for you in life. Even if it meant I would have to let you go and do your own thing for a while."

"My own thing?" I asked, not really understanding what he meant by that.

"Aye, yo, I'm about to go outside to my car and smoke a blunt real quick and let you two catch up. I'll be right back." Naheim excused himself, still texting back and forth on his phone. Once he was out of the office, I looked back at Lyfe.

"What did you mean by doing my own thing?"

He licked his lips, and my pearl twitched. "Just what I said, your own thing. You needed to explore the world and do you. I knew you weren't ready for the type of relationship I wanted back then, and I also didn't think you were ready to be with a nigga like me."

"A nigga like you? What does that mean?"

"A street nigga. The same nigga you will more than likely be trying to keep out of jail. I was just getting started in the game, and I needed a girl who was willing to break a few laws if need be. I wouldn't have asked you to do anything like that for me. Not when it could have jeopardized your chances of becoming a lawyer."

"So you just make that type of decision for me?"

"Yes. And, honestly, if I had to, I'd do it again."

Stunned by his admission, I decided to change the subject about our past relationship and move on to something else. What happened between us was years ago, and I'd slowly gotten over that heartbreak. Although the feelings I kept trying to deny were starting to resurface, I knew I had to keep them at bay for the time being.

"So how's married life?" I asked, going through a box that had a few important files in it.

He shrugged his shoulders. "It is what it is. Can't expect too much when you're not married to the person you should be married to."

I opened my mouth with the intent to ask another question but closed it back shut when I couldn't come up with anything else to ask. What he just said kind of threw me for a loop and had me a little curious as well.

"Um, if your wife isn't who you wanted to be married to, then why get married at all? Why go through the whole process of buying a ring, having a big engagement party, and then this lavish-ass wedding, just to admit that you're not married to the right person?"

Lyfe stood from his chair and walked around to my side of the desk. The look in his eyes was one of determination, yet lust—all rolled into one. Pulling my chair back, he grabbed my hand and lifted me from my seat and pushed me against the wall. His hard body so close to mine, I could feel his heart beating through his chest. I tried to keep my head down because I knew if I looked up, what I'd wanted to do since he walked into this office would no doubt happen, and I didn't want to start anything between us right now, especially if he was still married to ole girl. I placed my hands on his chest to push him back a little, but he grabbed both of my wrists and pinned them above my head, and then lowered his lips to my ear.

"I went through that whole process because the person I should have married deserved so much more than what I could have given her at that time. I went through that whole process because I knew that if I would have begged you to stay like I wanted to, I would've ruined not only the friendship between Heim and me, but I would have ruined your life. I was young, dumb, and out there in these streets doing what I had to do to get to where I am today, and now that I have everything that I could possibly ever want, there's only one thing missing." His lips lightly brushed across my cheek and down my jawline until he got to my chin and softly pressed his lips against it, nudging my head up to look at him.

I swallowed the lump in my throat and tried to speak but couldn't.

"Do you know I flew out to Los Angeles?" he asked, looking me in my eyes. I slowly shook my head no, kind of shocked at what he just said. "I flew out there the night before I got married. Because in my heart, I knew I wasn't marrying the right woman for me. I went to your apartment, but you weren't there, so I had Kiko trace your phone to find out where you were. When I found you, you were at some little Italian restaurant on a date with some nerdy-looking nigga. I damn near lost it when I saw him kiss you on the lips and you smiled. He whispered something in your ear and then gave you some small box that was wrapped in some paper. You tore it open, and when you saw whatever it was that he bought you, your face lit up, and it was in that moment that I realized with me being as heavy as I was in the game at that time, moments like that, seeing that type of happiness all over you, would be far and few. That look you had on your face that day deserved to be on your face every day, and at that time, I knew I wouldn't be able to do that for you."

He kissed me on the spot behind my ear, and I felt my body shake. "But . . . but . . . You could do that for *her?*" I asked, voice barely audible.

"No, because she wasn't looking for that kind of love. Sarai was happy with being that ride-

or-die chick who would do anything for me, no questions asked. In return, all she wanted was that hood glory and to be feared by the same people who feared me."

"But you had to love her in some way. You . . . You gave her two kids."

"Whom I love dearly, but that doesn't mean I was in love with her."

"Lyfe, I can't—"

He kissed the side of my mouth. "You can't what?"

"I can't be—" I started to say but stopped when his mouth crashed down to mine, and his tongue invaded my mouth. I tried to find the strength somewhere to push him away, but my mind was saying one thing while my body was totally saying another. When his free hand slid around my waist and down to my ass, where he gripped it and pulled me closer in to him, the moan I'd been trying to hold back slipped from my mouth and into his.

"I've missed you, Savannah," he said between kisses. "And I'm going to do everything to make us right now that you're back in my life."

I wanted to believe what he was saying, but I wasn't too sure if it would ever be true. Especially if his wife wasn't feeling the same way he was when it came to them finally parting ways.

Lyfe and I were so into that spine-tingling kiss that neither one of us heard when Naheim walked back into my office.

"Nigga, what the fuck are you doing?" His tone was a little snappy. "Get the fuck off my sister. I already told you what you needed to handle before you even step to her. Until then, she's off-limits."

"I heard you the first time you said it." Lyfe slowly stepped away from me, but not before placing one last kiss on my lips and smiling. "What's up, Heim?"

"Man, look, we need to go. Kiko just called and said they finally found ole boy who was shooting in the club that night. Some little nigga who they've never seen before. They waiting on us to get there before they do anything to him."

My eyes traveled over to my brother. "Uh, you do know you are in a law office, don't you? Talking about going to kill somebody."

"And what that mean? Sis, you already know my get down. Now that you're back, who do you think I'm going to call if I ever get jammed up?"

I laughed and moved from in front of Lyfe and back over to my desk, wiping the sides of my mouth. "Boy, bye. I will need that $5,000 retainer fee before you even think about getting me to represent you. Now, both of y'all get the hell out since you're not going to help me finish unpacking the rest of my shit."

"I'm sorry, Savvy, I was on my way back in to help, but then got the call." He kissed me on my cheek. "I'll come back this weekend and help you out. I promise."

"Okay. Wait, not this weekend. I forgot I have a date. Maybe on Monday?"

"A date?" Lyfe asked, a scowl decorating his handsome face. "With who?"

"Nigga, get out of her business and let's go," Naheim interrupted. "I already told you, dead that other situation; then you can question her like that. Until then, she free to date and see whoever the fuck she wants to see."

"Now, isn't that the pot calling the kettle black? Does that same sermon you just preached apply to Reign too?" I asked my brother, laughing at the scowl that was now on his face.

"Don't get your girl fucked up, Savannah. I'll check on you later on tonight. There's a chili burger, fries, and Coke for you in the bags. Whatever is left over, throw it away or save it for later, okay? And tell my baby to answer the phone when I call." I nodded my head, ignoring that last part and watched my brother walk out of my office. Lyfe, who was still standing on the side of my desk, was staring a hole right through me.

"Yo, whoever you going out with this weekend, dead that shit after you get that free meal, or I'ma make sure you never hear from that nigga again." I smiled, which pissed him off a little more. "I'm not playing, Savannah. Play with me if you want. It's a lot of shit you don't know about me that you will soon learn. But you better make sure you let that nigga know—or *I* will."

"Let him know what? That I can't date him because I'm about to start fucking back with my first love who just happens to be married?"

"I don't give a fuck what you tell him, just as long as his ass loses your number." And with that said, Lyfe turned around and walked out of my office leaving me hotter than I just was after that kiss and contemplating on telling Hash to really lose my number—or not.

Lyfe

"Aye, what was all that about back there?" Heim asked as he hopped in the passenger seat of my new Audi R8 I just picked up this morning. "I thought we already had this discussion about you not stepping to li'l sis until after you end whatever it is you have with Sarai."

I waved him off. "You know as well as I do that the shit between Sarai and I has been over for a long time now."

"Does *she* know that?"

I thought about his question, and although my wife and I knew that the marriage we had was quickly dissolving, at times, it seemed like she wanted to try to work things out. Maybe back in the day and if Savannah never moved back to Charlotte, I may have felt the same way too, but after years and years of the arguing, lies, cheating, and her sneakiness, I was just flat-out done with whatever Sarai and I once had. Of course, we would have to be civilized with each other to coparent our children, but knowing Sarai, that might not be such an easy task.

"Nigga, she know our marriage isn't what it used to be, and she knows that my feelings for her have never been 100 percent. I brought up the notion of us getting a divorce a couple of years ago."

"And what happened?"

I shrugged my shoulders. "Just never went through with it. I brought it up, she somewhat agreed. I had the paperwork drawn up, but we never signed them."

Heim sent a text out on his phone, and then looked at me. "Do you think she will go for that shit now? I mean, Sarai probably was okay with it when she thought it was a mutual decision. But you know women, man . . . Once she finds out that Savvy had a little to do with it, she's going to go crazy."

I jumped on I-85 North, heading to the warehouse where Kiko and the rest of his team had the cat who shot up my club. Normally, I wouldn't get down with this part of the game, but because this muthafucka could've hit Savannah with his no-aiming ass, I made it my business to handle this nigga myself. Pressing my foot down on the gas a little harder, I zipped along the highway like I was on a mission, thoughts of Savannah and those soft lips on my mind. It took everything in me not to throw her on top of her desk and fuck the shit out of her, but I knew Heim would more than likely walk back in at any minute. I didn't know what it was about Savannah, but I couldn't get her out of my system for nothing. Years had passed, and I'd had my countless share of women, even married one, but not one of them could get me to forget about her, and as much as I had a feeling she would deny it, I could tell that she hadn't stopped thinking about me either.

"Aye, you OK, man? You can daydream when you in the car by yourself, but with me in this muthafucka, nigga, I'ma need you to keep your eyes on the damn road." Heim laughed, breaking me from my thoughts of his sister. "What you over there thinking about anyway?"

"Shit, nothing really. Just hoping whoever this nigga is we about to handle tells us something."

"I feel you on that. And I hope the nigga talks fast. I got shit to do after this."

I looked over at Heim. "Shit like what? I hope it doesn't involve Peaches's crazy ass."

He laughed and shook his head. "Crazy ain't even the word to describe her ghetto ass. I wanna drop her and try to do right with Reign, but I can't. As much as I hate that hood rat attitude she has, that shit is a major turn-on to me. Especially when she rolls with me sometime to pick up—"

"Nigga, please don't tell me you have her ass rolling around with you when you do the pickups and drop-offs?" I interrupted, already feeling my attitude shooting up to ten.

"Sometimes when Kiko has Man and Brutus doing other shit, I take her with me."

"So not only does her ass know where all of our dope houses are, but she knows the locations of where we keep most of the money and the majority of our product?"

He waved me off. "Man, you sleeping on Peaches. I'm telling you, she real sick with her gun and could be a good asset to the team. I don't know why you won't let her head up that little storage setup. It's not like we about to have a lot of traffic over there. We just need another place to stash our shit."

"I don't want her to head up nothing in our operation because I don't trust her ass. And on some real shit, you shouldn't either. She don't move right to me; never has. Any bitch that tries to fuck your homeboys or family is not to be trusted in my eyes."

Heim smacked his lips. "Man, you just need to give her a chance. I'm telling you, we can trust her. If she slips up and some shit even seem suspect, you know I'll kill that bitch with no questions asked. I mean, the head is out of this world, and the pussy is good, but I don't love her ass. Don't like her mama too much neither, so I wouldn't feel shit if it ever came down to me having to handle her."

I nodded my head and continued to focus on the road as I thought about everything my nigga just said. I still didn't trust her ass, but if he felt like she would be a good fit and could handle the little storage setup, then I would give it some thought. I planned on having that new storage facility opened up next week and needed to have it staffed as soon as possible. Yeah, putting her on would require a little more thinking on my part, but right now, it would have to wait.

Pulling up into the warehouse, I whipped my ride through the front of the empty parking lot and pulled up in the back, behind Kiko's black Denali. Heim and I both exited the car at the same time and walked through the small metal door on the side of the building. As soon as we stepped over the threshold and into the dimly lit space, I could see a young boy hanging from the steel beams in the ceiling by his arms, slowly spinning around, his face showing no type of emotion or fear at all.

"So this the little muthafucka that got to blasting in my club, huh?" I asked to the few faces standing around, but not really looking for an answer.

"Yeah, this little bastard tried to blast at us too when we kicked the door in, but Man did some karate shit and kicked the gun out his hand," Kiko laughed.

I walked over to him with death in my eyes and looked closely in his face. His dark eyes slanted a little as he stared back at me with the same look. I smirked and chuckled a little, thinking about how much heart the young nigga had. Reminded me of myself when I was around his age. Never showing fear to anyone. Wasn't much good in that shit, though, but it made me the man I am today.

Tired of the silent threats being sent to me through his eyes, I snatched the duct tape from his mouth. "What's your name?" I questioned, anger all over my tone.

"Fuck you."

"Oh, shit. Little nigga got heart." Heim laughed.

"A little. But let's see how much heart he has when I place my gun between his eyes," Kiko added, pulling his piece from behind his back.

"You good, Kiko, I'ma handle this one," I cautioned.

"But, Lyfe—"

I raised my hand, cutting him off. "I know it's your job to dispose of our threats and problems, but this one was kind of personal to me, so I'll handle it."

Without saying another word, Kiko placed his gun back behind his back and stepped over to the side, allowing me to walk past him.

"Now where were we?" I asked, walking over to the wooden table that held various tools used for torture. A coppery smell of fresh and old blood mixed with the musty smell of the warehouse filled the air. I picked up a long thick link chain and wrapped it around my hand several times, leaving about three feet hanging off, but not before putting on the plastic jumpsuit that would keep the blood spatter from ruining my clothes. I turned around back to the boy and had to laugh at his face now. The fearless look he had a few seconds ago was gone.

"Please don't do this," he begged. Tears began to roll from his eyes while his lips started to shake.

"Don't do what? And what happened to all that bass you had in your voice a few minutes ago when you said fuck me?" I gritted, slowly circling around his hanging body. The fresh stench of urine now added to the air.

"Lyfe, please don't kill me, man."

"Please don't kill you? Oh, so now you wanna talk?" I looked up to the little nigga who I could tell already knew what his fate would be if he didn't say anything, but still managed to shake his head no with the little bit of heart he must've had left. "No, huh? Well, suit yourself," was all I said before I started to forcefully swing the chain on every part of his body. Blood began to pour from his nose when I whipped the metal links across his face, the sound of some bone cracking when I landed a few hits to his chest.

"Ahhhhhhh! No . . . no . . . Ahhh," he screamed out in obvious pain, which, ironically, sounded like music to my ears. I looked over at Heim and Kiko, who kept turning their heads away with every lash. They had seen me beat niggas on the regular, but none as brutal as this.

"Damn, nigga, you gon' bust his shit open until you see skull or something?" Heim asked on the verge of throwing up. The nigga didn't have a problem pulling the trigger, but couldn't stand the sight of open flesh and blood.

A little winded, I stopped swinging the chain and caught my breath. Pulling a Cuban cigar from my pocket, I lit it up and took a few puffs.

"That shit just took a lot out of me. I wonder if this nigga feels like giving me his name yet."

"Yo, what's ya name, homie?" Kiko stepped up and asked. "I know you don't want to go through another round of that shit."

He raised his head, blood dripping over his eye from the deep cut above his eyebrow. "It's, it's Quick. My . . . My name is Quick," he managed through tears.

"Quick, huh? How old are you, Quick?"

He began to cry a little harder, knowing that his life was about to be over. Did I feel sorry for the nigga? Hell no. Just like he didn't feel sorry for shooting my shit up. The only thing that he could do now was answer my questions to try to prolong his pending death.

"I'm nineteen, bruh, please don't kill me. I'm sorry, I swear," Quick begged.

"Yeah, nigga, I agree with you. You're one sorry-ass nigga," I laughed, blowing smoke in his face. Turning back to the table, I laid the bloody chain on top of the plastic tarp and grabbed a container of sulfuric acid. "Who sent you to my club?"

"Man, he gon' kill my mama and my sisters if I tell you."

"Who is *he?*" Heim asked, walking back from the corner where he was throwing up.

Quick slowly shook his head. "I already know you're going to kill me either way, and I'm not about to let my mama and sisters end up the same way."

My eyes traveled over to Heim who had the biggest smile on his face. "What the hell you smiling about?"

"You know his little ass reminds me of you."

I nodded my head. "I thought the same thing too, but this nigga could never be me."

"Why you say that."

"Because had it been me walking into that club, I wouldn't have missed," I said as I doused Quick's body with the sulfuric acid. "Feels good, doesn't it, nigga?" I taunted. Quick was yelling in excruciating pain, and I was getting a rush making his ass pay for what he had done. There's no remorse for a nigga trying to bring another black man down in my books, and his ass needed to be taught this lesson. After about an hour of continuous torture, Quick's body just hung from the steel beams lifeless. "Handle that," I tossed over my shoulder looking at Man and Kiko as I walked out of the warehouse, Heim right behind me.

"You know he probably would've given us a name, right?"

"Probably, but he had already wasted enough of my time. I'm pretty sure something will come up, and whoever is gunning for us will try again."

Stripping out of the plastic jumpsuit, I bunched it up in my hand and threw it down the chute that led to the incinerator, followed by the gloves and the white button-down shirt that I had on.

"You think whoever it is will try again?" Heim asked as we walked to my car. "If so, I might get someone to shadow Savvy around now that she's back in town. You know I'll fucking die if something happened to her behind me. That's why I kind of wished she opened up her firm out there in Los Angeles. At least until I got out of the game and no one would try to use her as a way to get to me."

What Heim had just said ran through my mind, and I couldn't agree more with having someone shadow Savvy around. Sarai and the kids too, until we find who is after us and rectify the situation. "Yeah, hit Kiko and tell him to get somebody on Savvy, Sarai, and my kids. You might wanna have him put someone on Reign's house too, just in case. I'll hit Bryant up and see if his contact has heard anything, and when I go to this meeting with Cody, I'll see what the word on the street is."

Heim nodded his head and sent a text to Kiko. Pulling out of the warehouse parking lot, my mind shifted back to Savannah and what she could possibly be doing right now. Just thinking about the way her body looked in them tight-ass jeans and thin-ass tank top had my dick rising up a bit. I wondered if she was still at her office setting shit up or was she back at home. Maybe I should stop by and spend a little more time with her before I headed home. I could use a little of the peace and serenity she provided before I went to the hell Sarai had me in.

"Aye, you think Savvy still at the office?"

"Why, nigga?" Heim asked, cutting his eyes at me. "Shouldn't you be taking your ass home to spend some time with your *wife* and kids? I could've swore you just hopped off a plane a few hours ago from being gone a week."

I laughed. "I did, but what does that have to do with anything?"

"Like I keep telling your ass, handle your shit at home before you step to my sister. I ain't playing with your ass, nigga. Don't end up looking like that fool Quick fucking with me."

"I ain't gonna look like shit. Especially with the way your ass was throwing up all over the place back there." We laughed. "Naw, but for real, I heard you the first time you said it, and

I hear you now. I won't step to Savvy until after I leave Sarai." Sticking my hand out over the center console, I waited for Heim to smack his hand in mine. Once he did so, we pulled in for a brotherly hug, and no other words were spoken.

Yeah, I just promised my mans that I wouldn't step to Savvy until this thing with Sarai and me was done, but that didn't mean I had to stay away from her. Until then, I guess I'd just head home and spend some time with my family. Well, my kids, at least.

Sarai

I looked up at the clock on the wall for the hundredth time, praying that my husband didn't walk through the door anytime soon. He'd been gone for a week and was scheduled to come back today, but I didn't know when he would show up. If Lyfe got wind of what I'd been up to for a while now, he'd probably fuck around and kill me for real.

"Bitch, will you hurry the fuck up. I'm not no drug dealer, and if your husband catch us in here, he's gonna kill me *and* you."

"Don't you think I know that?" I asked, sucking my teeth. "I do this shit all of the time, so stop tripping. And instead of standing there shaking like a fucking leaf and sweating like a ho in church, why don't you come over here and help me do this shit?" I yelled back at Desiree as I cracked open a freshly packed brick of cocaine, ignoring her attempts at changing my mind about taking some of Lyfe's stash. I chuckled, shaking the aluminum pan the cocaine was in and looked back at her scary ass. "Besides, Lyfe gave me a pass to do me whenever I needed to. He just don't know that what I'm doing is coming from *his* ass."

Desiree handed me one of the big black Prada duffle bags I had on the floor. "Your ass is playing with fire, Sarai. It's one thing to steal a couple'a dollars from your man, but this . . ." She shook her head. "Even I wouldn't do no shit like this, and you know I'm all about my money."

I rolled my eyes and continued to fondle the coke. Desiree didn't understand shit between my husband and me, and I wasn't expecting her to. Yeah, to someone on the outside looking in, it would seem as if I was stealing from Lyfe, and in a small sense, maybe I was. But it wasn't like he didn't give me permission to. Lyfe always told me that if I ever needed to make some extra money, I could tap into his stash and sell some work to my two brothers. The problem with that was, the pass that he gave me to dip into his stash was years ago, before we got married and had kids. Plus, my oldest brother Roc was locked up doing life, and my other brother Hillz was dead. With them no longer in the picture, it forced me to sell coke to these other niggas out in the streets that I knew. In any event,

Lyfe wasn't aware of what I'd been up to, and I wasn't planning on stopping anytime soon. The money was way too good to give up and had my personal account looking right. Just in case his ass tried to bring up that divorce bullshit again, I wanted to be sitting on a nice little nest egg to tide me over until I found the next nigga to come up on or finally put my degree in accounting to work.

I started to fill the duffle bag. "Well, see, that's the difference between me and you, Desiree. I'm not gonna steal a few measly dollars and be satisfied. If I'ma rob a bank, I'ma rob a *big* bank."

"But you're not robbing a bank, Sarai, you're robbing Lyfe."

"Desiree, when I said—You know what?" I shook my head. "Never mind. Just hand me the other bag so I can put the rest of these pans in there." I don't know why I continued to remain friends with her ditzy ass. But what could I expect? Desiree fell from the same tree as her dumb-ass cousin Peaches, and I was friends with her first.

Back in the day when my brothers and I moved from Virginia to Charlotte, it was Peaches who I met in the beginning. My auntie, who we came to live with, stayed across the street from her people. One day while I was sitting outside on the porch, minding my own business, Peaches made it her business to come over to my aunt's yard to ask me who I was and to let me know that Billy Green from down the street was off-limits. Me, being the type of chick that didn't take too kindly to threats, cursed her ass out six ways to Sunday. We verbally went back and forth for about ten minutes before I got tired of all the yelling and slapped the shit out of her. Needless to say, we fought right there on my aunt's front porch until my brother Roc and her cousin Skeet broke us up. We stayed enemies for about four weeks before we decided to say fuck it and just become friends. Roc and Skeet started hanging around real tough, so I was around her ass all of the time anyway. Not too long after that, Desiree moved in with Peaches and her family, and she and I started to hang out. By the time we got to high school, Desiree and I were glued to the hip and doing normal things teenagers did while Peaches was in the face of whatever nigga was hot at the moment.

I gotta give it to Peaches, though, it was because of her that I met Lyfe. The nigga she was fucking with at the time had a party at his house and Desiree and I decided to go. We were sitting around drinking and laughing for a few hours when Lyfe, Naheim, and the rest of their crew walked in. I'm not gonna lie, each one of them niggas was lookin' right and could've easily gotten my number, but there was something about Lyfe that stood out to me more than the rest. I mean, it wasn't love at first sight or anything like that, but something about him did have me feeling all tingly on the inside. Lyfe was fine as hell back then and keeping it one hunnid. My husband still had it going on. You don't know how many bitches I had to check or damn near put on life support behind his sexy ass. I didn't play when it came to my man, even though I knew he didn't love me like I loved him.

With me, it was all about a respect thing. Lyfe respected me as his wife and never brought any of his outside affairs to my face, and I respected him and continued to stay that down-ass bitch he pretty much groomed me to be. I shook my head just thinking about all the shit I've done for that man. He'll never find another like me.

"Are you almost done?" I heard Desiree's shaky voice ask.

"Here." I handed her one of the duffle bags. "You hold this one, and I'll grab the other two."

"What do you want me to do with this?"

I looked at this bitch like she was crazy. "What else, Desiree? Help me carry it out to the car. I'm going to drop a few deliveries off today and do the rest in the next couple of days."

"So you just gonna drive around with all this cocaine in your car? What if the police pull you over?"

Standing up from my crouched position on the floor, I stood to my full height and straightened my pants out. Looking at myself in the full-length mirror in our closet, I made sure the rest of my outfit was in place before I smoothed my hand over my jet-black hair which was in a sleek ponytail. Picking up the two duffel bags, I headed out of my room and down the short flight of stairs with Desiree hot on my trail.

"Where the kids at?" she asked, bumping into me as she frantically looked around.

"They're at my aunt's house. Why?"

She shrugged her shoulders. "I don't know. I'm just used to seeing them running around the house whenever I come over."

"Girl, you already know when Lyfe is gone, our kids are too. It's the only way I can handle my business. Especially with these niggas callin' all times of the night for this shit."

We walked into the four-car garage, and I popped the trunk to the Model S Tesla Lyfe bought me for my birthday a few months ago.

"Why you asking all these questions? You working for the feds now or something?" I eyed

Desiree as she handed me the duffle bag that was in her hand. Best friend or not, if I even *thought* she was talking to the law, I'd kill her ass before she could blink. And just to remind her that I wasn't unfamiliar with the feel of cold metal in my hand, I pulled the small nine I had stashed in the side of my trunk and cocked it back.

"Why the hell you cocking that gun back and shit?"

I wanted to laugh so bad at the look on her face, but I needed Desiree to see how serious I was about my freedom, just in case she was out here feeding information to the law. "I'm just making sure the clip isn't empty. Never know when I may have to use it." My eyes connected with hers, hoping she took heed to my silent warning.

"I hear you and all, but can you put that shit away? I'm already risking my life in here with these stolen pans of cocaine. I don't want you to accidentally shoot me too."

"Bitch, please. You already know my aim is on point." I laughed, putting the last bag in the trunk and finally changing the subject. "What's up with Peaches? Have you seen her lately?"

I could tell by the way that Desiree's breathing began to slow down that she was relieved by the subject change. "Naw, not since she started fucking with Naheim real heavy. She did call me the other night to ride out with her to some girl's house, but I was already in bed."

"Did she say whose house it was?"

"Some chick that Naheim keeps running back to . . . Summer, Autumn, something like that."

"Reign?"

"Yeah, I think that's her name."

I smacked my lips and rolled my eyes at the mention of that bitch's name. I mean, Reign and I had never had any real beef, but I knew Lyfe had some type of history with her best friend, who was now living in California. Anytime I asked him about her, he would always tell me that it was none of my business. I tried to get some info on the bitch from Reign one time when we were at Lyfe's club together, but she acted like she couldn't tell me shit either. The only thing I knew about the girl, besides her being Reign's best friend, was that she was Naheim's sister and she was going to school to be a lawyer. Never met her or anything. Didn't even know how she looked.

Anytime she was in town, it was like she dipped in and dipped right back out. Didn't stay for long periods of time or anything. Kind of like she was trying to dodge seeing somebody. I don't know. As long as she didn't bring her ass back around here trying to break up what Lyfe and I had going, then I was good.

"Peaches is gon' fuck around and get the shit beat out of her one day if she keeps rolling up to people's houses like that," I said to Desiree as I hopped into the front seat of my car. She opened the passenger side and slid in.

"I keep telling her that, but she won't listen. I don't know what Naheim did to her ass, but he got her acting way out of character." I plugged the location to my first drop-off in the GPS. "Oh, did you hear about what happened at the club last week?" Absently shaking my head no, I continued to listen to Desiree speak. "Some nigga came up in there shooting, and they had to shut the place down."

Pulling out of the garage, I hit the button on the remote to close the door. "How you know that?" I didn't remember Lyfe mentioning anything about a shooting before he left. Normally, he shares that type of shit with me, but not this time. *Hmmmm.* What the fuck was up with that?

"Peaches told me. Said the nigga was aiming for Lyfe and Naheim but couldn't shoot worth shit." She paused for a second, and I could feel her eyes on me, so I turned my gaze to her.

"What?"

"How are things with you and Lyfe?"

"Great. Why?" I lied, a fake smile plastered all over my face.

She smacked her lips. "Keep it real, Sarai. Y'all good or what?"

I could feel my eyes becoming a little misty, but I wasn't about to let her see me cry. "You know, things between Lyfe and I are good. They haven't been the best, but we're good."

What went on between my husband and me was none of her business. I did tell her some things here and there, but she didn't need to know that we haven't been getting along for some time now and that he and I had been arguing for the last few months like crazy. So much so that we were sleeping in separate rooms. Something was different about him, and I couldn't put my finger on it. A part of me wanted to say fuck it and give him the divorce he's been asking for, but I just couldn't let this lifestyle go. Having all these perks of being married to the biggest supplier in Charlotte was addicting. I've been queen-pin for a while now, and I wasn't ready for it to stop.

"Has he brought up that divorce shit again?"

"Yo, why you asking me all of these questions? You know something I don't about my husband?

You about to serve me some papers or something?"

"Naw, I was just going to tell you to keep your eyes open. Peaches told me that he had his attention focused on some girl on the dance floor the whole night. She didn't get to see who it was, but she thinks it was Naheim's sister."

"Naheim's sister? Isn't she in California?"

"Not anymore. According to Peaches, she just moved back into town. That's who Lyfe and Naheim gave the party for that night."

I shook my head as we pulled up to the destination. Something about Naheim's sister being back in town had me feeling some type of way. Even though I didn't know her, I knew that her presence was going to potentially be a threat to my marriage and all that it held for me. And I'd be damned if I let the next bitch take the lifestyle I'd worked so hard for.

Savannah

"Maybe it's best if we end whatever it is that we have right now, Savvy. I mean, you a nigga's heart and all, but I don't want you to miss out on making your dreams come true."

"But my dreams include you too, Lyfe. Don't you see that?" I cried. "There are plenty of colleges around here that I can go to. UNC, Duke, FSU—Look." I gathered up all of the college acceptance letters from my bed and shoved them in his chest. "I've been accepted into every one of them. Just tell me you want me to stay. Please, babe, just tell me you don't want me to leave."

My wet eyes watched as Lyfe went through a roller coaster of emotions of his own. But I knew the minute he looked at me with a blank stare on his face that his decision to break up with me was final. "Look, I didn't want you to find out like this, but," he closed his eyes and let out a frustrated breath, "I've been seeing somebody else. And shorty kind of got my attention."

I shook my head, confused. "Seeing someone else? Who is she? Do I know her?"

"No, you don't know her, Savvy. What I look like fucking with somebody you know?"

"Is that supposed to make me feel better?"

Lyfe stepped back from my reach and grabbed his keys off of my dresser. "I didn't say it to make you feel any type of way. I told you that so that you can see that going to California is the best choice for you right now. Forget about me. Forget about us. Go handle your business and make something of yourself, ma."

My heart literally fell to the bottom of my stomach. A life without Lyfe? I waited years for him to look at me the way that he did now, and three months into our relationship, he wanted to send me off, heartbroken and without him? I walked back into his space, only for him to create more distance. Why was he doing this me? To us? Lyfe told me that I was the first and probably will be the only girl he'd ever loved. But what kind of love was this? It felt as if he was trying to hurt me on purpose. Was he lying? Was he really seeing another girl besides me? The tears that were falling from my eyes began to cloud my vision. The idea of him being with someone else had my blood pressure rising and my throat going dry. My stomach started hurting, and my chest started to ache. Before I knew what was happening, my breathing began to pick up, and I couldn't catch my breath for anything.

"Savannah," Lyfe cried, urgency in his voice. "Baby, are you okay?" His arms circled around my waist, and he pulled me into his chest, his scent invading everything around me. The minute my body connected to his, I closed my eyes and could feel my lungs start to slowly expand, allowing the air I was trying to catch a few seconds ago to enter my body. Lyfe kissed the top of my head and pulled me closer to him. It felt like I was in his arms forever and everything he'd just said was a lie—but then reality hit me hard when he spoke again. "I'm not good for you, Savvy. At least not right now. Maybe once you graduate and come back, we can give us another try. Until then, you need to handle your business and forget about me."

"But I don't want to be without you. We can make this work, Lyfe. I'll fly home every other weekend. Come back every winter, spring, and summer break. I'll even forgive you for talking to that other girl."

Lyfe grabbed my chin and lifted my face up so that I was staring into those bright eyes of his that made my heart swell every time I looked into them. "Ma . . ." Pressing his forehead to mine, he shook his head. "You will always have my heart. No one but you. Remember that." After kissing me on my lips one last time, he walked out of my bedroom, my heart, and my life without another glance. I sat in my room for days and cried. I called and texted Lyfe maybe a thousand times and never got a response. The day before I left, I tried my luck one last time, hoping he would answer and just tell me to stay, but instead of his sexy and low voice, I was met with that automated bitch who likes to tell you when someone's number has been disconnected.

"Uhhh, hello?" Reign snapped her fingers breaking me from my thoughts.

Ever since the kiss Lyfe and I shared in my office a couple of weeks ago, I'd been thinking about him and the relationship we had before I left. The way he kissed me that day felt as if he still had the same amount of love for me now as back then. I knew he said I would always have his heart, but that was kind of hard to believe seeing as he married the same chick he confessed to cheating on me with.

"Uhhh, I know you hear me talking to you, Savannah. Don't tell me you're over there thinking about Lyfe's ass again."

"Like you weren't thinking about Heim a second ago when I was talking to you?"

She rolled her eyes and plopped back down on my couch. "Ain't nobody thinking about your dumb-ass brother. I told you, I am totally over that nigga. Peaches can have his bitch ass."

I heard her talking, but I didn't believe a word Reign's ass was saying, although I was kind of surprised when she told me that she and her neighbor had exchanged numbers and had been talking for a little while now. But I still didn't believe her. Reign may have been trying to get over my brother, but we both knew that Heim wasn't about to let that happen. Not as much as his ass has been questioning me about Reign and what she'd been up to. Even with Peaches's scheming ass still in the picture, he wouldn't let my girl go. Hopefully, it worked out for them. If not, as long as Reign was happy, I was happy, whether she was back fucking with Naheim or someone completely new.

My phone buzzed on the coffee table, and I picked it up, giddiness all over me. For the last hour, I had been flirting, going back and forth with Hash, while trying to catch up on the few episodes of *House of Cards* that I missed. I could feel Reign's curious eyes on me, but I didn't care. Picking up my glass of wine and taking a sip, a small smile crossed my face as I read the message that was just sent. Hash sure did know how to keep a smile on a girl's face. And just to think, I almost passed him up, thinking Lyfe and I could pick up where we left off.

"Who got you smiling like that?" Reign asked, throwing a piece of popcorn from the big bowl she had on her lap and hitting me on the cheek.

"If you must know, it's Hash."

Slowly nodding her head, Reign focused her eyes back on the TV screen, but not before stuffing a handful of the buttery popped kernels in her mouth. I could see the question on the tip of her tongue dancing around in her head, so I wasn't surprised when she spoke again. "So you really gon' continue talking to him after Lyfe told you to stop?"

"Lyfe doesn't run shit but his mouth. He can kiss my ass and any other part of my body where the sun doesn't shine."

Reign laughed and shook her head. "You planning that boy's funeral, and he don't even know it."

"Funeral? Girl, bye. Lyfe isn't worried about me and who I'm seeing. He was just talking crazy, that's all."

"If you say so."

I grabbed a handful of popcorn from the bowl and threw a few pieces into my mouth. Reign's comment was playing over in my mind. Would Lyfe really try to do something to Hash if I continued to see him? Naw. It had been a couple of weeks, and he hadn't said anything about it. Nor had Naheim, and he knew that I'd been out on a few dates with Hash. Hash even came and helped me repaint a few walls in my office and do some other cosmetic maintenance to the large space. Heim was there a few times too. Granted, they didn't really say too much to each other. My brother had seen him around, and I was sure he'd mentioned it to Lyfe. Reign didn't know what she was talking about. I was the furthest thing from that man's mind.

We sat and watched a few more episodes of *House of Cards* until our stomachs started to growl. Not feeling like cooking anything to satisfy our hunger, we opted for some pizza.

"The food should be here in about thirty minutes. What do you want to watch until then? I don't want to start another binge session until the pizza gets here."

"Let's watch that episode of *A Different World* with Tupac when he played Piccolo. That's my favorite one," Reign suggested.

I scrolled through Netflix until I found the show, and then turned on the episode she was talking about. While the opening credits were rolling, I decided to see where Reign's head was really at when it came to my brother.

"Has Heim called you today?"

"Thirty-two times. I'ma start calling his ass Magic in a minute."

I laughed. "Leave my brother alone. You should answer at least one of his calls to see what he has to say. You never know, it might be what you want to hear."

"That's the problem, Savannah. Heim is always telling me what I want to hear, and I fall right for that shit. Not this time, though. If that nigga wants me to come back to him, he has to prove to me that he's ready for the type of relationship I want."

"And what type of relationship is that?" I never questioned Reign or Heim about their situation, but I was kind of curious on where she thought they would be in the future.

Reign poured herself another glass of wine and downed the whole thing in one gulp. After filling up her third glass, she slouched down on the couch with a sad look on her face. I knew she was really missing Naheim, but I also knew that she was tired of his bullshit. His ass knew damn well Peaches coming to her house was a straight violation, which should've resulted in him checking the fuck out of her and kicking her ghetto ass to the curb, but for some reason, he was still fucking with her.

"I used to think that Naheim and I would fall in love, get married, and have a tribe full of babies. And on some real shit, he told me that he thought the same thing. But now, I'm not too sure if I see a future with Heim. After going through all of this bullshit—the jumpoffs, almost baby mamas, bitches who think that just because they sucked his dick that he was only exclusive to them." She shook her head, and her eyes became misty.

"Savvy, I love your brother. I really do. But I'm tired. I'm so fucking tired of all of the lies, the cheating, coming and going when he pleases. I . . . I . . . I can't do it anymore. And you know what the funny thing is?" Reign looked at me, and I just took a sip of my wine, silently telling her to continue. "Even after all the shit he's done to me, I *still* love him. Still would carry his child if he asked me to. But, I see now that I deserve better. I want better. I need better. And Heim isn't ready to give me that."

I rose from my seat on the couch across from Reign and sat next to my best friend. When she started to sob uncontrollably, I wrapped my arms around her and pulled her into me. Her small body shook so hard, it caused my own to vibrate a little. After what seemed like ten minutes of her getting everything out, Reign corrected her posture, wiped the last few tears that had fallen with the sleeve of her shirt, and put a smile on her face.

"That was the last time I plan to shed any kind of tears for your brother. From now on, if they aren't tears of joy, you won't see them coming from me." The doorbell rang, and Reign got up from her seat. "I have a ten in my wallet. Put that with your money on the pizza. I gotta go to the bathroom right quick."

"You sure you okay?" I asked, concerned for my friend and heart.

She nodded her head. "I'm good. Now hurry up and go pay the pizza man. I'm hungry as hell."

I watched Reign until she disappeared to the back of my home, with her cell phone nestled in her hand. I wondered if she was going to call her new friend, the neighbor, or go and read the text messages I was sure my brother has sent to her. Reaching into her bag, I removed the ten-dollar bill and then went to retrieve the rest of the money from my purse. The doorbell rang again, and I almost snapped. If this fool wanted a tip, it would be wise for him to have a little patience. I walked toward my front door, but not before glancing at myself in the mirror. Pulling at the cheeky track shorts I had on, I made sure my ass wasn't hanging from the bottom and that the white tank top I had on didn't give the delivery guy too much of a peepshow. With my hair in a high bun on the top of my head and a makeup-free face, I opened the door with the money already out, expecting to see some young, acne-prone, high school dude with a shitty atti-tude, but stopped dead in my tracks when those light brown irises connected to mine.

"Lyfe—" breathlessly left my lips. I don't know what it was about his eyes, but those damn things got me every time. He smiled the only way he does, and I felt my insides start to moisten up. He looked sexy as hell right now, and I couldn't even deny it. The last few times I ran into Lyfe, he was dressed all businesslike, with a suit and some shiny loafers to match. But right now, he was dressed down and looking like the boy I met on my twelfth birthday, just a little older.

He licked his lips, and I watched as his eyes roamed over my body's entire frame from head to toe. When his gaze stopped at my breasts, I knew he saw my pebbled nipples through the thin cotton tank.

"You always answer the door like this?"

"Not really. But I thought you were the pizza guy, so it was going to be quick. What are you doing here?"

"I gotta have a reason to come see you?"

"When you're married, yes."

His eyes looked over my shoulder and right to the table with the two glasses of wine. "Why you not inviting me in? You got company or something?"

I looked over my shoulder at what could've been a date night scene, and then back to Lyfe. What did it matter if I had company? He wasn't my daddy or my man. Those eyes continued to survey my body, and I could feel the hotness building at my core. Crossing my arms over my traitorous breasts, I put all of my weight on one leg and stared back at him.

"How can I help you, Lyfe? Did you need anything? Is Heim okay?" I started to panic. "He told me that you guys were chilling at the club tonight."

Lyfe chuckled at the frantic look on my face. "Heim is good. They're at the club right now, and I was there too. But I wanted to come check up on you and see how everything is going with the office and all."

This nigga wasn't slick. The same way he had been texting me with those good morning and good night text messages is the same way he could've checked on me now. The jiggle of keys behind me told me that Reign was back in the living room, but what I wasn't expecting was to see her fully dressed and walking out of my house with a big smile on her face.

"Where you going? I thought we were chilling tonight. You know I open up my office Monday, so this will more than likely be the last weekend I get to hang out with you."

"We can do lunch sometime during the week, and I got a key to your shit, so it isn't like I can't let myself in whenever I want to," Reign said. She turned to Lyfe. "Hey, bruh, what you doing on this side of town?"

"Trying to get my girl back."

Was this fool serious? How was he trying to get me back when he had a whole family not too far from where I lived? Get my girl back, my ass. Like I said before, I'm not no home wrecker, and he had me fucked up if he thought I was going to be, even if that kiss last time snatched my soul and took it hostage. Nope. Not me. Besides, I was enjoying this thing I had going with Hash.

"Well, all right, then, bruh." Reign dapped him up. "Take it easy on my girl." She winked at him and then smiled back at me. This heffa wasn't slick either. Pretty convenient how he showed up at my doorstep thirty minutes after she walked to the back of my house with her phone. I didn't win all those cases while I was interning back in California being naive. Being a lawyer meant that you had a sixth sense sometimes and could smell some bullshit from a mile away. "Call me in the morning, girl. I'm sure we will have lots to talk about."

Reign walked off laughing, and I knew right then I had been set up. His ass must've started to text her when I did not respond to any of his texts earlier.

"So can I come in or nah?"

Rolling my eyes, I stepped back and allowed Lyfe to walk in. When he walked past me, his cologne had me weak at the knees.

Get it together, Savannah. I tried to pep myself, but the more I inhaled his scent, the weaker I became. Taking off his tan blazer, my eyes scanned over his broad shoulders, the muscles in his back, and the ones in his arms. Milk and life had obviously done his body good. The white V-neck he had on clung to every bicep and ab you could think off, while the white jeans sat low on his hips with a belt the same color as his blazer. The all-white Louis Vuitton boxing sneakers set the outfit off just right and had Lyfe looking sexy as hell. Obviously on his grown-man shit. A far cry from the young nigga who dumped me.

He sat on the couch, and I followed suit, sitting on the love seat across from him. We needed some distance between us, or wasn't no telling what could happen. My phone buzzed. He picked it up, snatching it right from my grasp. I could tell he didn't like whatever message Hash had just sent me, because his facial expression turned dark.

"Yo, you still talking to this nigga?"

"Mama gotta have a life too," I responded, throwing a few pieces of popcorn in my mouth.

He squinted his eyes and looked at me. "You fucking this nigga?"

My hand was midway to my mouth with some more popcorn, but I stopped when I heard what he asked.

"Who *I'm* fucking should be of no concern to you. Especially when you—"

He cut me off. "Got a wife at home. How many times are you going to remind me of that?"

"As many times as it takes for you to leave me the hell alone and go home to her. Why are you over here again? Besides questioning me about who I'm fucking."

He smirked, and I hated my body for reacting to that shit. "You ain't fucking that nigga."

"How you know?"

"You've never been a good liar, Savvy. I don't know how you became a lawyer. I could just look at you and see right through your bullshit."

I shrugged my shoulders, not caring about what he could do back in the day. Picking up the remote, I scrolled back through Netflix until I found *House of Cards* again. I was just about to play the next episode when Lyfe asked me where the bathroom was.

"I'm pretty sure you been in this house just like Heim did before I moved in, so I already know you know where it's located."

He smiled and stood up. Again, my traitorous body betrayed me. "But I want you to show me." Sticking his hand out, he stood in front of me and waited for me to take it. Lyfe's ass knew what he was doing, but I kept telling myself to remain strong around this man. He'd always had the ability to make me putty in his hands, and I didn't think that part of our lives had changed.

Pushing his hand out of the way, I stood up on my own and tried to walk past him, but stopped when his arm snaked around my waist.

My heart started to beat fast, and the hairs on the back of my arm began to rise. I licked my lips and tried to control my breathing, but his face inching closer to the side of mine caused my lungs to quicken their pace. When his soft lips grazed my ear, a low moan escaped my lips. I moved my head over, trying to dodge the next kiss to my lobe, but all that did was expose my neck which he latched on to the minute I absently gave him access to it.

"Lyfe . . ." lightly floated out of my mouth. "What . . . What are you doing?"

His growl on my neck caused my nipples to harden even more. "Tell me you don't want me and I'll leave you alone. Tell me you didn't feel anything when we kissed in your office, and I'll leave you alone."

I tried to open my mouth and object to something he was saying, but nothing came out. A chill ran down my body, causing goose bumps to decorate every inch of it. I tried to step out of his embrace because I knew if I didn't, that we would cross a line we weren't ready for, but when he turned me to face him and took my lips into his, any thought of being a home wrecker flew out of my mind and through the window.

I was a little hesitant at first, but when his tongue invaded my mouth to find mine, it was like I was under a spell when they finally connected. Whatever emotions he was trying to convey behind this kiss could be felt throughout my entire body, and I had no problem accepting it.

"I missed you," he mumbled against my lips.

"I missed you too," I finally admitted back.

"I'm only with her because of the kids, Savannah. Nothing else. You are the only one I've ever loved and would ever give my love to. Nobody else, baby." Pulling me closer to him, Lyfe's hand traveled down my back and my ass until they were on my thighs. Lifting me from the ground, I parted my legs and wrapped them around his waist as our lips connected again. What we were doing was so wrong, but my heart, mind, and pussy didn't want to understand.

"Where are you going?" I asked as he started walking through my home and toward my bedroom, eyes open, but our lips still connected.

"To show you what time it is and write my name all over that pussy. Change your number in the morning, and I better not hear anything about that nigga comin' around you after tonight. You understand?" When I didn't respond, he bit my bottom lip, only to suck it when I whimpered from the pain. "Don't play with me, Savvy. I'll kill you and that nigga if you even let him sniff my pussy."

"I heard you," I moaned as his finger slipped into my wetness. I didn't even feel him pull my shorts to the side. Rotating his fingers just the way I liked it and hitting my spot, I could feel myself about to come. Wrapping my arms tighter around his neck, I lay my head on his shoulder and screamed into his neck as my juices coated his entire hand and my orgasm finally stopped. There was no turning back now. I was officially about to become a home wrecker.

Lyfe

"I don't wanna be a home wrecker."

Savannah kept repeating this over and over again as I kissed her beautiful body from head to toe. The thing was, she could never wreck a home that was already on the verge of falling at any minute. I had love for Sarai because she'd been down with a nigga since we started fucking around, but the shit was dead and been dead for some time now. I hardly stayed at the home we shared not too far from Savannah. The only reason I still did show my face was for my seeds. I tried to make it in the morning to see them off to school or in the evening to help them with their homework and spend a little time with them before they went to bed. But other than that, I was at one of the other homes I owned around the city. My attention focused back on Savannah when I felt the wetness from her tears on the side of my face. I hated to see my baby crying. Shit reminded me of the day I broke up with her.

Savannah had always been hardheaded, and I knew that if I didn't dead our situation that she would've stayed and probably would've lost out on the education she had now.

I pulled my face back and looked into her wet eyes. Savannah always told me that my shit did something to her, but I felt the same way about her dark orbs that couldn't hide her feelings about me. She was always able to look inside of me and see some shit most niggas and bitches would never see. This girl was my weak spot, and she knew it. I'd do anything for her and wouldn't think twice about it. Like this fly-ass condo she was living in right now. I picked it out and paid cash upfront for it. Didn't want her living in that middle-class area where Reign was, so I contacted the realtor she had been working with and had her show Savvy this condo in Ballantyne West. She didn't know that the down payment and monthly payments she was making went directly into an account I had set up for her a while ago, and she would have access to it whenever she found out.

Wiping away her tears with my thumb, I kissed the spot that they last touched, and then her nose.

"Don't cry, baby. You know I hate to see you cry."

"It's been years since you've seen me shed a tear."

"Physically, yes, but it doesn't stop me from seeing them in my dreams whenever I close my eyes at night." I wasn't lying either. That day I literally broke Savannah's heart played over and over in my mind. I'd tried to block it out, but nothing ever worked.

"Lyfe, I just don't want to be hurt again."

"And you won't," I assured her, pulling my shirt over my head and removing my pants and boxers. I stood in front of Savannah completely naked, and I could tell that she appreciated every inch of my body. I didn't work out every day, but I did eat healthy and tried to get a few physical activities in my routine during the day.

Before gently laying her back on the bed, I removed the thin-ass tank top she had on, and then the small pink shorts that did little to nothing to hide her thick thighs and round ass. I appraised her body the same way she did mine and could feel my dick twitching with every inch my eyes consumed. Her dark skin was so smooth and soft to the touch. Her breasts were full and sitting upright. I traced the contour of her flat belly with my finger and watched her body shiver. When I placed my hands on her wide hips, her legs opened, inviting me in. I nestled my body between her soft thighs and kissed her lips again. The faint scent of the cocoa butter she rubbed into her skin penetrated my nose. She raised her chin, and I kissed it. Then I made a light trail down her jawline, neck, and chest until I reached her Hershey's kissed nipple and took it into my mouth.

Savannah moaned, and I could feel the pre-come from my dick slowly dripping onto the bed. Her fingers found their way to my head where she applied a little bit of pressure with a squeeze whenever my tongue flicked over her sensitive breast. Removing her hold on my dick to avoid coming too fast, I sat back on my haunches, still admiring her beautiful frame. Crossing her legs at the ankle, I pushed them toward her face, exposing her dripping wet pussy and heart-shaped ass. Her scent had me on a different kind of high, and all I wanted to do was indulge in the aroma more. The second I had her fully exposed to me, I went headfirst into my new home and latched on to her pearl, causing a rumbling moan to escape her throat.

"Fuck, Lyfe. What the fuck!" she screamed as I continued to suck the soul and everything else I wanted from her body. This was the first time I'd had Savannah's essence in my mouth, and I knew from this point on that I would be the last to have it.

Her body shook from her second orgasm, and she tried to move from my hold, but I locked her thighs under my arms and took her into my mouth again. Sticking my long tongue into her hole only intensified the third orgasm, and I welcomed every drop of her come into my mouth.

"*Mmmmm,*" I moaned against her glazed lip. "You taste so fucking good, baby." Savannah tried to say something in response, but couldn't due to her throat being completely dry. After filling my appetite with a little more of her sweetness, I crawled back up her body and positioned myself back between her thighs. Rubbing my head against her slick folds, I wasn't surprised at how wet my dick was when I looked down at it. Returning my gaze to her eyes, I lowered myself down and slid into her before she could inhale again.

"*Ssssssss,*" I hissed the moment her tight walls gripped my dick and sucked me deeper into her being. The soft cushioning of her walls felt good as fuck and had my shit getting harder by the second. Savannah felt the exact same way she did all those years ago when she gave herself to me for the first time. I already knew that I would have to keep Bryant's ass on speed dial and his retainer paid up from now on. If a nigga even looked at her for a second, I was killing him, just so the muthafucka could know that she was off-limits. I sat still for a few, trying to gather myself together and think about anything but the way her hot, wet, and snug pussy felt on my dick. I knew that if I started stroking her like I wanted to, I would be nutting in no time.

"Don't make me come," I whispered into her ear, as she squeezed her muscles. When Savannah started to rock her hips underneath me, the idea of making love to her got tossed out the window, and I began to drill into her like my life depended on it.

"Oh . . . my . . . Gawwwd . . . Lyfe . . . Oh my God, baby," she screamed as I moved my hips from left to right. I was digging for oil and wasn't going to stop until I hit gold. Her fingers dug into my back, and I knew I would have scratches all over it. I didn't give a fuck, though.

"Fuck, Savannah, you feel so fucking good. Your shit is golden, baby," I growled, picking up my pace.

Before I knew what was happening, Savannah wrapped her legs around my waist and flipped me over on my back, my dick still embedded deep into her love. My eyes rolled to the back of my head when she started bouncing up and down and rotating her hips around in a circle.

I grabbed her titties and squeezed her nipples, just to be rewarded with a preview of the nut I knew she was chasing. Gripping her waist, I kept her in place on her throne and started lifting up and fucking her back. Her eyes closed, and her head fell to her chest. I could hear her mumbling something, but I couldn't make out anything she was saying. I smacked her hard on her ass, and the sound echoed in her dark room.

"Ride my shit, Savvy. Show me how much you missed me," I egged her on, planting her feet flat on the bed. She rested her hands on my chest and started bouncing on my dick faster and harder. Our bodies were slapping against each other so hard, the loud clapping noise had my ears ringing.

"I'm about to come, Lyfe. Baby, I'm about to—"

I cut her cry short by pulling her down to my chest and capturing her lips into mine. Wrapping my arms around her body, I pressed deeper into her and continued to deep stroke her pussy until I reached my own climax and released my seed all in her belly. My toes were still curling long after my dick had started to go limp, but it was a good feeling. Just the feel of her walls coated with my come and still gripping my shit now had my body still vibrating.

"Shit." I heard the shake in my own voice.

Savannah, whose head was turned away from me, looked at me and smiled. "That was . . . that—"

"That was the only kind of sex you get when two people truly love each other," I finished her sentence. A somber look crossed over her beautiful face, and I already knew what was on her mind. Pushing a loose strand of hair behind her ear, I kissed her on her eyelids, and then forehead.

"I already know what you're thinking, and, no, Sarai and I have never had sex like that. In fact, she and I haven't had sex in a while. When I go to the house, it's strictly for the kids and to go into my safe. Anything else," I shrugged my shoulders, "I wouldn't know about. Sarai could have a whole other nigga living there, and I wouldn't even know it."

"But still, Lyfe—" she tried to argue.

"But still nothing. We've been apart for long enough, and I'm tired of being married to a woman I shouldn't have married in the first place. But you already know how I am about family, Savannah, so I will never fully turn my back on Sarai. She's done a lot for me over the years and is the mother of my children, but other than that, you don't have anything to worry about. I doubt if she will even get mad when she finds out about us. She never has before."

Savannah sat up on my lap. Dick still being gripped and held in place. "Wait a minute, so you've been cheating on your wife this whole time?"

I shook my head. "Not the whole time. In the beginning, I tried to make it work. Tried to force myself to fall in love with her to forget about you, but I couldn't do it. My heart has always been yours and will always be yours. No one else's," I assured her and kissed her on the lips. She blushed. "A few years after we got married, I had sex a couple of times with other women, but nothing ever like you and I have."

"And she knew about those women?"

"She found out about them."

"And she was okay with that?"

"Yes and no. As long as they never disrespected our home or children, and she never saw me out with them, she would be okay."

Savannah shook her head in disbelief. "Wow, your wi—I mean Sarai is better than me. I would kill a bitch over you. Fuck being disbarred and all that other shit."

I bit my bottom lip and smiled at what Savannah had just said. Although I would never allow her to get her hands dirty like that, it was nice to know that she would kill for me. Her admission had my dick coming to life inside her.

A small, sexy moan floated through the air when I reached my full length.

"You know your pussy now belongs to me? I don't want anyone within five feet of it."

She giggled and wrapped her arms around my neck. "I have clients, both male and female. I don't know how that would work."

I pushed into her, and she started to rock her hips. "You'll find a way, or I'll shut that shit down."

"But baby—" she moaned.

"But baby *nothing*. Now shut up and ride this dick so we can get a couple of hours of sleep before I have to go handle some business." And just like that, my baby rode me until I was filling her womb up again. I made a mental note to get with Bryant sometime during the week to draw up those divorce papers for me and Sarai. I was pretty sure she'ld sign those papers without a problem as long as I left her ass with a large sum of money and at least one of the houses.

"Daddy, Daddy, Daddy!" Ramair and Sakina yelled, running up to me when I walked through the door to the home Sarai and I shared. Ramair, my oldest, was six, and my little princess, Sakina, just turned four last month. Despite the growing wedge between Sarai and me, the love that I had for my kids was unexplanatory. I spoiled them rotten, and in all honesty, they were the only reason why I stayed with Sarai this long. My childhood wasn't a stable one growing up, and I didn't want my kids to experience the same things I did at their ages.

"What's up, babies? Daddy missed y'all," I said, picking Sakina up and giving Ramair a pound.

"We missed you too. What did you bring us back from New York?" Ramair quizzed with his hand out.

"Boy, you tryin' to hustle me? I didn't get y'all nothing," I told him while putting Sakina down and walking into the kitchen where I was surprised to see Sarai preparing breakfast. Normally, one of the nannies would be in here making my kids something to eat before they were sent off to school, but today, I guess Sarai didn't have anything else to do. I took a second and looked at Sarai while her back was turned to me. No doubt she was a beautiful woman and down for whatever, but that was never enough to make me fully love her. My heart always belonged to the chocolate beauty I just left, not the Sanaa Lathan look-alike I married. The moment she turned around with a bland expression on her face, the atmosphere surrounding us quickly changed.

I sighed. "What I do now, Sarai?" I asked walking up to her and giving her a kiss on the side of the face. I never wanted my kids to know that we were going through some problems, so I played nice in front of them. Sarai knew what the deal was, though, so I know she didn't feel the love behind that kiss.

"I was hoping that we could all sit down and have breakfast as a family. It's been awhile, you know?" She turned the bacon over in the skillet and poured some pancake batter into the waffle maker.

"Where's Araceli? You gave her the day off or something?"

She rolled her eyes. "You act like I don't take care of my kids."

"Never said that you didn't. However, you normally have a little help 80 percent of the time."

Whipping the eggs in a large bowl, she sprinkled some cheese, green onions, and tomatoes in the mixture. "So are you eating with us or what?"

My phone began to vibrate in my pocket at that moment. Looking down at my screen, I couldn't help the smile that formed on my face when I opened the picture Savannah just sent of her lying in bed. The sun was hitting her face at an angle that had her looking like an angel. The rays caused her dark eyes to look more like a rich brown. The satisfied smile on her face had my dick slowly waking from its comatose state.

My Heart: I miss you already. Can't wait to see you at dinner.

I forgot all about us going out to dinner tonight. With the phone calls I received from Heim, Kiko, and Bryant on the way here, us going out tonight totally slipped my mind. I was still staring at the picture when Sarai cleared her throat. I picked my head up from the phone. She was standing on the other side of the island looking me dead in my eyes. "I guess you won't be staying after all," she spoke, shaking her head.

Not one to bullshit around, I shook my head no, confirming what she had already predicted.

"Kids, run upstairs and get washed up and ready for breakfast," Sarai ordered. I knew she wanted to have a quick word with me outside of their presence. Once they disappeared up the stairs, Sarai turned back to me with her arms crossed over her chest and a frown on her face. "I need to ask you something very important, and if you have an ounce of love in your heart for me, you'll be truthful with me." She undid her apron and turned off the fire under the bacon.

"You wanna do this now?" I asked, already knowing where this was going.

"What did I do to you, Lyfe? What have I ever done so hideous that you barely can stand to look at me?" I was kind of shocked by her questions. And for a moment, it kind of seemed like she really cared about the way our marriage has been going these last few years.

"Yo, we not about to do this right now. Besides, you already know what it is, man. It's not you. You didn't do nothing."

"So what's the reason for the distance between us? We hardly say two words to each other when we're in this house, and I can't remember the last time you made love to me."

"Come on, Sarai, you looking into this way too deep. It ain't that serious, and you know that. Where the hell is this coming from anyway? And making love? When have I *ever* made love to you?"

Honestly, I couldn't think about anything Sarai was doing wrong in our marriage besides not being Savannah. She managed all three nail salons on a day-to-day basis. When she felt like it, she came home, cooked, cleaned, and tended to our children. Never have I seen her looking relaxed or loose. Sarai stayed dressed and with a made up face. Light brown skin, hair always done, and a set of C cup breasts that complimented her thick frame. On a scale of 1 to 10, she was a strong 9, and that was after giving birth to my two children. A straight showstopper. I couldn't and wouldn't deny that I loved her, I just wasn't *in* love with her. That right belonged to Savannah.

"Before you leave this house tonight, I need you to know that I love you and whatever it is that you need me to do to fix this—us—just tell me, and I will do what I have to do to help things get back to where they were. Just don't give up on me without giving me a chance, Lyfe," she pleaded, right before the kids ran back into the kitchen. "Go ahead and get out of here."

I walked up to her nodding my head. "We'll talk more about it later," I said, leaning in and giving her a kiss on the lips. My phone when off again, but instead of answering it, I decided to turn it off altogether. I didn't care to be disturbed for the next couple of hours. The streets and Savannah would have to wait until I ate this home cooked meal with my kids and their mother. Hopefully, nothing too serious popped off until then.

Reign

Pulling into my driveway, I sighed and thanked the Lord that I was finally home. Working these long-ass hours these past few months has really been draining and had me ready to quit. If it wasn't for all of the bills I had coming in every month, I probably would've put in my two-week notice a long time ago. There was a nice little balance in my savings account that I had been building since I first started working when I was sixteen and probably could've lived off of for a few years. But with me paying all of my mama's bills as well as mine, that money would be gone in no time, and I'd be forced to find another job.

Laying my head back on the headrest, I closed my eyes and sighed again. All I needed was a big glass of chardonnay, a couple of sleeping pills, and a few hours of sleep and I would be good. But, I had a date to get ready for, and I didn't want to be late. I looked over at my neighbor's house, who just happened to be my entertainment for the night, and smiled. Ever since the morning Peaches came to my porch tripping on Heim's sorry ass, my neighbor and I have been getting more acquainted. When he first asked me for my number, I fronted him off and just kept it at a casual hi and bye whenever we would see each other in passing. But one morning, while I was in the grocery store looking for some breakfast food, he and I bumped into each other in the cereal aisle and had been texting and talking on the phone ever since. Tonight was our first official date, and I must say, I was a little excited.

Grabbing my briefcase, shoes, and jacket, I got out of my car and walked barefoot to my house. Flipping the light switch on as I entered, I threw everything in my arms on the ground and walked straight to my kitchen. I took the bottle of chardonnay that I didn't finish yesterday straight to the head, not stopping until every last drop was gone. I'd been drinking a little more since Heim and I broke up, trying to cope with my broken heart someway. I knew drowning my sorrows in liquor wasn't the right way to go, but it was all that I had at the moment. Talking to Savannah about me and her brother's problems was out of the question, and my mother, well, let's just say she never liked Heim from the beginning. He was always *the boy who was going to break my heart* in her eyes, so I knew I'd get no sympathy from her.

Reaching for the second bottle of wine in my fridge, I cracked it open but poured it into a glass this time. Sipping wouldn't get me too drunk before I went on this date.

Walking through my living room, I went straight to the bathroom and ran water in the bathtub. Testing the temperature with my hand, I made sure it was just right before I plugged the drain and threw one of my bath bombs inside. I stripped out of my black pencil skirt and brown lace blouse before sitting on the toilet and looking at myself in the mirror. At twenty-eight, I still looked like I was no older than sixteen, but my grown-up body made up for that. Balancing my wineglass in one hand, I took a wipe from off of my vanity with the other and removed the little bit of makeup that I had on my face.

My house phone rang, but I let that shit go right to voicemail. I already knew who it was and wasn't about to waste my time or energy on his lies. Since I blocked him from calling my cell phone, Heim has been trying to reach me in any way that he could, whether it was showing up at my job unannounced or coming to my house in the middle of the night, banging on my front door. Because he wasn't the type of dude that most people would say no to, I knew me rejecting him this time around was throwing him off his square a little bit. But I needed Naheim to understand that I was finally tired of his bullshit and was done with him and everything we ever had.

Turning the water off, I stepped into my free-standing tub; one of the many modern features I added on when I had the inside of my home remodeled, and moaned. The scorching hot water already had my body relaxed and feeling like I was in heaven. I stayed submerged in the water and soaked for about forty-five minutes before I got out, dried off, and moisturized my skin with my favorite body butter. I already had what I was going to wear laid out on my bed, so all I needed was a cute pair of shoes to go with it. Deciding to go with comfort, I slid my feet into my gold Tory Burch sandals, and then pulled the green ruffle hem romper over my body. After spraying a little spritz of perfume on my neck and wrist, adding a few pieces of jewelry to match, and brushing back the few strands of hair that were out of place, I coated my lips with some nude lipstick, and brushed my eyelashes with a few strokes of mascara and headed out for my date.

Leaving my cell phone purposely behind, I walked over to my neighbor's house and knocked on his door, ready for whatever he had planned. I waited for what seemed like five minutes before he appeared before me looking good enough to eat.

"Good evening, Reign. I'm glad you could join me tonight." He offered his hand, which I took and held. "I hope you like Chinese."

"I do. Did you have your mind set on a certain restaurant or did you want me to pick?" I figured with him being new to the area, he wasn't going to be familiar with what Charlotte had to offer cuisine wise.

He licked his lips and smiled. Damn, even his chuckle was sexy. "I thought it would be fun for me to cook for you tonight instead." Stepping back, he gestured with his free hand for me to walk in, while he offered me a glass of red wine with the other. I gladly accepted the sweet Merlot and took a sip as I entered his home. The minute I set foot inside the living room, the aromatic smell of ginger, garlic, shallots, and sesame oil hit my nose, causing my stomach to growl. "I'm glad you're hungry. I didn't know what your favorite Chinese dish was, so I made a few different ones." He tilted his head. "This way."

Placing his hand on the small of my back, we walked through the rest of his living room and down a short hallway that led to a beautifully decorated dining area and open kitchen.

"Who decorated your house? It's very nice." The layout was similar to mine, so I knew he had two bedrooms, two bathrooms, a den, and an extra room that could be used for office space or an extra bedroom. Although his kitchen seemed a little bigger than mine, they still were pretty much the same.

His back was to me as he flipped something in a pan. "I actually decorated myself. A little something I picked up on during my travels."

While he continued to mess around with the food on the stove, I looked around and admired his style and eye for interior design. Garnet reds and emerald greens were the main color scheme, followed by gold accents placed throughout. There were stainless steel appliances in the kitchen and modern but masculine furniture everywhere else. The one thing that really caught my eye, though, was the baby grand piano in the corner of the den. Walking over, I slid my fingers down a few keys, causing him to turn away from what he was doing and smile.

"You play?"

I shook my head. "Not really. I learned a couple of songs when I was younger, but never really picked up on it. You play?"

"I do. My grandmother played for the church I grew up in back home."

"Where's back home again?"

"Baltimore." His accent was really cute. "You from Charlotte?"

"Born and raised."

"That's cool." He turned his attention back to the stove. "So Ms. Reign, what do you do for a living?"

Walking over to the window, I looked out at his neatly trimmed backyard. Other than a built-in barbecue grill and a nice seven-piece patio set, his backyard was pretty plain. There was a dog run off to the side, but I didn't see a dog in sight. I walked back over to the kitchen and pulled a stool from under the breakfast nook.

"I'm a marketing manager for a company called The Devine Group."

"Sales, brand development, and multimarketing campaigns, right?" I nodded my head impressed by his knowledge of some of my job qualifications. Heim couldn't tell you anything about what I did except that I worked in the big-ass glass building downtown.

"You must know someone who works in the same field as me, right?" I asked, popping a grape in my mouth from the tray of fruit he placed in front of me.

"Not really. I thought about going into marketing when I was in college, but I went toward something else." He looked at my empty glass of wine. "Would you like a refill?" Chewing on another grape, I simply held my glass out to him, and he smiled. "I'm glad you like the wine. While I was in Whole Foods today, I asked about five different women what flavor they would recommend to make a good impression on a first date."

"So you wanted to impress me, Mr. Monroe?"

He rested his hip against the counter and crossed his arms over his chest with a smirk on his handsome face. The white dish towel he'd been wiping his hands with was draped over his shoulder. Evidence of his hard work in the kitchen decorated a few spots, so I knew he was working hard on our dinner. My eyes traveled down his fit physique and back up to his face again. Monroe was almost the same size as Heim, but I could tell by the size of his biceps that he had a little more muscle on his body. The silver necklace around his neck had a small cross hanging from it, which told me that he was a little religious. I wasn't really a fan of the color blue, but the navy, long sleeved casual Polo shirt he had on looked good on him. Paired with some dark washed jeans, blue Nike slides, and a half apron, Monroe looked sexy as fuck and could cook for me anytime.

"Do I get brownie points or something if I was trying to impress you?"

I smiled. "I don't know about brownie points, but I am feeling you a little more for that effort."

He bit his bottom lip, and my knees buckled. "So you feelin' the kid, huh?"

"The kid's got my attention."

We stared at each other for a minute, both content in whatever this was building between us. I wasn't looking for anything too serious right now, and Monroe knew that, but I had a feeling that it wasn't going to stop him from trying. He knew all about my past with Heim and the shit that he put me through over the years. When I asked Monroe if he thought that I was stupid for putting up with all of Heim's bullshit for so long, he simply told me that I was a woman in love, and he couldn't fault me for wanting to make something work that I felt was worth fighting for. He also said that although he would've never treated me that way, he could understand why Heim was having such a hard time with letting me go. Something about a man's pride and ego and all that other fuckery. But I didn't give a shit. Heim had fucked me over for the last time, and I was not going back. Peaches and all the rest of the hoes he was fucking around with could have him and keep his ass. I was done. And I meant that.

"Well, the food is ready. Take a seat at the table, and I'll bring everything out."

"You don't need any help?" I asked, walking over toward the stove and admiring all of his hard work. Beef and broccoli, combination fried rice, vegetable chow mein, and some fried crab rangoon were on the menu. The big wok he had just fried the wontons in was still hot and sizzling.

Grabbing my shoulders, Monroe walked up behind me and guided me to the glass table with the large plush chairs in his dining room. Pulling out my seat, he made sure I was good and situated before he went back into the kitchen and brought our dinner out. After making our plates, refilling our glasses with wine, and saying a quick grace, we dug in.

"Wow. You really cooked your ass off. Did you go to school or something for that?" He and I have talked over the last few weeks, but never got into what we did for a living.

He wiped his mouth with his napkin and took a sip of his wine. His dark eyes roamed over my face with an appreciative glance, and I blushed. "No, I didn't go to culinary school. However, if you call having to sit in the kitchen while my mother and aunts prepared Sunday dinner and food for other occasions where we would have big meals, then I guess I did."

"Okay. So what is it that you do? I see you leaving in the morning at the same time as me sometimes, but then, you don't get home until real late most nights. I know you're not a dope boy or anything like that." I looked at him again and shook my head. "Naw."

His face became serious. "What makes you say that?"

I shrugged my shoulders. "You don't strike me as one. I mean, I grew up in the hood, so I know what a dope boy looks like."

"Dope boys have a look, huh? So what do I look like to you?"

I shrugged my shoulders again. "I don't know. An accountant or something."

A hardy laugh escaped his throat which made me smile and become slightly embarrassed. Obviously, my assumption of his career choice was wrong, and his ass thought it was funny as fuck. Monroe took another sip of his wine and sat back in his seat. His pecan complexion looked smooth under the dim light. Looking back at me, his full lips were now in a curled smile with that one dimple in his right cheek on full display.

I bit my bottom lip trying to at least control my raging hormones a little bit, but this sexy muthafucka was making it so hard for me. I told myself that before I started any type of sexual relationship with the next man that I would at least try to get to know him a little bit at first. Had I used this same thought process before jumping headfirst into the situation between Heim and me, my body, heart, and mind would probably be a whole lot better right now.

Running his fingers over his neatly trimmed beard, Monroe tilted his head to the side, and then back up again. I got the feeling that he was contemplating on whether to tell me what his job occupation really was. Stuffing a piece of broccoli in my mouth, I enjoyed the sweet and savory taste of the beef sauce and waited for him to tell me something. Instead, I got hit with a question I wasn't really expecting.

"Is that what your ex-boyfriend is? An accountant?" I had to laugh at that one. If only he knew. "What's so funny?"

Wiping my mouth with the napkin, I sat back in my seat, belly full and too stuffed to move another inch. "Does he look like an accountant to you?"

"He could be. I don't base what people do off of their looks because that shit can be deceiving." He stood up from his chair and began to gather our dirty plates, but not before going back to his question. "So what does he do?"

"I thought tonight was about us getting to know each other better. Why you so interested in what my ex does?"

"I'm not *so* interested. I just wanted to know the type of dudes you like to date and whether I fit into the fold."

"But you asking questions like you the feds or something," I laughed but stopped when Monroe's body froze in place the minute the words slipped from my mouth. My eyebrows furrowed. "Wait a minute. *Do* you work for the feds?"

He placed the plates back on the table and turned toward me. "If I did, would it be a problem?"

Would it be a problem? I asked myself. I mean, I liked Monroe, but what we had was still new and could easily end without anyone's feelings getting hurt. But then again, if I did continue to see him, would his intentions on getting to know me be strictly for that reason, or could it just be a front to get information on the people that I associated with. I always hoped that those niggas would get tired of this street life and just turn it over to somebody else and start to live a normal life. But that was like wishing on a star. Niggas like Lyfe and Heim loved making that fast money and became addicted to it once they got to a certain way of living. I tried to get Heim to invest into a few companies over the years to clean up his money, but he always told me that he had someone handling that. Which I learned was code for one of his bitches already looking into it for him. So many thoughts were running through my head and with all the wine I drank tonight, I couldn't think straight.

"Hello . . . Reign? Are you okay?" Monroe lightly shook my shoulder, grabbing my attention. Squatting down next to my chair, our faces were so close that I could smell the wine on his breath.

"I think I should go." I tried to stand up, but he sat me back down.

"Not before you answer my question." His dark eyes stayed on mine.

"What question, Monroe?"

He looked down at the space between his legs, and then back at me. "Would it be a problem if I did work for the feds?"

"Honestly, I really can't answer that right now. I'm not too sure what your real intentions are with wanting to get to know me, if you want me to keep it real."

He grabbed my face between his hands and kissed my lips. Closing my eyes, I reveled in the softness of his lips. "I assure you that my intentions are to only strictly get to know you. In the case that anything ever comes up, which I doubt it will, please know that I won't have a problem telling you the minute I know."

From the look in his eyes, I could tell that he was being truthful, but there was still something in me that needed some time to think about this. What would Heim think if he found out that I was dating a nigga who worked for the feds? I shook my head. Who gave a fuck what Heim thought? Monroe could tell that I was having an internal battle with myself. So instead of asking me his question again, he kissed me on my lips and then walked me to his front door.

"Whenever you make up your mind, you know where to reach me, Reign. I would really like to be given a chance to get to know you. If not, I hope you eventually find what you're looking for, whether it's with your ex or someone new."

With one last kiss on the cheek, I walked out of Monroe's house and across the lawn to mine. When I reached my door, I turned around and waved at him, already knowing he was still there watching me.

Entering my house, I went straight to the kitchen and grabbed the bottle of chardonnay from earlier and poured me a glass. I had a lot to think about and a lot to lose if I did give Monroe the chance to get to know me. So far, I was impressed and interested. But on the other hand, I shook my head. As much as I hated this nigga and wanted him out of my life, it killed me how every decision I had to make in my life always came back to Heim's ass.

Naheim

With heavy eyelids, I leaned back farther into the comfort of Peaches's widespread legs as I sipped the remainder of my drink. The heat flowing from her center only added to the sweet feeling of her gently massaging fingers that were busy working every ounce of tension from my hard frame. I held the blunt out and over my shoulder so she could take a long swig. Placing it back in my mouth, I allowed the feeling of pure pleasure to take over as I lay back against her breasts and closed my eyes.

See, this was what people couldn't understand about my feelings for Peaches. Although she was as ghetto as they came and probably mad as fuck at me right now for running behind Reign, it didn't matter. She was always ready and willing to please a nigga, wrong or not. Yeah, she did all that cussing, fussing, and showing out, but all that did was let me know that she was in need of some attention and some dick. Which is one of the reasons why I booked the Presidential Suite at the Ritz Carlton for us. Today, I planned on giving her both to shut her up for a few days and keep her in line, and to give me some time to finally see what the fuck was up with Reign. I'd been calling her ass for the last few weeks, with little to no response at all. I tried to get Savvy to put in a good word for me, but that didn't even help. I really missed my baby, and I needed her back in my life.

Yeah, I know that I was in a room with Peaches right now, but that didn't stop me from thinking about Reign's short ass and how much I'd missed her. Especially with Bryson Tiller's "For However Long" playing in the background. This was one of the songs Reign always played whenever she was in the kitchen cooking me dinner or whenever she was in her living room trying to put some presentation together for work. It's funny how you miss the little annoying things that someone does when they aren't really fucking with you like that.

My mind was so gone and in its relaxed state thinking about Reign and how much I missed her that I didn't feel when Peaches released her grip on my shoulders and pushed me up a bit, removing that added heat from between her legs on my back. Giving me a kiss on the neck, she rose to exit the Jacuzzi.

"Where the fuck you think you're going? I know you don't think you're finished, do you?" I asked, seriously wanting her to return to the task even though my thoughts were of Reign. I glared defiantly in her direction.

"Damn, if it's all right with you, I was going to get me something to drink." Sucking her teeth, she shook her head as she glared back at me with her hands on her shapely hips. "Damn, nigga, you so spoiled at times. I don't know why I treat you so good when all you do is treat me so bad." Swishing across the room with water dripping from her naked frame, she winked over her shoulder, shooting a seductive smile my way.

"You *know* why you treat me so good."

"Oh, yeah?" she questioned, pouring a drink. "Why is that?"

"Because I give you this good dick."

Peaches laughed. "True. It's because of that *and* the fact that I love you."

I sat back in the Jacuzzi, hoping Peaches didn't start tripping about me not saying I loved her back. Her ass already knew what we had going on had nothing to do with love, so I didn't understand where all that shit was coming from. We didn't really go out anywhere, never really spent any quality time together outside of fucking and making this money. Where she got love out of that, I really didn't know. Don't get me wrong. I had love for her, but it wasn't in the same way that she loved me.

Peaches was a good worker, and I really liked having her on my team. She'd been constantly hounding me about giving her a little more responsibility in our operations, and I felt like she'd proven herself enough. My nigga Lyfe, on the other hand, was totally against that shit. When I suggested that she head up the storage spot we just opened, he quickly nixed that idea and went with one of the workers that had been down with the team for a while. I knew Peaches's past was shady with all the jacking niggas and setting them up, but her ass knew better than to try me. I wasn't breaking her off like I tried to do Reign plenty of times, but Peaches knew not to bite the hand that was feeding her. Since she started fucking with me and making this money, her ass moved into a house, bought two fly-ass rides, and wore all of the Gucci, Prada, and Louis Vuitton that she could afford. Before I put her on, her ass was living in the projects with her cousin Desiree and a host of roaches and bedbugs. She would be a fool to go back to that shit over stealing some crumbs.

Relighting my blunt, I puffed on it a few times before putting it out and saving the rest for later. My eyes traveled back over to Peaches, and I shook my head. The sight of her perfect, heart-shaped ass swaying fluidly to the music had my attention wholeheartedly and my mind on the wetness between her thighs. The immediate return of tension that began to throb in my center was begging to be taken care of. Realizing that she needed to massage my shit, sooner rather than later, had me smiling in anticipation. As my dick continued to get harder and harder, it dawned on me the other reason why I kept Peaches around. I never got tired of sexing her horny ass. I mean, I loved making love to Reign, but not even her sex compared to the wild, uninhibited shit I experienced with Peaches. Girly was down for anything, whether it was sucking, fucking, licking, or a threesome. Whatever sexual fantasy my mind could come up with, she was with it. If I could get Reign to be as freaky as Peaches's ass, I would stop fucking with Peaches completely and try to be in a committed relationship with my baby.

"I'm back, spoiled ass. I brought you another drink too." Placing the cup on the side of the Jacuzzi, Peaches' eyes filled with lust as soon as she saw my shit sticking out of the water. "Umph, umph, umph. What do we have here?" she asked, reaching down to grab the head. Running her hand up and down my considerable length, she licked her lips.

"Damn, ma, ain't no use in wasting them licks," I joked, before reaching up and pulling her back into the warm water. Peaches giggled and then straddled my legs at the ankle while stroking my man up and down. Resting my head back against the wall, I couldn't do anything but close my eyes when she leaned over and forced nearly every inch of my dick to the back of her throat and started humming. Her mouth was so warm and wet that I almost nutted prematurely.

"Damn, slow down, ma, before this is the only way you get this dick tonight," I joked.

Frowning playfully in response, Peaches twirled her tongue on my dick one last time before she turned her back to me and slowly began to sit down on my shit. After swallowing me inch by inch and gasping for breath, Peaches swirled her hips in a slow, rhythmic manner, while making her inner muscles grip and release me.

Clasping my eyes tightly together, I massaged her soft ass cheeks, while savoring the feel of her warm, pulsing insides. Each time she raised her hips, it became more and more obvious why I fucked with her crazy ass. It was the way she worked her inner muscles that had me gone. Nearing her climax, Peaches leaned flush against my chest as she increased her movements. Becoming vocal, she pumped up and down harder while frantically tweaking her nipples.

"You love this pussy, don't you? Don't you, nigga?" Yelling loudly, she bit her lip in a state of half-hysterical pleasure. "You're so big, Heim. Oh . . . God . . . nigga, you're soooo big!"

Rising up to meet her, stroke for stroke, I pumped back with a pistonlike urgency. Water from the tub was splashing all over the floor, but I didn't give a fuck. "You're damn right, I love this pussy," I grunted through clenched teeth, feeling my toes curling up. Unsuccessful in my attempt at holding back, the combination of the tightness I was immersed in and her loud moans sent me over the edge. Grabbing her hips, I slammed her body down on my own and shot my fluids deep inside her.

Reaching a leg-trembling orgasm at the force of the deep, hard invasion, Peaches yelled out, "Yes! Oh, yes, Heim!" before grinding down hard one last time and matching my orgasm. I could feel her thick nectar releasing all over my now semi-hard dick and lap. Turning back to face me, Peaches kissed my lips and moaned, a satisfied smirk on her face.

"You always make me come like that," she whispered in my ear before she got back on her knees and began to lick both of our creams off of me. "We taste so good together, baby." When she tried to kiss me again, I turned my head and her lips connected with my jaw. I rocked with Peaches in some ways, but that wasn't one. The only pussy juices that had ever been in my mouth were Reign's, and that wasn't about to change just because I enjoyed the look of nastiness on Peaches's face almost more than the feeling of her tongue and juicy lips.

"You know better than that," I warned. She pouted, and I tapped her ass. "Start the shower so I can wash myself off and then order us some room service or something."

Peaches smacked her lips. "Heim, we've been fucking for over a year now. When will it be my turn to feel you sucking on my shit?"

I looked at her like she was crazy. "Peaches, you already know I don't get down with anyone else like that but Reign. You will *never* feel my lips on your pussy. If you feel some type of way about that, you already know what you can do, right?" Rolling her eyes, she stood up from my lap and started the shower water. "Now, unless you want to cut our session short, I suggest you fix that attitude and go do what the fuck I said."

"Whatever, nigga. You gon' eat my pussy one day, believe that."

I laughed at her retreating back. "Turn into Reign and that just might happen."

The door slamming let me know that she was more than likely going to be in her feelings for the rest of the night. But all I had to do was let her sit on this dick again and all would be well. After washing my body clean, I wrapped a towel around my waist and walked into the suite. The television in the living room was on, but Peaches was nowhere in sight. I walked back to the master bedroom and found her laid out on the bed dozing off. Because I wanted to dip out for a few hours, I silently dressed in my clothes and canceled the room service order she had put in. Making sure I had my gun, phone, and keys in hand, I left our room and headed to my car.

As soon as I pulled out of the crowded parking lot, my phone rang.

"What's up, little sis?"

"Hey." Her voice wasn't the cheery, playful one that I was used to, so I was already on alert.

"What's up with you, Savvy? Why you sound like that?"

She sighed and became quiet for a second. "Have you talked to Lyfe?"

"Why? What's up?" Her sounding sad, calling me, and asking about my nigga wasn't a good thing.

"I just haven't been able to reach him, that's all. I've been calling him all week, and he hasn't returned any of my calls. Is he out of town again?"

I could've lied, but I chose not to. Lyfe was my boy, but Savvy was my sister. "The last time I chopped it up with him, he was at the house with Sarai and the kids." The line was so quiet, I thought she hung up. "Hello?"

"Yeah, I'm here." I could tell by the tone of my sister's voice that she was in her feelings, so I decided to change the subject.

"How's everything going at the office?"

"It's cool. I got a few cases in court next week, and I've gotten a few referrals from some of my associates I still keep in contact with out in California. So, so far, business is good."

"That's what's up, baby sis. I'll stop by your house sometime this week, and we can have dinner or something. I'll bring the drinks, and you cook the food."

Savvy laughed. "Nigga, why I always gotta cook? It's your turn to make some shit."

"If you don't mind eating frank and beans or some microwave macaroni and cheese, then you got that. You know those are the only specialties I know how to make."

"Oh, I know all too well. I used to hate when you would call yourself 'cooking' for me when I was younger. I was so glad when one of your little ho-ass girlfriends came over to impress me or when Reign's mama would send us the leftovers from their house."

Just thinking about Reign's mama's cooking had my stomach growling. Ms. Gertrude knew she could burn in the kitchen. Taught my baby a few things too. I missed those Sunday dinners I used to go to at her parents' house or the big family gatherings they used to have over the holidays. I used to give Reign a hard time about me going, seeing as we weren't an official couple, but I always made my way there. Especially when her Aunt B made that 7 Up cake or the three-layer caramel cake. I needed to get our situation right before I missed out on any more of her family's cooking.

Savvy and I talked on the phone about some family shit until I made it to my destination. After promising to let her know if I came in contact with Lyfe, I got off the phone and was ready to get out of the car but stopped when I saw a shorty who looked real similar to Reign on her neighbor's porch, all in some nigga's face talking, smiling, and then giving him a hug.

My gut was telling me that ole girl I was looking at was Reign, but my heart didn't want to believe it. Her moving on to someone else was never in the plans, and her ass knew that. She was supposed to wait for me like she always does because eventually, I would get my shit right. Seeing her all in the next nigga's face had me feeling some type of way.

Pulling out my burner phone, I called her shit back-to-back and watched as she ignored each and every one of my calls. I wanted to get out and question her about being at that nigga's house in that short-ass green outfit and the gold sandals I bought her for her birthday last year. Had it not been for the text I just received from Kiko about some detectives coming around and asking questions, her ass would've been telling me what was really going on, but I started my car up and headed out to our meet up spot. If the pigs were coming around again, that meant that there was another snitch in the crew, and we couldn't have that shit again. Reign's ass was saved for right now, but best believe when I came back, she and that nigga would have to answer to me.

Lyfe

It had been a long couple of weeks, but I felt it was well worth it. Sarai had been in her feelings lately, and although any other time she would have had to just get over it, now wasn't a good moment to have her unsteady. Besides the fact that Savvy and I had gotten back into each other so quickly, Naheim and Kiko had been blowing me up about some detective coming around asking questions about me and the shooter that night at the club.

And as if that wasn't enough, my attorney Bryant had been calling me too about a sealed federal indictment that could come down at any moment. It looked like that nigga Toby had been working with the feds for quite some time. I wasn't sure how much he knew of the inner workings of our organization; however, it was enough to have them sniffing around. He was really under Naheim's side of the business, and I was hoping that he didn't see too much.

But after seeing how Heim trusted this bitch Peaches with so much, I wasn't sure how close or far he had kept Toby. A nigga wasn't shook, but I did know that now wasn't the right time to have Sarai rethinking her loyalty and commitment with all of this shit about to come down on me. Spending time with her and the kids for the last couple of weeks to get her on point was a definite must. Although not being able to hear Savvy's voice had been killing me, I knew where my heart was, and I just hoped that she knew as well.

The vibration of my phone brought me back to the road. So consumed with my thoughts, I had nearly missed my exit to Graham Street, but quickly answered it.

"Yo, what up?" I asked after pressing the phone icon on my steering wheel. Naheim's loud voice came through the sound system.

"Nigga, what's up is where the fuck you at? We been trying to reach you for some days now."

"Chill out, playboy, I'm pulling up as we speak," I responded with a laugh. My partner was something else with his always late ass, and here he was now questioning me.

When I walked into the club, I could tell by their faces that the cops had my people a little on edge. I knew that what I was about to drop on them wouldn't help ease their minds much either. But I needed everybody, especially my inner circle, to be on point if shit actually did hit the fan.

Standing behind the bar, I poured myself a drink as I listened to my top enforcers bring me up to speed on the homicide detectives that were now working the disappearance of the alleged shooter case. Although we had tried to destroy the DVD from the surveillance cameras, it was just our luck that a second streaming feed was backed up by the security company. The cops had acquired that footage and identified the shooter as Qunell Perkins aka Quick. We still didn't have the full details on who he really was and who actually sent him, but that was the least of our worries right now. After Kiko, Heim, and everyone else finished filling me in, I dropped the information on them that I had received from my attorney earlier.

"Well, we also got another situation." I downed the shot in my cup and poured me another. "I got an urgent call from Bryant a couple of days ago, and according to him, there's a sealed indictment with a few of our names in it."

"Is this from that Toby shit?" Kiko asked, and I nodded my head, letting him know it was. I looked over at Heim.

"So how concerned do we need to be, my nigga?" I asked, hoping that he didn't allow Toby access to too much of our operation. His long delay and the raising of his brow began to worry me. So I asked a second time, "How concerned should we be, Naheim? We need to know something so we can handle it accordingly."

"The bitch nigga knew enough," Naheim finally answered. He turned his back and started texting on his phone. I wasn't going to dig any further at the moment because I knew how sensitive my boy could be when he felt like he had fucked up and was being called out in front of people. So I left the other questions for a later time.

"Well, I think we need to lie low for the next few weeks. At least until Bryant learns more or the feds make their move. Everybody straight on bread, right?" Kiko and Naheim nodded their heads yes, and so did a few other people. "Well, good. Let's cancel the coke and the boy for the time being and just keep the weed pumping. That way, we keep some money in our workers' pockets without as much risk. Okay?" Once we were all in agreement with what the new schedule was going to be, everyone filed out of the club, leaving me, Heim, and Kiko to discuss some other business.

"Niggas been calling you for some weeks now. Where you really been, Lyfe? Either Savannah been sexing you down, or Sarai done hopped on your dick again," Kiko joked.

"Nigga, don't you ever let me hear you talking about my sister like that, playing or not." Heim finally looked up from his phone. "Have some respect for that one."

"Naheim, shut your ass up. I got the highest respect for Savannah, and she knows that, so why you frontin'?"

"I'm just making sure niggas respect my sister, that's all." Cutting his eyes at me, Heim sat down on a stool and started playing with his phone again.

I stepped from behind the bar and into Heim's space. "You got something you need to get off your chest?"

A frown crossed his face as he looked me in the eyes. "What's up with you and Savvy? Didn't I tell you not to step to her until your shit with Sarai was dead? And don't even try to open your mouth to say it's not what I think. My sister can't lie to me for shit. Who you think she's been calling the last couple of weeks trying to get in contact with you? Asking if I've seen you or not?" Heim stood up from his stool and was now face-to-face with me. "I swear to God, Lyfe, you better keep that bitch of yours on a leash once this shit between you and my sister hits the fan. Knowing Sarai, she's going to nut the fuck up once she realizes Savvy ain't one of those broads you normally just fucked and threw away in the past."

"Regardless of how you feel about Sarai, she is still my wife, so you need to respect her as such."

"And you need to respect my sister, nigga. You and I have never been in disagreement out of all the years we've been grinding together, but don't make that shit change."

"All right, all right, all right, niggas. Let's calm this shit down," Kiko interrupted. "We got way more important shit to worry about than this man's dick," he laughed. "Or your suppressed feelings, Heim."

"Suppressed feelings? Nigga, you've been watching Iyanla again, huh?" Heim joked.

"Aye, you can learn a lot from that sista. You see how I've calmed down with my temper. I mean, I'll still kill a muthafucka, but it has to take a little more than stepping on my shoe to do it now."

Kiko looked at both Heim and me. "So are we good? We've come too far to start tripping on each other now."

My eyes traveled to Heim, who was not only my partner, but my brother. Shit between us has never gotten this heated, and I didn't want it to start. He was right, I shouldn't have stepped to Savvy when I did. But I couldn't help it. I stuck out my fist for Heim to pound. "We good?"

Nodding his head, he dapped my fist. "Yeah, we good. But, aye, I'm about to roll up out of here and handle this business. If y'all need me or anything goes down, hit me on my cell. I'll see y'all later on tonight."

"Tell Reign we said what's up, nigga," Kiko yelled to his back laughing.

"Fuck you, you Boris Kodjoe-looking mutha-fucka."

"I don't know why he just won't leave that girl alone and let her move on with her life. Reign ain't fucking with that nigga like that no more anyway."

I grabbed my keys off of the bar counter and started for the exit. Next stop was to Savvy's house to try to see where I stood with her. I had every intention of going over there and lying about where I had been the last few weeks, but I didn't see any point in that. If we wanted our relationship to work out, Savvy had to understand the methods behinds some of this madness, and I had to be considerate of her feelings.

I knew I would've been at her front door every day had I not heard from her in a couple of days.

"Is everything on for tonight?" I asked Kiko as we walked outside to my car. "I still want all the businesses to continue running like any normal day. Make sure you tell Germ to have our section in the VIP stocked with alcohol and a couple of your niggas from the security team walking around all night. This is the first big event we've had since the shooting, and I want everything to run smoothly."

"I got you, Lyfe. What if Sarai calls trying to get in? You know with an event this big, her and her girls normally fall through. Especially if she knows you'll be here."

I thought about Sarai coming out tonight since I planned on bringing Savannah with me as my date. I knew she wouldn't act a fool in public to save face, but Desiree and Peaches were a different story. "Make sure their names aren't on the list. The event is invite-only, so make sure whoever is at the door knows that."

Kiko nodded. "Where you 'bout to go?"

I slid into my car and rolled the window down. "To make things right with my girl."

Kiko smiled. "Heim gonna kill your ass, watch—if Sarai don't do it first."

I didn't even respond back to him as I pulled out of my parking space and headed toward Savannah's office. Hopefully, she didn't have any client meetings today because we really needed to talk.

"Welcome to Zaher Law Firm. How can I help you today?" the cute receptionist at the front desk asked as I walked into Savvy's office building. I looked around at the newly painted walls, oversized plants, and modern furniture that now occupied the lobby area of the office. Everything looked neat and professional, way different from the empty space it was the last time I was here.

I removed my glasses from my face and smiled. "Hi, I'm here to see Savannah."

She blushed and looked at something on her computer. "Do you have an appointment with Ms. Zaher? I don't see anything on her schedule for this time."

"No, I don't have an appointment. I'm just stopping by to see her."

"Uhhhh, well, Ms. Zaher doesn't see any new clients without an appointment. If you like, I can schedule for next week. There's a 10 a.m. and 11:30 a.m. slot open."

I heard Savannah's sweet laugh come from behind her door. "Is she in there with a client?"

"I can't tell you that, sir."

"Well, can you tell her that I'm out here?" I asked, voice slightly raised. I didn't get what the big problem was for her to pick up the phone and tell Savannah that I was here.

She looked at me with a little fear in her eyes. "Uh, Mr. Montoya requested that they not be disturbed."

Mr. Montoya? There was only one mutha-fucka that I knew with that last name, and he wasn't about to start running shit around here. I walked from in front of the receptionist's desk and headed to Savannah's office door.

"Sir, you can't just go back there."

"Watch me," I snapped, venom laced all in my tone. I told this nigga to stay away from Savannah the last time I saw him, and here he was, all in her face again, having a private, do-not-disturb meeting in her office. I could tell from the flirty laugh I heard Savvy just make a few minutes ago that their conversation didn't consist of just law talk.

Sidestepping the receptionist, I reached Savvy's door and opened it without knocking. The first thing I saw when my body entered the room was Savvy and Hash embraced in a hug.

When her eyes landed on me, there wasn't an ounce of fear in them. Instead of breaking away from his hold like I assumed she would, Savvy lingered in his arms for a few seconds longer, then pulled away and kissed him on his cheek.

"Thank you for lunch, Hash. I really appreciate it."

"No problem, baby. Maybe we could do this again, say tomorrow night?" Hash looked at me and smirked. "You still owe me for moving those big-ass sofas and chairs in the lobby from the truck."

"I do. Let me think about it and get back to you, okay?" She touched his cheek with her open palm, and he grabbed her wrist and kissed it.

"Call me when you get in tonight."

"I will."

"No, she won't. Now get your fuck-boy ass out of here," I hissed through clenched teeth.

Hash looked at me and tilted his head but didn't say anything else as he walked out of Savvy's office with the receptionist right behind him. Closing the door, I rested my back against it and looked at the woman who had my mind about to go crazy. Seeing Hash with his arms around Savvy's body had me feeling some type of way and almost committing a murder right here in her office. But I already had a lot of bullshit trying to take me down. I didn't want to add a homicide to that list.

Savvy walked back around to the seat behind her desk and started to clean the mess that she and Hash made with lunch. Once she had everything in the tiny trash can by the back window, she opened her computer and started to type something like I wasn't even there. I knew she was going to be mad at me, but I wasn't expecting it to be on the level of completely ignoring me. But I guess that was what I deserved, seeing as I treated her the same way these last couple of weeks. Blowing a frustrated breath from my mouth, I wiped my hand down my face and started to plead my case.

"Savvy, let me ex—"

"Why?" she asked cutting me off, eyes never leaving the computer.

"Why what?"

"Why are you here?"

"That's what I was about to tell you."

We sat in silence for a few minutes. Her fingers rapidly pressing hard on the keyboard keys. "I'm waiting."

"Look, Savvy, the only way this will come out right is if I just keep it one hunnid." I licked my lips, nerves slightly rattled. "I've been going through some shit that might not only jeopardize my freedom, but the people around me as well. And I had to make sure that *everybody* was on point just in case some shit goes left."

"When you say *everybody,* that includes your wife as well?"

"You already—" She held her hand up, cutting me off.

"Does it include your wife as well?"

I stood up from the door and walked farther into Savvy's office. My eyes looked around at the decor in here, which was just a smaller version of the one in the lobby. Everything white with silver and pink accents. Her desk was even new. Instead of the dark old-school one I helped bring in, she now had one of those glass desks with the white top and the big plush tufted office chair to match. Pictures of her during her college years scattered on the wall, while pictures of her, Heim, and I sat in little silver frames on her desk. I picked up one of the pictures and smiled. It was the one we took inside of the restaurant Fahrenheit for Savvy's sixteenth birthday. The same night we shared our first kiss.

The receptionist's voice coming over the intercom broke me from my trip down memory lane. "Ms. Zaher, your next appointment is here."

"Tell them I'll be with them in a second." Savvy's eyes finally left her computer screen and turned to me. "Since you can't answer my question, this conversation is over. Could you please do me a favor and leave my office so I can get some work done?"

"Not until you give me a chance to explain."

She looked at the gold watch on her wrist and then rolled her eyes. "You have two minutes, Lyfe, so don't waste them."

I smiled at the little attitude she was trying to give me. There was no doubt that she was in her feelings and upset, but that didn't stop her body from becoming aroused the closer I stepped to her. I could see her nipples through the thin blue blouse she had on. The white polka dots did a good job disguising it, but if you were looking hard enough, you could see them hardening by the minute. Then the red knee-length skirt she had on did little to hide the scent of her arousal. I could smell her from where I was standing, and it had my dick hard as hell. As much as I wanted to bend her ass over her desk and fuck the shit out of her, I had to calm myself down and get to the real reason why I came here.

"To answer your question, yes, everybody includes Sarai. But it's not for the reason that you think. I just found out that the feds and some local detectives are snooping around trying to find some information on a few cases that may or may not involve me. If, by some chance, I am charged, you already know with your profession how important it is to have a spouse's loyalty, regardless of whether you want to be with them. And if Sarai is the key to me staying a free man, I'm going to do whatever I have to do to make sure she and I are both on the same page."

Savannah's brows furrowed. "The feds and local detectives? What do they have on you? And does any of this involve my brother?"

"The thing with the detectives, I don't think so. But on the sealed indictment, I was told that a few names were on there. Heim's may be one of them."

"Shit, Lyfe. Why didn't you tell me this when you found out? I could've been on top of shit already." She picked up her phone and dialed a number. "Do you know who's over the cases?"

"No, I don't, and you don't need to worry about that either. My attorney and his team got shit handled and will take care of everything, should anything happen."

"You say that as if I couldn't handle a case like this if I got the opportunity."

"I'm not saying anything like that. I know you can do that, and much more." I walked around to the back of her desk and pulled her up from her seat, wrapping my arms around her. "Do you forgive me for being MIA these last couple of weeks? I promise it won't happen like that again."

Savvy looked me in my eyes, trying to make sure I was telling the truth. She always said that my eyes gave it away whenever I was lying, but I never believed that shit. "Did you fuck her?"

I shook my head. "No. All we did was spend time as a family and do family shit. I slept in the guest room or in my kids' bedrooms on different nights."

She looked into my eyes again. "I believe you, Lyfe. But next time, you better call, text, or something. I was going crazy not knowing where you were or hearing your voice."

"Me too." I kissed her lips, and we both moaned at the same time. "Can a nigga get a little of that sweetness between your legs? I know you said I had two minutes, but call and tell your receptionist you need an extra ten."

Savannah laughed and pushed me back. "You can have some tonight when you come over for dinner."

"Don't you have plans with that bitch-ass nigga Hash?" I asked, being funny.

"You jealous?"

"Naw, but didn't I tell you to stay away from that nigga? He's a snake. Don't have him around here anymore."

She nodded her head. "So what do you want for dinner?"

"Nothing," I said as I pulled her back into me. "I want you to come out to the club with me tonight. We're having a listening party for a local rapper, and I want you to be my date."

"You're serious?"

"Why wouldn't I be?"

"I mean, that's kind of big taking me out and shit. I thought you wanted to keep shit low until you and your wife officially separate."

"I do. But you won't have to worry about that tonight. This party is invite-only. So neither Sarai nor anyone she knows will be there. Just a lot of out-of-towners, local DJs, industry reps, and shit like that."

My phone started to vibrate in my pocket like crazy. When I took it out and looked at the caller ID, it was Sarai.

"Go ahead and answer you phone so I can get to my clients. I'll see you later tonight, okay?" Savannah said as she walked me to the door. My eyes went down to her ass, and I couldn't help but to grab it. Pulling her back to my chest, I kissed her neck, and then the spot behind her ear.

"I'll see you later," I whispered before kissing her one last time.

As soon as I stepped into the lobby area, Sarai was calling my phone again. I knew she had to be up to something; it was the only time she called me back-to-back.

"What's up, Sarai?"

"Where the fuck you at?" she snapped into the phone. It had only been half a day since I'd left the house, and here she was with the bullshit again. I made a mental note to stop by before I went out tonight, just to show my face and settle her nerves. I couldn't wait until all this shit was over, because going back and forth between Savvy and Sarai—something had to give.

Kwan

Reaching into the ashtray, I pulled out a partially smoked blunt and lit it. Savoring the smooth taste, I leaned farther back in my seat, blew out a cloud of smoke, and turned the music all the way up. I was halfway to Charlotte, and even though I was high as hell, driving throughout the night had me tired as fuck. With no one to talk to, I was finding it hard to stay awake due to the boredom I was experiencing.

It had been a long time since I'd taken this trip down 85, especially as a free man. Some spots looked exactly the same, while others were a bit new to me. However, I was getting closer to my destination, and I couldn't wait to touch down. Lazily rolling my eyes over the highway, I switched lanes, cutting off the compact four door that was now behind me. The driver blew his horn a couple of times and yelled something out the window, but I wasn't worried about shit he was saying. I had somewhere to be and more than a few people who I needed to see.

Taking a few more pulls of the blunt, my mind began to play back everything that was about to happen now that I was home. The strong desire to not only reclaim my former empire, but to also reclaim the only woman I had ever truly cared for was top priority on my list, and not in any particular order. There was also that little "incident" involving my brother that upped this situation tremendously. When I found out a few days ago that Quick wasn't going to be accompanying my girl for my release, my heart damn near shattered into pieces. Through my whole six-year bid at Butner Federal Correctional, that was the one image that had kept me sane. But now, thanks to these niggas Lyfe and Naheim, I had lost both. Yeah, I had a lot of shit to take care of now that I was home and wasn't nan nigga gon' stop me from taking back everything that was once mine.

With my foot leaning heavily on the gas pedal, I blew out another cloud of smoke and glanced over at Scottie's loud-snoring ass. Since my brother or girl wasn't able to come welcome me back the right way, I was stuck with him. I mean, it was good seeing my nigga after all this time, but I would have rather made this return trip with someone else. Muthafucka took a whole bottle of Hennessey to the head on his way here and didn't save me a drop. As soon as he stepped out of the car and gave me a pound, his ass blacked out and has been gone ever since.

Looking at the time on the dashboard, I couldn't help the smile that formed on my face. According to my calculations from earlier, we should be arriving in the city by daybreak, and so far, we were on time. Just one more stop to refill the tank and stretch my legs and I'd be one step closer to handling those bitch-ass niggas Lyfe and Naheim, as well as getting everything in my life back in order. The Queen City awaited my return, and who was I to deny her, her king?

An hour later, I pulled up in front of an address that I had embedded in my mind. After months of receiving letters and packages, I made sure to memorize it just in case I had to pop up on a muthafucka like I was about to do now. This bitch had me really fucked up if she thought that not coming to get me was cool. Obviously, those six years of me being gone must've fogged up her memory or something, but I was going to remind her of who I was today. Taking one last pull of the blunt, I snuffed it out and then placed it back in the ashtray. The loud snoring from the passenger's side was getting louder, and I was almost tempted to let him continue to sleep, but this nigga was about to wake up. Riding around with me, Scottie needed to be awake so that he could watch our surroundings while I went to handle this business. I hit the sleeping nigga on the side of his face, causing his head to hit the window. "Get up, Scottie, we're here."

Squinting his sleep-filled eyes, I watched as this nigga stretched his arms and looked around. "Where we at?"

"Where the hell you think we're at, fool? We're in Charlotte, nigga."

"Charlotte?" Sitting up to get a better view of his surroundings, Scottie scanned the area. "What part of the city are we in? Because this don't look like the hood, my nigga."

Frowning at his foolish question, the thought came to mind that not even he was ghetto enough to not recognize where the hell we were. But the truth was, he didn't. Like a lot of young street niggas, Scottie had never been far from our hood. So there were places in the city that were like a foreign country to him. The area didn't consist of boarded up or abandoned houses, grass and weeds as tall as your front porch, niggas sitting outside smoking and shooting dice, bitches patrolling the block with the tiniest clothes on looking for the next dope boy to come up on or their badass kids outside doing what those bad hood babies do. We were in an area far from the hood we grew up in, so I could understand him not being familiar with it.

"This Ballantyne, youngin. I gotta holla at an old friend right quick, so get over here in the driver's seat and don't take your Allen Iverson ass back to sleep. You know these white muthafuckas around here will call the police on your ass quick assuming you're out here burglarizing somebody's house," I warned, hopping out of the car. Hopefully, his ass stayed up and didn't call any attention to himself. I had a feeling I might be here for a while, especially if my baby is really happy to see me.

Deciding to surprise her ass on my arrival, I walked around to the back door and wiggled the knob. Of course, it was locked, but I was already expecting that, which was why I had Scottie to bring me this little tool kit. Pulling the kit from my back pocket, I worked my magic on the door and had it popped open within a few seconds. I walked into the dark house already knowing my way around, thanks to the layout my boy sent me awhile back. There weren't any other cars in the driveway, so I wasn't scared of another nigga being here. However, I did have my gun cradled in my hand and ready to bust if the opportunity presented itself.

Creeping down the hall, I checked the first two rooms I walked past. Both were empty. My curiosity did pique a bit, though, when I saw that one of the rooms was decorated for a little boy. There was a twin-size bed underneath the two windows with an Avengers comforter neatly over the top. Character paraphernalia was hanging on every wall while all sorts of toys and trucks were spread out over the floor.

I could feel my blood start to boil as my eyes roamed over the neatly decorated room. Not only was this bitch fucking with the enemy, but she had a baby by the nigga too. No wonder she'd been avoiding my calls and coming to see me in the last year and a half. Money stayed on my books, and the letters and packages came like clockwork every month, but she never mentioned anything about having a baby on me.

I closed the door to the room, making sure not to make any kind of noise and continued down the hall. Entering into her bedroom, the smell of the vanilla scent she always wore circled around my head and invaded my nostrils. My dick began to swell as I thought about her thick hips and the way she used to ride my dick, smelling like that sweet scent. Eventually, I would be dipping in her pussy again, but tonight . . . Tonight, I needed to remind her of who I was.

Walking past her canopy bed and over a pile of clothes and shoes that more than likely belong to the nigga she'd been playing house with, I stood outside of the cracked bathroom door and admired my baby's naked body. Standing in front of the mirror looking at herself, I silently watched as she bounced her titties around with her hands, and then started to wind her hips and move her lips to the song she had playing from her phone.

"But baby, don't get it twisted. You was just another nigga on the hit list, tryna fix your inner issues with a bad bitch. Didn't they tell you that I was a savage?"

As mad as I was at Peaches, I couldn't deny that she was sexy as fuck. Flawless brown skin, big brown eyes, full, pouty lips, and a body that most of these funny-shaped bitches would kill for. On top of that, she was a hood chick, with a nigga mentality, and down for whatever. What real nigga would ask for anything more? That's why when I heard about what she had been doing in the streets and who she was fucking with, I couldn't fathom it.

She turned toward the door and was just about to walk my way, but stopped when her phone that was sitting on top of the closed toilet rang. I could tell by the conversation that she was talking to Naheim's soon-to-be dead ass.

"Where the fuck are you at? I don't wanna hear that shit, Heim. I've been calling you for the last few days. When are you coming home?" She smacked her lips and rolled her eyes. "I know you don't fucking live here, and I'ma keep questioning your ass. I don't give a fuck about any of that. You better not be at that bitch Reign's house. I still owe her an ass whipping from the last time. No, I'm not about to stop talking about that ugly-ass troll-looking bitch. What the fuck does she got on me? Well, nigga, if she has your heart like that, why you runnin' up in me every chance you fucking get? Fuck you, Heim, you can kiss my ass." She became quiet for a minute.

"Did you ask Lyfe about me taking over that spot for you? I know that nigga don't like me. What does that—Come on, Heim, you know I need to pay my bills and shit. I know you give me money, but it's not enough. Job? Are you serious? I don't give a fuck what that bitch Reign—You know what? Call me later, and you better come see me before the week is up or I'ma come looking for your ass, nigga."

I didn't know whether to be mad at her begging this nigga to come see her or at the fact that she still fucked with this nigga knowing that I never fucked with him or Lyfe's bitch asses like that. I never questioned anything Peaches did, but the way she was just talking to this nigga sounded like she really cared about him or was falling in love. My mind began to wonder as I watched her immerse herself into the sudsy water and lay her head back on the pillow with her eyes closed. The same song was on repeat and started to play again. Was my savage now turning into the prey? Did she really want that white horse and carriage with another nigga?

The candles that were lit around the bathroom had a relaxed setting going on for her and was probably helping her get over the argument she just had with that lame nigga, but I was about to break that shit all the way up. Pushing the door open, I stepped fully into the bathroom and slammed my gun on the sink, causing a loud pitch sound to resonate through the room. Peaches' eyes flashed opened and landed directly on me. Bringing her hand from out of the water, I wasn't surprised to see the pink .380 dripping wet and pointing directly at me.

"Damn, don't I get a hug or something?" I jokingly asked. With her fingers still wrapped tightly around the gun, Peaches stood up from her seat in the tub, water and soap slowly sliding down her curvy and thick body. My eyes traveled to her shaved pussy. Peaches was always working with a little fatty down there, but with it now being hairless, my second favorite place on earth was looking plumper than I remember.

"Put the gun down, LeNora. We both know you're not about to pull the trigger." I shook my head and smiled. "Quick to pull, but never the first to shoot. Didn't I tell you moving like that will get you killed every time?"

"You also told me that I was the only woman you ever loved, but we see how *that* turned out."

"It's been six years, Peaches, and you still bringing Shawna up." Shawna was Peaches' old road dog back in the day. Setting niggas up and taking niggas for their money was the life they lived by and how I actually met them. During one of Peaches's and my breakup periods, Shawna and I fucked around for a minute. I'm not even gonna front. The pussy was good, and her head was out of this world. Not better than Peaches's, but pretty close. And on some real shit, I probably would've still been fucking around with ole girl. But the bitch tried to set me up, and I couldn't deal with a disloyal bitch. Especially if I was fucking her.

It only took two hours for me to find out that she had her baby daddy and a few of his buddies run up in one of my houses and take some money and dope, which was crazy, seeing as I used to break her ass off left and right. Needless to say, neither she nor her baby's father was alive to do that shit again. I had love for the bitch, but not enough to keep her walking around, like robbing me was the way to go.

Peaches stepped out of the tub with her gun still trained on me. I picked up the plush blue towel behind me and handed it to her. "You still gon' point your shit at me, huh?"

"Until you tell me what you're here for . . . then, yeah." She tried to put on a brave face, but I could feel the fear radiating from inside of her. Taking the towel from my hand, she started to dry off her body. Eyes still on me. "You look good, Kwan. Those six years did you good."

I smiled and nodded my head, but not in acknowledgment of the compliment I had just received. A few things were going through my mind in regards to Peaches' life, and I was having a hard time figuring out what I was going to do. Peaches had been real disloyal these last few years, and I was conflicted about how I was going to handle the situation. I could kill her now and move on to the next bitch, but then, I would have to train that one to be the type of girl I needed by my side, and I didn't have time for that. If I decided to let Peaches live and somehow managed to get back into her head, she could be an important piece in reclaiming my drug empire and enacting my revenge. There were so many decisions to make and not enough time. Whichever way I decided to go, I just hoped Peaches could forgive me for how she ended up in the end.

"Had you come to see me in the last two years, this muscle and weight gain wouldn't have been a surprise for you. Did you miss me?" I asked, looking down at my tattooed arms and flexing my fingers. The minute she saw her real name blasted on the back of my left hand, she gasped and walked over to take a closer look. Placing her gun next to mine, she reached her hand out and took mine into hers, admiring the tattoo I got a little while back.

"Kwan, you know I missed you. I've missed you every day since you been gone. No matter what I've been up to, baby, you were always on my mind. Always. That's why I stayed putting money on your books, sending letters, and having those packages delivered. I was out here getting it the best way I knew how. You believe me, right?"

I thought about the one-sided conversation I overheard her having with Naheim. "If I needed your help with getting everything back that was taken from me, would you be down?"

She looked up at me and swallowed the lump in her throat. "Wha . . . What did you have in mind?"

"Aren't you fucking with that nigga Naheim?" Her body froze and a look I've never seen before crossed her face. She was in love with this nigga.

"What does Heim, I mean Naheim, have to do with any of this? It's Lyfe who makes all of the decisions. He's the one that's in charge. Naheim just does what Lyfe says. He's nobody."

The fact that she was willing to downplay Naheim's role in their whole operation told me everything that I needed to know about her feelings for this nigga. I smiled and rubbed my chin. Yeah, I would use her ass to get all the information I needed on these niggas and fuck her whole life up in the process. A much harsher punishment than killing her off the bat.

I grabbed her by her neck and pulled her closer to me, face in a scowl and nostrils flaring, playing the role I needed to play. "You love this nigga or something? You his ride-or-die bitch now? I thought you would always be mine, baby."

She quickly shook her head. "No. I don't love him, Kwan. Naheim is just a mark. I'm trying to get in good so that I could learn everything I needed to learn to rob his ass blind. I . . . I don't love him." She broke eye contact with me and looked down at the ground. "Everything I've been doing is for us. That's the reason why I sent Scottie to go pick you up instead of me. I couldn't chance someone seeing me with you, and it getting back to Heim. He would never trust me then."

She looked back up at me and pressed her body next to mine. "We've been through way too much for me to bail out on you now. I know you haven't forgotten how good we once were together," she stated desperately, trying to turn the charm on now. "I still love you, Kwan, and not even you can be angry at the woman who loves you and will doing anything to make sure that you're back on top. Even if that means sleeping with the enemy."

Before I could even respond, Peaches' pouty lips were on mine, and my dick was getting hard. A nigga hadn't had any pussy in six years, and I was ready for some in a real way, but her ass wasn't about to get off that easy. Peaches needed to be punished, and there was only one way I could do that without killing her right now. Pulling my shirt over my head, I let her remove my jeans and boxers next. My dick sprang directly into her face and mouth the minute she lowered herself to her knees in front of me. Grabbing the back of her head, I shoved my dick down her throat as far as it could go. I could feel her nails clawing at my thighs to pull back, but I didn't. Tears were streaming from her eyes before I yanked her head back, and my dick out of her mouth.

"Stand up and bend over the sink," I instructed as I moved out of the way, stroking my shit.

Rolling her eyes at me, Peaches got up from her knees and did as she was told. Spreading her cheeks wide, I spat in my hand and rubbed the head of my dick with it. I needed my shit to be sloppy wet for what I was about to do.

"Hold it open, baby, just like that," I said from behind her, as I positioned myself and dick with her asshole. Before she could protest, I pushed into the tight little hole until my dick completely disappeared.

"What the fuck?" Peaches screamed. When she tried to move, I pulled her arms behind her back and held them in place. "Kwan, that shit hurts." Ignoring what she was saying, I began to pound into her.

"Please! Ohhh! Ohhh! Kwan! Ohhh, stop. Kwan—please stop!" Peaches cried out loudly, in a hoarse, quivering voice. With tears clouding her eyes as her body forcefully crashed into mine, she begged and pleaded with her insides raw and flaming. "Please take it out, Kwan! Oh my God—you're killing me!" she yelled.

I continued to chastise her as a slightly hysterical chuckle erupted from between my tightly clenched teeth. I was giving Peaches a mercy fuck she would never forget. Her eyes went wide as hell when I let her know that I wasn't following behind that nigga Naheim. Nah, she was going to have to give me what no man had ever had and take it. I continued to force myself into her tight ass over and over. Feeling my approaching climax, I closed my eyes and slammed into Peaches hard and fast.

Whimpering her pleas between grunts, she had to swallow in order to force down the vomit that threatened to find its way to the surface. Her torture came to an abrupt end when she felt me shoot my load deep inside her, followed by a loud, satisfied groan.

"Thank God," Peaches barely spoke above a whisper as she slumped against the bed.

"Now, *that's* what I call some good ass," I commented, pulling my dick out and slapping her roughly on her massive, right cheek. "You saved that good, tight shit for daddy, didn't you?" I taunted, wiping myself on her thick towel. I decided to fuck with her a little bit.

"I got a good mind to get me some seconds on that ass." I laughed at the fear that showed on her features as she raised up from her slumped position and began backing away with wide eyes and her palms held outward.

"Stop tripping. I was only playing. I got shit to do right now, but I'll take a rain check for later." Kissing her forehead, I looked around the bathroom for my discarded clothes.

As I moved around, I could see Peaches nervously standing frozen in place from the corner of my eye. The pain she felt coursing through her rectum was displayed across her face. I could tell she wanted to say something but decided to keep that shit to herself. Picking up my clothes and putting everything back on, I took her cell phone off of the toilet and punched in my new number.

"Call me later on tonight so we can meet up sometime this week and talk."

With tears streaming down her face, she slowly nodded her head and took her phone out of my hand. "I really am happy you're home, baby."

"I know you are. I'll check in with you later, okay?" I didn't wait for her to respond. Picking up my gun, I tucked it into my jeans and left her in the bathroom by herself. Peaches knew shit was about to get real bad out here in these streets. With the prison bid behind me and my brother's recent murder, niggas were about to feel me. Naheim and Lyfe were killers, but they lived by rules and ethics—two things I didn't give a fuck about. If Peaches knew what was best for her, she'd play both sides if she wanted a chance to win and stay alive.

Sarai

"What I tell you? I told you he was fucking with her."

"Peaches, all that nigga did was go into a law office and come back out twenty minutes later. How does that mean he's fucking somebody in there?"

"It's not just somebody, Desiree. It's Naheim's stuck-up-ass sister. I'm telling you now, Sarai, Lyfe spending time with her is not a good thing. I don't know the extent of their relationship or whatnot, but if Heim has a problem with it, something ain't right. You know him and Lyfe see eye to eye on everything. But they beefing about something, and it's behind her. Whenever I ask him what's going on, he just tells me to mind my own business."

"And why wouldn't he? He's not going to dime his sister out to you or anybody else. You sound so dumb sometimes, Peaches. I will never understand what Naheim sees in your trifling ass."

"Says the bitch who tried to get with him first, but he curved for me."

"That's only because your ho ass was opening and closing your legs in the club that night showing him your burnt-ass pussy. You ever wonder why he still chases after that girl Reign instead of making you his girl? Because that nigga know you're not supposed to turn a ho into a housewife."

"Ho? Bitch, don't act like the majority of them broke-ass niggas from the projects ain't ran up in your tired-ass pussy. At least I get paid fucking with the niggas I pull."

"Or you just rob their asses before the voodoo dust you blow into their faces wears off."

"Voodoo? Bitch, please. You just mad that you can't snag a nigga with money like me."

Desiree shrugged her shoulders. "Not really. I'm good with the dude I'm fucking with now. He isn't big time like Lyfe or Naheim, but he makes a little bit of change."

I picked my phone up from my lap and tried calling Lyfe's phone again as these two continued to argue back and forth. He answered a couple of minutes ago, but when I cursed his ass out and asked him where he was at and what he was doing, he hung up in my face and hadn't answered my calls since.

"What's the nigga's name that you fucking with?" Peaches asked Desiree. We were sitting in my black Jaguar across the street from some spot called the Zaher Law Firm. I knew Naheim's sister was a lawyer and shit, but I didn't know she was doing it like this. When Peaches told me that Heim came in the house the other night going off about Lyfe and his sister, I wasn't really tripping. I knew they had a little relationship in the past, but I didn't think it was anything for me to worry about. Well, that was until I started thinking about my husband's behavior in the last two weeks. Normally when Lyfe stays the night for a couple of days, I could persuade him to have sex with me. This last time, however, I tried every trick in the book, and his ass would not budge. I even went as far as buying some new lingerie and serving him his favorite dinner in it and still nothing. One night I crept into the guest room that he was sleeping in and tried to unbuckle his pants to give him some head, but he swatted my hands away and turned on his stomach. I will admit, I was in my feelings a bit because Lyfe had never turned me down for sex before. I didn't care if he and I hadn't slept in the same house for months. I was always able to get a quickie or suck his dick until he busted in my mouth. But now, I couldn't even touch his ass, and there was only one reason that a nigga would turn down sex with his wife. Another woman had his nose open.

I knew this day would eventually come, but I wasn't ready for it right now. Lyfe and I had always thrown the divorce word around in the air, but neither of us had ever signed the papers. They would get drawn up and then thrown right in the trash. However, now, I was feeling like this time when he brought up us getting a divorce, he might actually go through with it.

I tried calling his phone again, and just like the last ten times, my calls continued to go straight to voicemail. I started to leave another message, but didn't, seeing as he hadn't listened to the last nine. I watched as my husband sat in his car for a few moments with the biggest smile on his face before pulling off and heading in the direction of his house on the other side of town.

"I thought we were going to follow him, Sarai," Desiree said, breaking me from my thoughts.

"Yeah, you got me in my all-black Prada outfit for nothing," Peaches added.

"Didn't nobody ask you what designer you were wearing."

"I know. But I wanted to make sure your hating ass knew."

"See, this is why—" Desiree started to say, but I cut her off.

"Will you both just shut the fuck up? Damn, I can't even think with you two cackling hoes going for each other's throat."

"Why we gotta be cackling hoes?" Peaches asked, and I just blankly stared at her stupid ass. See, this was one of the reasons why she and I stopped being so cool back when we were kids. I could only tolerate so much of her faux-sidity attitude in a day. Desiree was more laid-back like me, which was why we got along so well. Of course, she also had her airhead moments, but she was still cool to be around.

I stared at the law office building Lyfe just came out of. Something kept telling me to get out of my car and go and introduce myself to the bitch that had my husband denying me sex and smiling so big. But the other half kept telling me to pull off before I did something that would have me ending up in jail. Just as I was about to be on some messy shit, my phone dinged, alerting me of a text I just received. I kinda felt some type of way when I saw that the message wasn't from Lyfe. Had our relationship really come to this? That was a question that I would no doubt need an answer to, just not right now. There was a nice piece of change calling my name, and you know I was never one to say no to making a little money. Starting the car, I pulled off from the curb we were sitting at and headed toward the direction of my customer who stayed on the outskirts of Charlotte.

"So we not gon' go inside and be messy?"

"Everybody isn't as ghetto as you, Peaches. Besides, why should Sarai have to stoop to the level of a side chick like you to solidify her place in her husband's life? Everybody knows who she is and who she's married to. I'm pretty sure Lyfe wouldn't jeopardize the life of Naheim's only sister just for some pussy."

"Let's get one thing straight. I have never been, or will ever be, a 'side chick.' 'Second wife' or 'new boo' are the terms I prefer."

"Which all mean *side chick* in the book of hoes."

"Whatever." Peaches turned her attention to me. "You never said where we were going, Sarai. It looks like we're leaving the city."

"We are. I just need to make this drop-off; then we will be right back."

From the corner of my eye, I saw Desiree shake her head while Peaches played with her nails in the back. Desiree still didn't agree with me stealing coke from Lyfe, but that didn't stop her from helping me take it from the stash house or delivering it to some of my clientele. The stack I gave her after every drop was her motivation to come and why she sat her ass right there in that passenger's seat every time. Turning the radio up, we continued to cruise down 85 while Mary J. Blige's newest song, "Thick of It," blasted through the speaker.

"So, tell me who, who's gonna love you like I do? Who will you trust? I gave you too much. Enough is enough. Now we're in the thick of it."

"You know, I like Mary J. and all, but the bitch is so goddamn depressing sometimes. Does she have any happy songs on her CDs?"

"What? Like 'There's Some Hoes in This House'? I bet that's one of your favorite songs."

"Desiree, I'm not going to be too many more hoes. Cousin or not, I will beat your ass and bring you flowers to the hospital on the same day."

Desiree laughed. "I'm just saying. Obviously, these songs are written for people going through similar situations or can relate. Perfect example, Sarai and Lyfe. I think this song is exactly what they are going through right now."

Peaches looked at me through the rearview mirror, and my eyes connected with hers. When she saw the redness in mine, her hand gently squeezed my shoulder. "I apologize for being so insensitive about your feelings and what you and Lyfe are going through, friend. Personally, I hope you two never break up. Y'all are #relation-shipgoals to me and a lot of these other bitches out here. Desiree included."

I laughed and wiped the lone tear that escaped from my eye. "Girl, don't let our relationship be your goal. Everything that looks golden isn't always gold."

"And you should know that better than anyone else, Peaches. Because that nigga Kwan had your ass out here looking stupid fucking your little partner in crime while you were trying to make everybody believe that y'all was the perfect couple."

The minute Kwan's name slipped from Desiree's mouth, Peaches' whole body froze up. The slick expression on her face was now replaced with fear, which had her turning around and checking her surroundings.

"You okay, girl?" I asked. Her whole demeanor changed. She nodded her head, but I could tell that she was lying. "Why you lookin' like that?"

"No reason." She was lying. I knew her change in moods had to do something with Kwan, so I decided to dig a little deeper. We were almost at our destination, and I needed her to be calm and over the situation before we got there.

"When's the last time you went to visit Kwan? I know since you got with Heim, you really haven't been talking about him much."

She licked her lips and pulled out her phone and started typing something on it. "I . . . I . . . I . . . haven't seen him in some months. Last I heard, he was still in jail."

Just as she put her phone down, Desiree's dinged. She picked it up, read the message, and then squinted her eyes. Seconds after she sent her response, Peaches' phone dinged. Something was going on with those two that had something to do with Kwan. I didn't know what it was, but I could tell it was something that neither one of them wanted me to know about. I didn't care anyway. Kwan and I had only met once, so it wasn't like he and I were friends. I just knew him as Peaches's boyfriend, and that was it. He used to be kind of big out in Charlotte with the drugs and shit, but once Lyfe and Heim started coming up, Kwan ended up in jail and forgotten about by anyone that mattered.

While Desiree and Peaches continued to text each other back and forth, I kept my eyes trained on the road with thoughts of Lyfe and our kids on my mind. I never thought about how a divorce might affect my kids until now. Even though Lyfe didn't live with us the majority of the time, he was still real active in our children's lives. Never has he taken them for the weekend or had them spend the night at one of his other houses. We always stayed together, like a family should. The funny thing about this whole situation, though, I didn't know if it would be me or the kids more affected by the separation. Yeah, I talked shit about not caring if we divorce or not, but the real truth was, I did care. I loved Lyfe with everything in me and would literally die for his selfish ass. The problem was, he didn't feel the same way about me, and I knew that from the very beginning.

Pulling up to the trailer park homes, I passed the broken-down security gate and rode all the way to the back like my customer instructed. Looking around the messy and somewhat deserted area with watchful eyes, I reached down and made sure my gun was in my purse, just in case I needed it. I'd never been to this part of town, and most likely would never come back, but we were already here, and no turning back now. However, a funny feeling began to settle in my stomach, which was normally a sign for me. But with the amount of money I was about to make from selling this half a kilo of powder, it pushed that feeling all the way to the back of my mind.

"Aye, I'll give you an extra stack if you come with me in here and watch my back," I told Desiree as I pulled the 9 mm Taurus from my purse.

"Shiiiiid. You crazy as hell if you think I'ma go in there with you." She pointed to the old run-down yellow and white trailer sitting on huge concrete blocks. The grass was so thick and high that you could barely see the rotted out porch leaning a little to the left. A very malnourished dog was on a leash and lying in his small dog shack at the edge of the porch. "I don't know these people. They been done messed around and killed both of our asses."

"Ain't nobody killing nobody," I said more confidently than I felt. "As a matter of fact, keep ya scary ass in this car, and I'll take Peaches with me," I said, opening the driver's-side door and getting out of the car with the gun visibly in my hand. "You coming?" I looked back at Peaches and asked.

"Girl, you know I live for shit like this," she replied, cocking back the gun I didn't even know she had. "I do this type of stuff with Heim all the time, so I got you. And you don't even have to pay me."

Peaches stepped out of the backseat, clad in her all-black Prada outfit, while I stood next to her in a pair of hip-hugging jeans, a pastel-striped blazer, and some pink stiletto heels to match. My hair was parted down the middle and hanging bone straight. Makeup flawless as always with jewelry on my neck, fingers, ears, and wrists that probably cost more than the land all of these old-ass trailers sat on. Walking down the broken brick path, I carefully climbed the porch and knocked on the door a few times with the butt of my gun, duffel bag hanging over my shoulder.

"There she goes," Jack smiled, opening his door for me and Peaches. "Who is this other lovely lady you have with you today?"

"What's up, Jack? And who she is, is none of your business. Just know that she's with me."

Jack lustfully eyed Peaches' body up and down like she was a tender piece of meat. A nasty-sounding grunt escaped his lips when his eyes focused on the cleavage of her breasts. His gaze roamed over to me, and he smiled.

"Are you going to stare at us all day? Or can we get to work?" I asked, ready to get the fuck out of here.

"Let me see what you got in that little bag you brought with you. Now you know I only want the good stuff you normally have. If it ain't the chino, the white girl, or snow, I don't want it."

"When have I ever not brought you quality stuff?" Reaching into my back pocket, I pulled out an 8-ball and passed it to his junky ass. Even with the cut I put on it, the cocaine was still pure as hell. I watched Jack bust open the little plastic bag, dip his finger in, then snort some. Dipping his finger back in again, he rubbed the white powder in and around his gums. "Take it easy, Jack. You know my shit is raw."

Peaches and I both stood back when his eyes shot open like a deer caught in head-lights, and he couldn't stop talking or moving around and throughout the trailer. Jack was tweaking, going from speaking a million words per minute to a trillion words per second. One minute he would speak to me, then the next to himself. He spun around the trailer like the Tasmanian devil, throwing things around like he was looking for something. It was funny for a moment, but then I started to get that weird feeling in my gut again. Not wanting to stay any longer than what I had to, I stepped around Peaches and dropped the duffel bag on the small table in the corner.

"All right, Jack. Now that we know you like what I've brought, let's do business," I said trying to get his attention. When he waved me off and continued to move rapidly around his trailer, I repeated myself. "Come on, Jack. I already told you I don't have all day. Now let's finish this business so I can get back to my side of town."

"Business, business, business, *zzzing*. Let's do business. How much, how much, how much?"

Peaches laughed, and I bumped her in the shoulder to shut her up. I didn't need him to think that we were egging him on. "I already told you before I got here, muthafucka. Fifteen thousand for half a kilo. Nothing less. Now if you don't have the money, I can easily take my shit and bounce."

"If you got it with you, I got the money with me *zzzing*." Pushing through us, Jack practically dived onto his couch still humming some song I'd never heard before. When he came back from in between the cushions, my heart dropped at the sight of the gun in his hand aimed at me. I wasn't about to let him see that fear, though. "Leave the shit here and get off my property."

"Now you know I'm not leaving here without my money, Jack."

"Your money? You mean *my* money. And *my* drugs too. Now if you wanna live to see another day, I suggest you take your black ass on before I take something else," he said looking down at the spot between my legs.

I rolled my eyes in disgust. If this muthafucka thought for one second that I was going to give him some pussy, and then leave here without my money or drugs, then his ass had me sadly mistaken. I reached out to grab the duffel bag back when Jack let off a round, damn near blowing my hand off. On instinct, I lifted my piece and pulled the trigger at the same time as Peaches raised hers. The sound of two loud-ass canons echoed throughout the confined space and caused my ears to start ringing. I looked over at Jack, who was slumped over on his couch with two holes the size of grapefruits in his chest.

"We need to get the fuck out of here," Peaches yelled. "Wipe down anything you touched."

"I'm not going anywhere. This was clearly self-defense. He tried to shoot me first."

Peaches looked at me as if I was stupid. "Self-defense how? When the police see the kilo in your duffel bag and the fifteen thousand dollars with all this nigga's blood on it, they're going to know that this was a drug deal gone wrong. Fuck! I'm pretty sure someone heard all of those gunshots. We need to go *now*, Sarai."

I let her words sink in for a minute, and then jumped into action, wiping down anything I touched or came close to touching. Peaches was right. No cop would believe that this was self-defense. Not with the drugs and money in clear sight. After going over the table one last time, I grabbed my duffel bag, gun, and headed for the door. "I'm going to call Lyfe. He'll know what to do about this."

"And what are you going to say when he asks you what you were doing out here?"

"I don't know. I'll think of something."

"Something like what, Sarai? *Hey, baby, I've been stealing dope from you and selling it around town. Oh, and if that wasn't enough, I just had to kill one of my customers for trying to rob me,*" Peaches said, mocking me.

"Maybe. I've never lied to Lyfe about anything. So why start now?" When we made it to the car, Desiree was already in the driver's seat and ready to go.

"What the fuck happened in there? All I heard was a couple of gunshots go off, so I hopped in the driver's seat."

"So you were going to leave us?"

"If you bitches didn't walk out of that raggedy-ass trailer, I was. Y'all had five more seconds; then I was gone. What happened in there, Sarai?" Desiree asked. She was shaking and crying like her ass was the one that just got shot at. "See, that's why I didn't want to take my ass in there. I knew some shady shit was going to go down."

"Just drive this muthafucking car, bitch," Peaches yelled. "Who stays at the crime scene asking questions? We need to be getting the fuck out of here."

Putting the gear in drive, Desiree pressed her foot on the gas and hightailed it out of there, a trail of dust behind us. I pulled out my phone and started calling Lyfe, but I kept getting his voicemail.

"Fuck!" I yelled out in frustration. I needed a cleanup crew or something to go handle Jack's body before someone finds him.

"What's wrong now?"

"Lyfe still not answering his phone."

"Heim isn't either," Peaches added, looking in the rearview mirror and wiping the specs of Jack's blood off of her face.

"What the fuck are they both doing that they can't answer their phones?" I tried calling Lyfe again but still got no answer. Desiree handed her phone to me. "What are you giving me this for? I'm not calling my husband from your phone."

She shook her head. "Lyfe and Heim are at their club for some rapper's listening party. They probably can't hear their shit ringing."

"Okay. That still doesn't explain why you gave me your phone," I said, confused.

Desiree merged onto the highway. "While y'all were in there killing muthafuckas, I was out here scrolling down people's pages on Instagram. One of my homegirls is at the party and in VIP with Lyfe, Heim, and the rest of their crew."

"Bitches are always in their VIP. That's nothing new." Peaches was right. Those thirsty-ass broads were always up in Lyfe's section trying to get noticed, but they never did. At least not when I was there. I use to stomp bitches out every other night for being so disrespectful, but once it started happening every damn time we were out having a good time, I kind of got used to it.

"Look at the picture on my screen." Desiree unlocked her phone and handed it back to me while keeping her eyes on the road. I brought her phone up to my face and examined the picture she was referring to. As expected, one of her little jumpoff friends was in the VIP section at my husband's club, dressed in nothing but a piece of dental floss. She was smiling extra hard with a bottle of Patrón in her hand. Looking in the background, I didn't see anything too out of place until I started scrolling through her timeline. In one of the pictures, clear as day, I could see Lyfe sitting down with some dark-skinned chick on his lap and his tongue down her throat.

Even though his lips were on hers, I could still see the smile on his face.

"Who the fuck is this bitch?" I asked no one in particular when Peaches snatched the phone from my hand.

"That's Naheim's sister. I told you there was something going on between them. That nigga has never brought another girl out in public like that, let alone kiss them in front of the whole city. We should've gotten out at her office earlier and beat her ass like I said." Peaches handed the phone back to me. "So what you wanna do, girl? Hell, we already have one body under our belts. We might as well add another one."

My mind was reeling. Not only did I just kill somebody, now I had to deal with Lyfe and this bitch who somewhat must mean something to him. The one time when I actually needed my husband to be there for me, he was in the club that we own together, flaunting his bitch around. What was so special about this one over the others in the past? There was only one person who could answer that, and I was about to go see his ass.

"When you get to the city, Desiree, head down to the club. I need to make my presence known to this bitch and the rest of these hoes who might think shit like this is okay."

"That's what I'ma talking about, Sarai," Peaches exclaimed. "And don't worry. I got your back on this one too. If that little bitch Reign tries to jump crazy, I'ma handle her. I still owe her ass for last time."

I didn't say anything else as I closed my eyes to try to get a handle on the headache I could feel coming on. Hopefully, all of this could be handled without anyone getting hurt. Hell, who was I kidding? I was about to beat the brakes off of this disrespectful bitch's ass. Show her the real reason Lyfe chose me as his queen and not her.

Savannah

Pulling my comforter over my head, I prayed that whoever was banging on my front door would just leave me the hell alone right now. I'd been held up in my home for the last few weeks, physically and mentally healing from all of the shit that went down the night I finally got to meet Lyfe's wife for the first time. I always knew when she and I finally came face-to-face that it wasn't going to be pretty. But I never thought a grown woman could act the way she did. If it wasn't for Heim or Reign coming to my rescue, I think I would have been dead right now. I turned on my side and groaned. The two broken ribs on the left of my body were getting better, but I still had some time to go before they were completely back to normal.

Slowly sitting up in my bed, I reached over and grabbed the bottled water and pain pills that were on the nightstand. After popping a couple of those, I lay my head back on the head-board and closed my eyes, thankful that the loud banging had stopped. My phone vibrating on my nightstand grabbed my attention, but once I saw Lyfe's name flashing across my screen for the one thousandth time, I ignored it and got up from my bed, heading to the bathroom to relieve myself.

As I sat on the toilet, all of the events that happened that night at Lyfe and Heim's club a couple of weeks ago began to replay in my mind.

"Girl, what's going on with you and Lyfe?" Reign asked as we danced with each other on the dance floor.

I twirled around, making sure to shake my ass a little harder because I knew that he was watching. "What do you mean?"

"I mean, what's really going on with y'all? That nigga has not taken his eyes off of you since we got down here."

I shrugged my shoulders and twirled again. This time giving my back to Reign and looking up at Lyfe who was posted in the VIP section with a drink in his hand and his eyes glued to me. When he licked his lips and took a sip of the brown liquor in his glass, I could feel my body shake and goose bumps decorate my whole body.

"Bitch, did you just shiver?" Reign screamed in my ear with a laugh.

I continued my lustful stare at the finest man I'd ever seen and began to grind a little harder. My hands caressed the top of my breasts, then fell to my stomach and slid down to my pussy. Good thing I had on this body-hugging jean jumpsuit or else I'd probably be playing with myself right here on this dance floor. Lyfe, whose stare became a little more intense as it stayed on me, absently unbuttoned his suit jacket, and then leaned his body over the rail. The print from his dick pushing against his slacks left nothing to the imagination.

"Uhhhh, I'm going to need you two to get a room already."

I turned back around to Reign, a devious smile on my face. "I can't wait until Monroe fucks the shit out you so you can stop worrying about what I got going on."

"It's not that I'm worried about what you got going on, Savvy. If don't nobody else know, I know the history you and Lyfe have and how long you two have been in love with each other. The thing is, he's still married. Regardless of their living situation and how much time he's been spending with you, that man is still someone's husband."

"But they—" Reign stopped dancing and grabbed my shoulders, cutting me off, her eyes staring directly into mine.

"Savannah, you are my best friend, and I love you, but please don't turn into one of those women who put on blinders to the bullshit when they finally have the man that they want in their arms. You are too smart, beautiful, and independent to be someone's second. Lyfe is my nigga and all, but if he's dragging his feet with getting this divorce, I honestly think you should let it go and move on."

When I turned my head and looked over my shoulder at Lyfe, whose eyes were still trained on me, I let Reign's words sink into my head. The look on my face must've caused a bit of alarm because before I knew it, Lyfe was on his way down the stairs, pushing past his security team and walking on the dance floor straight to me.

"Is everything okay?" he asked, his eyes darting between mine and Reign's looking for answers.

"We good, Lyfe." Reign touched my shoulder and motioned with her head. "I'm about to go over to the bar and grab me a drink. Do you want one?"

"We have more than enough bottles open in VIP."

Reign shook her head. "I don't want any of that hard stuff right now. I gotta be sober enough to drive in about an hour. Got a late-night date."

"Awww, shit. My boy Heim finally got his girl back. Aye, and please stop depriving that nigga of some pussy because his ass be slipping when you ain't giving him none," Lyfe laughed.

Reign's eyebrows furrowed. "Fuck Naheim. He didn't get shit back. And as far as him slipping goes, you need to thank Peaches's pussy for that."

I didn't want to laugh, but as much as Reign tried to deny or disassociate herself from my brother, he still had an effect on her mind and heart some kind of way. Even with Monroe's fine ass in the picture, Naheim still had a way of making her feel some type of way. Once I gave Reign my drink order, she walked over to the bar and flagged down the bartender.

Lyfe grabbed my waist and pulled me close to his hard frame. My body, as always, instantly melted into his. Our heartbeats in sync beat as one. I lay my head on his shoulder and closed my eyes, tuning out all of the noise and everyone around us. When I wrapped my arms around his neck and pulled him closer to me, I felt that same shiver from a few minutes ago shoot down my spine, and I know he felt it because his grip on me became tighter. The love I've had for this man since the first day we met had me on cloud nine right now. And after all these years of us not being together, we were finally here, at this moment. The moment where I felt like I was his and his heart finally belonged to me. No outside voices in our ears, no wives playing in the background, and no other obstacles blocking our way. Just me and him. Lyfe and Savannah. The way it should've been from the start.

Sometime during the course of us being in the middle of the dance floor hugged up on each other, the music switched from upbeat tempos, to what we were swaying to now.

"Don't wanna make a scene. I really don't care if people stare at us. Sometimes I think I'm dreamin. I pinch myself just to see if I'm awake or not."

Lyfe pulled his body away from mine and stared into my eyes as Jagged Edge's song "I Gotta Be" flowed through the speakers, couples around us swaying to the beat. The whole atmosphere didn't even feel like a club anymore. All you could feel was love and happiness in the air. That was until Lyfe's body froze up, causing our movements to stop and his heated gaze stayed on something or someone behind me.

"Shit," slipped from his mouth, irritation crossing over his face.

"What's wrong?" I asked, my guard already up. The last time he and I were on this same dance floor, a shoot-out happened.

"Sarai."

"Sarai?" I thought about that name for a second. "Your wife? What about her?"

He licked his lips, eyes still trained on whoever was behind me. "My wife is on her way over here. And I can already tell by the look on her face that she's about to be on some bullshit."

"But I thought—" I started to say, but was cut off by Lyfe pushing me forcefully behind his back.

"Oh, so this is the bitch that got your nose wide open now, huh?" Sarai screamed over the music. Her pink blazer hitting the ground as she shrugged it off her arms. Our eyes connected after we both finished sizing each other up. She was a pretty brown-skinned woman who kind of reminded me of myself when it came to the way she dressed, but everything else was a huge question mark for me when it came to what Lyfe saw in her. Not only did he marry her, but he procreated with the broad. Heim told me she was a little loose at the mouth, but I didn't think she would act like this.

"Sarai, what are you even doing here?" Lyfe asked. His voice was low, but you could clearly hear the challenge in his tone.

"Nigga, fuck all of that bullshit. Answer the muthafucking question. Is this the bitch you fuckin' or not?"

Lyfe chuckled. "Why the fuck do you care if it is or isn't? You and I both know what it is. We don't even live together anymore. If it wasn't for my kids—Matter of fact, where are my fucking kids while you're out here trying to check me and embarrass yourself?"

"Embarrass myself? How? I'm not the one out here sleeping with a married man." Sarai pointed at me. "She is." Her lips turned up. "Savannah Zaher. Attorney at law. Peaches, would you want a home wrecker to represent you in any court of law?"

Peaches, who was dressed in all black and looked as if she had just come off of a jewelry heist, stepped forward. Long blond weave pressed bone straight and parted down the middle. Her arms were crossed over her busty chest, and her stance was very defensive while she smacked on the huge piece of bubble gum in her mouth.

"Hell, no, I wouldn't want this bitch to represent me—fucking her brother or not." Peaches' *eyes went to the side of me, and she smiled while waving her fingers. "Oh, hey, sister wife. Have you seen our man here yet? I've been calling him and calling him, but he hasn't answered any of my calls. Thought maybe he had you on your knees somewhere with that big-ass dick of his in your mouth."*

Reign stepped forward with both of our drinks in her hand but stopped when I grabbed her arm.

"Yo, this bitch can get it tonight. I'm about to knock her ass out." Reign's eyes went down to my hand on her arm, and then back up to me. "Why are you just standing here letting her call you all kinds of bitches, Savvy? Yeah, you in the wrong low key for being out here in public with her man like that when they aren't divorced yet, but that doesn't mean she has to disrespect you like that. You better check her ass."

I looked over at Lyfe, who had pulled Sarai to the side and was having some kind of heated hushed conversation, her eyes looking up to him as if she wanted to cry, and his looking down at her as if he hated the ground she walked on.

"It isn't my place to check her, Reign. That's Lyfe's wife, and he can handle her. Besides, I'm not about to lose my license behind beating her ass."

Reign dropped the drinks in her hands onto the floor, a loud crashing sound grabbing everyone's attention. "Well, good thing I'm not a lawyer, huh?" she stated before charging Peaches, who was talking to some other light-skinned girl that came with them and still talking shit.

Before I could get to Reign to break up the fight between her and Peaches, I felt my pony-tail being pulled behind me and my body being swung down to the ground. The six-inch stilettos I had on easily played a part into me losing my balance completely and meeting the shiny tile of the dance floor. I turned my body to try to get up but was kicked in my rib cage so hard that it became hard for me to breathe. Rolling over and holding my side, I tried to crawl out of the circle that was formed around me, but had no such luck when one of the girls kicked me again, giving the four hands open season on beating my ass. My screams, as well as the screams of the other clubgoers, could be heard echoing throughout the club.

Footsteps pounding on the floor of people trying to escape shook my body like an earthquake as the rain of blows continued to cover every inch of my body. I kicked my legs out, trying to stab anyone I could with my sharp heels, but was rewarded with my foot being twisted to the point that I felt my bone about to snap. Even with all of the bodies covering me, I still managed to get a couple of swings in while protecting the side of my body that was hit with that massive kick.

One by one, the girls who jumped me were being picked up and thrown to the side like rag dolls. When my vision was finally clear enough to look up, Lyfe's worried face was the first one I saw, with Naheim behind him screaming at the top of his lungs with Kinko and the rest of security trying to clear the place out and call the ambulance.

"Don't worry, baby. I got you. I am so sorry." Lyfe kissed my forehead, blood now on his chin and cheek. "All of them bitches is gonna pay. Trust me. Starting with Sarai's ass first."

I heard everything he was saying, but I wasn't trying to hear the shit at all. Me being bloody and on my way to the hospital with a possible concussion and broken bones should have never happened. Maybe Reign was right. I should have stayed away from Lyfe until he had officially gotten a divorce, but who's to say the same shit wouldn't have happened?

By the time we made it outside and to the ambulance, I was going in and out of con-

sciousness, Lyfe shaking my body and calling my name every couple of minutes to keep
me awake. After laying my body down on the
stretcher and kissing my head again, I expected
Lyfe to hop in the back of the emergency vehi-
cle with me, but I got the shock of my life when
he didn't. I tried to speak but was cut off by
the oxygen mask being placed over my face.
With his phone to his ear, we stared at each
other until the first door of the ambulance shut.
Before the EMT got up to shut the other, I was
able to hear a little of Lyfe's conversation, and
my heart broke.

"What the fuck was that? My place of business,
Sarai? No . . . No. What the fuck? You know I
don't want any kind of heat here, and you come
and do this. I don't give a fuck. Not only are you
messing with my money, but you're messing
with my livelihood. I don't want to hear any of
that shit. She doesn't matter right now. Take
your ass straight home, Sarai. No, I'm coming
there first. I'll meet you there in ten minutes."

When he hung up the phone, he blew out a
frustrated breath and regained his composure
for a second. He turned his body to walk in the
direction of the ambulance to say something to
me, but the EMT finally closed the other door,
slamming it right in Lyfe's face.

***

I tried to stop the tears from falling, but I couldn't. My arms were being weighed down as my side was being attended to. Instead of coming with me to the hospital, Lyfe was on his way home to talk to his wife. Instead of being there when I needed him, he was on his way to make sure whatever they had going on did not interfere with his money or livelihood. Yeah, maybe Reign was right after all. It was time for me to let go and move on, because it was obvious that as much as Lyfe said he loved me and wanted to be with me, there was still something about the woman he married, pulling him back in that direction.

I winced after wiping myself off and getting up from the toilet. It had been a few weeks since I suffered my injuries, and I couldn't wait to get better so that I could get that bitch Sarai and her little crew. Because I wasn't answering Lyfe's calls, it was Heim who told me that the females who jumped me were cousins and friends of Peaches and the other chick I now know as Desiree. According to my brother, he and Lyfe had already taken care of those girls by getting some of their friends to beat their asses ten times worse than they did me. When I asked him about Sarai and Peaches, though, he changed the subject and told me that whenever I talked to Lyfe, I would find out about that situation. There was no need for that, though, because I was going to come for those two bitches myself. They were able to get me good this time, but I swore on my dead parents' grave that I would be the one with the last laugh.

Walking back into my bedroom, I had just positioned myself on my bed to take another nap when there was another knock on the door. Since I was already halfway up, I decided to go answer it this time. Lyfe had stopped dropping by unannounced after the last two weeks of me ignoring his knocks. The only other person it could be would be the flower man who's been delivering me beautiful bouquets of Get Well Soon roses since a couple of days ago. I didn't know who they were from. But what I did know was that they weren't from Lyfe. The penmanship on the card was not his. Sorta looked familiar, but I couldn't remember where I'd seen it before.

"Who is it?" I croaked out as I got closer to the door, my socked feet sliding against the carpeted floor, everything my fingers rolled over, shocking me to the touch. With my midsection still bandaged up, I looked down at my purple tank top and black boy shorts, deeming them acceptable enough to answer the door. My hair, which was wrapped around my head and still in place, looked okay as I passed by the mirror hanging on my wall. Even with the bonnet hanging halfway on my shoulder, I still looked all right. "Who is it?" I yelled again. My hand on the knob.

"Uhhhhh . . . delivery for Savannah Zaher," the guy stuttered. He didn't sound like the other dude who brought me flowers, but I opened the door anyway. Figured it may have been his day off or something like that.

"Hey," I greeted when my eyes connected with a short, balding white guy, his striped shirt and faded slacks nowhere near the flower shop's uniform. I shut my door some and tried to reach for my bat, but was having a hard time leaning over subtly with my broken ribs. "How . . . how . . . can I help you?"

He wiped the sweat from his brow. His chubby hands reaching into the satchel that was draped across his round belly. "Are you Savannah Zaher?"

"I might be. Who's asking?" My eyes darted to the left and right.

"Well, my name is Jonathan Lewis, and this is for you."

I looked down at the manila envelope in his hand and grabbed it. "What's this?"

"You've been served. Have a good day, ma'am," he rambled out before turning around and high-tailing it away from my house. I watched him jump into the passenger side of a black-tinted Jaguar before it pulled off and disappeared down the street.

I looked down at the envelope that was addressed to me wondering who could be sending me any type of paperwork through the mail, let alone serving me. The only people who had my home address were Heim, Reign, and Lyfe. Three people who didn't have any reason to be suing me for anything.

Opening the package, I pulled out the paper-work and skimmed over it, dropping my mouth when I finally was able to see who it was from. Pure rage shot through my body as I read over everything the paper said. I closed my door with a slam and walked back into my bedroom as fast as I could, grabbing my phone off of the nightstand, scrolling down to Lyfe's name before pressing the call to connect. His line rang once and went straight to voicemail, so I hung up and called again getting the same results.

"Ugh," I screamed out in frustration, tears threatening to fall from my eyelids. "*Now* you don't wanna answer the phone after calling me a million times."

Reaching for my prescription, I popped two pain pills in my mouth and drank the last of my water, while making another phone call.

The phone rang about five times before she finally answered. "What's going on, Savvy? You need something?" Reign's voice flowed through the receiver.

"Tell me why this bitch is suing me."

I could hear Reign moving around and some papers shuffling in the background. I knew she was at work, but I needed to talk to somebody. "Who is suing you?"

"Lyfe's fucking wife."

"Sarai?"

"Yes."

Reign laughed. "Suing you for what? I don't mean to sound fucked up, friend, but didn't she bring some girls to the club to whip your ass? Not the other way around. Shouldn't *you* be suing her for pain and suffering or something like that?"

"Reign, I'm not joking. The bitch has filed a lawsuit against me for Infidelity and Alienation of Affection. Stating that I'm the reason her marriage is going down the drain and her husband has decided to leave her. Do you know what this can do to me? How this can affect my life if she wins this?"

"Savvy, I don't think she is going to really go through with this. Maybe it's just a scare tactic to get you to leave Lyfe alone. Have you talked to him? I'm sure he has to know about it if she drew up paperwork and had it mailed to you."

"I was just served. The bitch had me served, which means she wants to go through with this bullshit."

Reign was quiet on the phone for a second. "Well, what do you want to do? I'm pretty sure you can represent yourself if this goes to court, but do you really wanna do that? When is the court date?"

I picked the papers up and was searching through them when there was another knock on the door.

"Hold on for a second, Reign; someone's at my door again."

"Shit, you better not answer it. It might be another lawsuit from Sarai's heartbroken ass. Suing you to get a mold of your pussy so she can get a replica and make Lyfe stay." I didn't want to laugh, but leave it to Reign to come up with some funny stupid shit like that.

Because I had just popped those pain pills, I was able to make it to the front door in a little less time than before. Looking through the peephole, I noticed the frame of two rather large men dressed in black suits standing on my porch. When I opened the door, the one on the phone released whatever call he was on, and the other had his back turned to me.

"Uh, how can I help you?"

"Are you Savannah Zaher?"

"I am, and who are you?" They both flashed their badges at me, but the shorter Tom Cruise look-alike was the one to speak.

"We are Agent Morales and Agent Franks from the Federal Bureau of Investigation. Do you mind if we speak with you for a moment?"

"What is this in regards to?" I asked, coming out of my home and stepping onto the porch. My door was slightly ajar, just in case they said some shit I didn't want to hear.

The taller one, who was now facing me, took the shades off of his face and gave me a glare that I didn't understand.

"Ma'am, do you know a gentleman by the name of Lyfe Simmons? Owns a couple of clubs and local businesses around here in Charlotte."

"What business is that of yours?"

He smirked, his chubby cheeks turning a blush pink. "I see what this is about to be. You're going into lawyer mode on us, huh? All we did was ask you a simple question. Do you know the man or not? You already know we know the answer to that."

I stepped back into my home, already over this conversation. Although I was angry with Lyfe, I wouldn't tell the FBI anything about him. If he was in some trouble, that means Heim would be too.

"All right, gentlemen, this line of questioning is over. If you're not here to arrest me, then you already know what to do."

Tom Cruise nodded his head and handed me his card. "We understand. But you might want to let your brother and his 'business' partner," he used air quotes, "know that we're on to them and their illegal activities, and it will only be a matter of time before we have enough evidence to put them both in jail."

I looked at the card in his hand and stepped farther back into my home, closing the door in their faces and looking out my peephole until they left. Once they were in their unmarked car and pulled off from in front of my house, I blew out the breath I'd been holding and rested my forehead against the smooth mahogany.

First I got served by Sarai, and now the feds showed up at my house without giving me a warning and asking questions. Who would've thought reuniting with my first love would bring so much drama into my life? Lyfe wasn't worth me lying for or getting my career ruined over. I had a lot to think about. Help the one man who broke my heart into a million pieces or get ready to possibly visit my brother in jail for the next thirty years? Fuck! My life sucked so bad right now.

Sarai

I stretched my arm over the center console and handed the envelope of money to the server who had just jumped in the car. I thought I would have the perfect view of Savannah's face when she realized what she had received while sitting in the backseat, but the bitch closed the door before opening my gift. Lyfe would for sure make his way home once she called and told him about the lawsuit. The nigga still wasn't answering my phone calls or text messages. I even had the kids calling him from different numbers. But as soon as I took over the call, he would hang up or not say anything until I gave one of the kids back the phone. The shit was funny, because in the world of side hoes and mistresses, should I, the wife, be the one mad after finding out my husband was messing around with someone else? Shouldn't *he* be calling *me* all day and night trying to ask me for my forgiveness?

Although Lyfe and I hadn't been on the same wavelength for a while now, it still hurt to know that the love I'd always showed to and wanted from him was being given away so effortlessly to someone who hadn't been by his side these last ten years. Someone who lied to the police. Someone who risked their freedom by carrying drugs and guns for him. Someone who gave birth to not one, but two of his offspring. You'd think with all of the shit I'd put up with and done for him that he'd have some sort of respect for me. But, no, I literally felt like just another bitch in the street that he fucked with on occasion. Especially after this home wrecker Savannah came back into town.

My eyes wandered back up to the server, who was counting his stack of money with his fat, stubby fingers. I didn't know where Desiree found him, but I was glad she did. After I offered him a few dollars to serve these papers for me, and a small bag of that pure, he was more than willing to.

"So she didn't open the envelope at all?" I asked, rolling down the window, trying to get some air. The cheap cologne he had on was making my eyes water and smelled like gasoline.

"No. She just took it from my hand and looked at me for a second. I nodded my head and came back to the car after she started to close her door."

"Did she at least ask you what it was?"

He nodded his head, stuffing his envelope into his man purse. "She did. I told her it was some important information."

"God, I wish I was a fly on her wall right now," I said under my breath, eyes focused on the sidewalk traffic as we cruised down the street, headed to the gas station to drop this dude off.

"All right, man. Thanks for doing that little job for my girl," Desiree said as she pulled up into the BP station on Ballantyne Commons Pkwy.

"No problem. And if you ever need my services again"—he looked back at me and licked his lips, heavy wheezing coming from his chest sounding like a damn grizzly bear that just ran across the forest—"come find me. I'm always around." His milky white skin now had a red tint to it as his cheeks heated up.

I rolled my eyes and started playing with my phone. A few of my regulars had been hitting me up for some work, but after that whole trailer park incident, I'd been laying low. The police hadn't found any evidence at the crime scene, and there were no witnesses, so we were in the clear as of now. The only thing that could tie us to that murder was the guns that Peaches and I used, which were sitting in the glove compartment of my car. I made a mental note to finally get rid of those things before I got pulled over and the police found them muthafuckas.

"Earth to Sarai," Desiree shouted, her hands waving in my face, grabbing my attention. "Are you going to get in the front seat or are you going to stay back there like your ass is being chauffeured around?"

"Just drive. I don't feel like getting out right now."

She smacked her lips and then turned around in the seat. After reading and responding to a few texts on her phone, she pulled into traffic and turned the music down.

"So where to now?"

I looked down at a message from Kinko. Once again, Lyfe wasn't going to be able to pick our kids up from their after-school program, so it was left to me.

"Take me to the kids' school so we can pick them up."

"Lyfe still not fucking with you, huh?"

I cocked my head to the side, eyes on hers in the rearview mirror. "What does Lyfe not fucking with me have to do with picking my kids up?"

She shrugged her shoulders. "Did the school call? How do you know he isn't going to pick them up?"

"Because Kinko just hit me with a message saying that Lyfe had some business to take care of."

"That's what I'm talking about. Before that little club incident happened, the nigga at least called you when it came to the kids. Now, he just has one of his little workers relay his messages." She looked over her shoulder and switched lanes. "When was the last time you saw his ass?"

The night Savannah got her ass beat is what I wanted to say. But Desiree didn't need to know how bad my marital problems actually were.

"He was home a couple of nights ago," I lied. "We didn't speak much, but we spent some time together as a family for the kids' sake."

Her eyes connected with mine in the rearview mirror, and I could tell by the look on her face that she didn't believe me but wouldn't dare say shit. Desiree knew I was crazy as hell when it came to Lyfe and my image on these streets, and I would have no problem slapping the shit out of her while driving if she ever tried to question any of it. With a simple nod of her head, she left the subject alone and continued to drive toward my kids' school.

My mind started swirling around with all kinds of thoughts. What would I do if Lyfe really did present me with some divorce papers? Was I really ready to let go of everything we had even though we were more like partners than lovers? Would he really be happy with Savannah? What about the drugs? How will I continue to sell my shit if I don't have access to his dope anymore? The more I thought about everything that was about to happen, the angrier I became. Not only was my money about to slow dramatically, but my reign as queen of Charlotte would come to an abrupt end.

When we pulled up to my kids' school, all thoughts of my outside life ceased, and my mommy mode kicked in. Hopping out of the backseat, I ran my hands down the front of the tan, sleeveless, body-hugging dress I had on and made sure the strings on my Balmain Lace-Up Suede Boots were intact. After grabbing my clutch from off of the floor, I walked into the school with my head high, attitude on ten, and shades pulled over my eyes. I still had an image to maintain, and hoes still needed to recognize me as Mrs. Simmons, even if they've heard about or seen the ho my husband has been flaunting all around town.

***

I walked into my mother's kitchen where she was sitting down playing a game of spades with her next-door neighbor, Ms. Pearl. Thick clouds of cigarette smoke floated through the small space, and the smell of burnt hair lingered in the air. Open bottles of wine lined up on the counter, while half-empty glasses rested in front of my mama and Ms. Pearl. After grabbing a water out of the fridge, I sat on the stool at the breakfast nook and downed the entire bottle. I'd just got done helping my kids with their homework and was about to leave them at my mom's house and handle some business for a few hours.

"You look like you gaining some weight, girl," my mother spoke, pulling the cigarette from her mouth and blowing smoke in the air. "What you out here stressing about?"

I twisted the cap back on the empty water bottle and threw it in the trash. "I ain't stressing 'bout shit. You know I'm living the life I've always dreamed of living. I'm not wanting for nothing. Got the cutest and smartest kids in the world, and I'm married to one of the finest and most well-known men in Charlotte. Why would I be stressing about anything?"

Ms. Pearl laughed, her deep, raspy voice laced with amusement. "Girl, you need to stop all that lying. Me and ya mama may not be in these streets anymore like we used to, but we still hear 'bout the thangs going on around here."

I stood up from the stool and walked around the counter, washing my hands. When I looked up, my mother's eyes were on me. "What?"

"So you not gon' tell me why you've been bringing these kids over here every day for the last couple of weeks? Why you have them all day every day and Lyfe doesn't?"

"Mama—"

She took a pull of her cigarette and blew the smoke from her nose this time, shuffling through the cards in one hand and picking up the book she just made with the other. Big pink rollers were fixed in her hair with a silk scarf tied loosely around the top.

"Don't 'Mama' me because you sitting around here lying about this stress-free life you have when it's anything but. When were you going to tell me that Lyfe done found him another woman?"

"Because he hasn't."

"Bullshit," Ms. Pearl screamed and laughed, her round belly shaking like jelly in the muu-muu she had on. Her hair was in rollers like my mama's, but hers were the spongy black kind that didn't leave a hair dent in her wig.

"That boy running around here with whatchu call its sister." She pointed at my mama. "That fine little chocolate boy Lyfe been friends with. What's his name again?"

"You talking about Naheim?" my mother asked. Her questioning eyes looking at me.

"Yeah. That's him. Fine-ass Naheim. If he liked old pussy, I'd give that fine-ass nigga a run for his money. But he too busy humping on that loose gal Peaches." She shook her head. "That boy ain't gon' learn until it's too late with her. Especially with that knucklehead Kwan being out of jail. I seen them the other day trying to sneak around and not be seen. But you know ole Ms. Pearlie sees all and knows all."

"Nosy ass," I said under my breath, but my mama heard me.

"Don't be mad at Ms. Pearl because she telling your business. Now, what's up with you and Lyfe? Are y'all finally getting a divorce, or are you gonna keep pretending like you guys are this happy couple while he out here got you looking stupid and shit?"

I ignored my mama and grabbed my purse. I had let Desiree use my car while I was spending some time with my kids and now she was back. We had to go to the stash house and get a few kilos to sell to some of my clientele, and then get rid of these damn guns.

"So you just gonna ignore me, Sarai? You don't wanna hear the truth, huh?"

I stopped in my tracks and turned around to my mother, anger in my eyes. "What fucking truth don't I want to hear, Mama? That my husband cheats on me? Well, I already know that. He's been doing it for years, so this is nothing new."

"He's been doing it for years, true, but he's never had his hoes in the public eye. Heard he was all hugged up with that girl at the club you both own. He's even been seen out to eat with her at different restaurants. When a man starts to not care about the consequences of his actions, that means he doesn't give a fuck about you or your feelings anymore. You said he's been cheating for years, right?" I started to answer, but she cut me off. "Then why are you still there, Sarai? Is it for the money? I know it can't be that, because you've been stealing from that man and selling his shit on the side." I furrowed my brows, stunned at what she just said. My mama held her hand up. "And before you fix your mouth to tell that lie, please know that I'm not dumb, Sarai. Plus, you sold some shit to Pearl's grandson not too long ago." Her hard eyes stared me down.

"Since when did you start selling drugs? I've always taught you to snag a drug dealer, not be one. What happens if you and Lyfe get caught up? The feds already been around asking questions. You don't think they have people watching y'all right now?" She shook her head and took another pull of her cigarette. "Girl, you need to do better. Since he don't want you no more, then you move the fuck on. If you don't want to get you a job and take care of yourself and your kids, you go out and find you another drug dealer. Them niggas come a dime a dozen. Don't let Lyfe be your downfall. All he sees is that girl he messing with now. You aren't anything but his baby mama now. That's it; that's all. Get out while you can and just let that nigga go. He's not gonna change for you because he doesn't love you in that way. Find you someone who is willing to go above and beyond just to make you happy, okay?"

I didn't even know I was crying until I felt the first tear fall down my cheek and land on my chest. Slowly nodding my head, I wiped the remaining tears away and walked out of my mother's house. Their loud laugh echoed in the background as I shut the door and ran out to my car.

"You okay, girl?" Desiree asked as she backed out of my mom's driveway. "You look like you were just crying."

I pursed my lips and ignored her, my eyes looking out the window and my mind going over everything my mother just said. Although the things she said about Lyfe were all true, it would still be hard for me to just up and leave—especially with my reason for leaving being behind another chick. I would lose any respect I ever had from these muthafuckas on the streets. Bitches feared me and niggas wanted to be like me or with me. If they ever found out that I was run off from one of the biggest dealers in the game by a fucking lawyer, they would surely laugh at me. I couldn't let that happen. I *wouldn't* let that happen. I would kill Lyfe myself before I ever let him make me look like one of these dumb broads he usually toots and boots.

My phone ringing in my hand grabbed my attention. It was from an unknown number and butterflies started going off in my stomach. Just that fast I was wishing and hoping for Lyfe to be calling my phone. To at least reach out to me and see how I've been doing and to show that he cared at least a little bit. I mean, I knew he was probably still upset with me for having some of Peaches's homegirls fuck his little bitch up, but he had to see where I was coming from. His ass probably would've shot up the whole club if I was there with some other nigga grinding on his lap and kissing him all up on the dance floor. It was all about respect, and that shit he was doing at the business we owned together was disrespectful as fuck. And instead of me getting my hands dirty, I did what any queen would do—have her minions fuck shit up for her.

"You not gon' answer your phone? That might be some money."

I looked down at my screen as it went black and lit back up when the unknown number called again.

"I think it might be Lyfe."

Desiree looked at me, and then down at my phone. "He changed his number or something? That number isn't programmed in your phone, is it?"

"Nah. But he usually calls me from different burner phones. Especially when a new shipment is coming in."

"Well, are you going to answer it? This is the third time he's called."

I tried to hide the smile on my lips but couldn't. I fucking hated how this man could still cause me to get all giddy and shit, and I know his heart is with someone else. Curious to know why he was calling so much, I finally answered my phone.

"Hey," I said in my most syrupy sweet voice.

"Hey to you." I took the phone away from my ear and looked at the screen, trying to see if I recognized the number, because I sure didn't recognize the voice. "You still there?"

I put the phone on speaker. "Who . . . Who is this?"

When I looked at Desiree, a look of confusion crossed her face, and she turned her head.

"Who I am doesn't matter right now. But it will soon enough."

"Okay. So what do you want?"

"I heard you're the woman to see in these streets. Heard you got that good shit rolling through the city."

"Nah, sir. You have the wrong number. I'm just a housewife who loves to stay at home and cater to her husband and our kids."

"A husband who hasn't been home in weeks?" I opened my mouth to say something, but couldn't. I looked at Desiree, and her eyes were glued to the road. "Now, how can you cater to him when he's not even there?"

"Look, I don't know who this is, but what goes on in my house with my husband and me is none of your concern. Now, if you could so kindly lose my number. Please don't call this phone again." I was just about to hang up when he stopped me in my tracks with his next statement.

"I can help you get rid of that little problem your husband seems to be so attached to, but only if you help me with something first."

"Something like what?"

He chuckled, and my body started to tingle. "I'll get with you in a few days. Don't change your number and answer your phone on the first ring the next time I hit you up," was all he said before releasing the call and my screen going black.

"What the fuck?" I said to Desiree, who was still sitting quietly in the driver's seat. We were almost at the stash house. "What the hell is your problem? Why are you acting so weird all of a sudden?"

She shook her head, the long ponytail at the back of her head swaying from side to side. Her layered bangs covered damn near half of her face. Dressed in all black, Desiree looked like she was ready to put in some work, except her ass was only along for the ride to be my driver as I made these deliveries. The way she hightailed it out of that trailer park after I killed ole boy had me easily promoting her ass. I didn't think there would be a next time, but just in case I needed to make a hasty getaway, I had her to get me to safety and out of the police reach.

I squinted my eyes, staring at the side of her face. Desiree knew something but didn't want to say anything. The way her hands were gripping the steering wheel and had her knuckles turning white told me that. I wasn't going to push now, but I knew eventually she would say something. She always did. Desiree couldn't hold water for shit. Well, except about this mystery dude she's been fucking with.

"So, you ready to make this money?" I asked, changing the subject. The relief she gave the steering wheel showed me that she was now at ease.

"Yeah. You know me. As long as I ain't gotta touch the shit or go in the house to get it, I'm good. I'm more scared of Lyfe finding me in his stash house than the police finding me at a drop-off location."

I nodded my head in understanding. "So where's Peaches? Have you heard from her?"

Peaches had also been missing in action ever since the club incident. After Reign beat her ass again, she'd been laying low trying to let her face heal up.

"She been running behind Heim trying to get him not to leave her. When he found out that the girls who beat up his sister were her friends, he smacked the shit out of her ass and kicked her out of his house. Told her that she was the dirtiest bitch he ever met and slammed the door in her face. Threw all her shit out of his second-story window, and then called the police on her ass for trespassing," Desiree laughed. "I don't know why she thought Heim would forgive her for that shit. I mean, that was his sister. And then there's that shit he got going with Reign." Desiree shook her head. "How you claim to be so in love with one person, but can't stop fucking the other?"

The question was rhetorical, so I just sat back and continued to listen to her ramble on. Right when we were getting ready to get off of the interstate and head to the house, a police siren from an unmarked car went off and flashed its lights at us.

"Shit," I hissed as Desiree pulled to the side of the road. "What the fuck did you do?"

Her eyes and movement were frantic. "I . . . I . . . I didn't do anything. All I did was switch lanes. You don't have any drugs on you or in the trunk, do you?"

I looked down at my skintight dress and small clutch. "Does it look like I have anything on me? I was going to change when we got to the house. The only thing in the trunk is the black

Prada bags, and those are empty. Nothing in the backseat or under the seats and nothing in the glove compartment but my insurance . . ." I trailed off. "Shit shit shit!"

"What? What's wrong, Sarai?" Desiree's cries damn near had me shook, but I knew I had to get my shit together before the cop walked up to the side of the car and asked us to roll our windows down.

"I forgot to get rid of these guns."

"What guns?"

"The ones me and Peaches used that day in the trailer park."

"Oh my Gawd! I'm going to fucking prison. See, I should've listened to Ms. Pearl and stopped fucking with your ass. She told me you would bring me down with all of the bullshit you've been doing."

"First of all, fuck Ms. Pearl, and you can tell her I said that. Second of all—" I looked in the side mirror and saw a man dressed in a nice-ass Italian suit walking on my side while another was slowing creeping up on Desiree's. "Second, you just need to shut up and let me do all the talking. My tags are up to date, and my insurance is active, so we're good on this end. You said you didn't do anything illegal so this is probably only a routine stop or them being nosy because my windows are so dark."

I took the guns out of the glove compartment and put them in the safe under the mat. After making sure everything was straight in the car, including Desiree, I had her roll down both of our windows.

"Good afternoon, ma'am," the one on my side spoke first. "I'm Agent Morales, and my partner over there is Agent Franks, and we're with the Federal Bureau of Investigation. Do you mind if we speak with you for a second?"

"I do, to be honest. I was in a bit of a hurry. I have to go pick up my friend, and then go pick up my kids."

"We understand that completely, ma'am. But we just wanted to ask you a few questions."

"Pertaining to what? I didn't know the FBI pulled people over now. Did we forget to turn our signal on when switching lanes back there?"

Agent Morales smirked. "No, this is not a traffic stop. We just wanted to ask you a few questions about your husband Lyfe Simmons, if you don't mind."

"I actually do. Like I said before—" I looked at Agent Franks who was looking in my car, "I was busy and have things to do. If you have any questions, feel free to contact my lawyer. I'm sure he will be able to assist you with anything you need."

"Is it the same lawyer your husband uses?"

I nodded my head. "Yes. Bryant has been our lawyer for years."

"Bryant?" Agent Franks scoffed. "I thought Mr. Simmons told us he was represented by a Savannah Zaher. I know you've heard of her," he stated with a smirk.

I could feel my body start to shake from the anger pooling at the core of my belly. "Unfortunately, you are mistaken. Savannah Zaher is just an associate of my husband who doesn't represent either one of us. Now, if you'll excuse me, I have to go get my kids."

Agent Morales tapped the top of my car. "We will talk later. Oh, and don't forget about that friend you said you had to pick up too."

I plastered a fake smile on my face as I rolled up the window on my side and told Desiree to pull off. These muthafuckas had me fucked up bringing that bitch's name up. She would never defend me—or anyone else for that matter—once I got done with her. I would just have to deal with Heim and whatever aftermath came with him if he ever figured out that I was the one who killed his sister. Hopefully, I'd get that call from ole boy much sooner than later to see what he had planned.

Lyfe

"You've reached the voicemail of Savannah Zaher. Leave a message after the tone, and I will call you back at my earliest convenience."
Beep.

"Savvy, baby, this is me again. Give me a call as soon as you get this message. I just want to make sure everything is all right with you. Please."

Releasing the call. I placed my head against the headrest of my seat and closed my eyes. For the last few weeks, Savannah had been ignoring all my calls, texts, and pop-up visits. She even had Reign lying for her. The crazy part about everything was, all I wanted to know was if she was okay. I knew I fucked up by going to handle Sarai instead of jumping into the ambulance and riding to the hospital with her, but I needed to get some shit clear with my soon-to-be ex-wife before she had me putting a bullet in the middle of her forehead. Yeah, she was the mother of my children, which had me overlooking a lot of the shit Sarai had done, but enough was enough. It was time for her and me to sit down and really get this divorce shit done. With her, Savvy, my product, and other business going on, I was being pulled in so many directions. I needed to get shit in order.

"Where to next?" Kiko asked from the front seat of the truck. We were in front of Savannah's home, waiting for her to pull up from wherever she had gone. But after being posted up for about two hours with no view of Savannah in sight, it was time for me to go take care of a few things before I turned in for the night.

I wiped my hand over my face. The wild hairs from my grown out beard and mustache scratched my palm along the way. I'd really been off these last few weeks and couldn't blame anyone but myself.

"Yo, take me to the house. Sarai should be at the salon right now since it's Wednesday." I looked at my watch. "I need to get some more of my things and those extra kilos I had there."

"Extra kilos? In your house?" His eyes connected to mine, and I nodded my head. "You really slipping, Lyfe. You never take the work to the place you lay your head. That's the first door the feds kick down once they find enough evidence to get a search warrant for you."

"Yeah, man. I know. I've been meaning to move it for a while now, but it kept slipping my mind. Now that I know these pig-ass mutha-fuckas are going around asking questions about me and Heim, it's time for me to move it out of there."

"How much you got stashed at the house?"

"Enough to get a few life sentences."

"Damn, man." Kiko shook his head. "Should I call Heim and have him meet us there with the van?"

I thought about what he asked for a second. Heim and I haven't really been on speaking terms. Not since the night Peaches, and her homegirls jumped Savannah. He and I spoke when it came to business and shipments com-ing in, but other than that, I didn't know what Heim had been up to lately. When I tried to ask him about Savvy a couple of days after she was released from the hospital, he and I almost came to blows, but Kiko and a few of the other security guards at the club broke it up.

Did I regret being all over Savannah in the spotlight? No. Would I do it again? Honestly, yes. Savvy was my heart, and although we'd been going about starting our relationship back up again the wrong way, that didn't change the way I felt about her. Sarai knew what it was too. That was why I didn't understand her coming down to the club and showing her ass the way she did. I mean, no, I'd never been out and public with another woman like that, but she knew it was bound to happen. Wife or not, I wasn't going to let that intimate moment Savvy and I shared on the dance floor pass me by. Holding her in my arms like that reminded me of the old times when we were younger before she went off to college. That feeling of her belonging to me and only me was a feeling I lived for and would die for in the same breath.

"Yeah?" I answered my ringing phone, my mind still running with thoughts of Savannah.

"Aye, shit's all good over here." It was Heim, and he was letting me know that the shipment of heroin that was scheduled to come in today was already here.

"Okay. Where they going?"

"To the new joint."

"Peaches?" I asked, hoping he still wasn't going to allow her to run the storage facility we bought to store our product in between packaging and selling it.

"What about her?"

"I hope you fired her." The line got quiet. "Heim?"

He blew out a breath. "Aye, look, man, because it was such short notice, we weren't able to hire anyone new. So she's going to work for a week or two, and by that time, we will have someone else running that spot."

My hand clenched my cell phone tightly. I didn't trust that bitch Peaches for shit, and I thought Heim would feel the same way after finding out it was her homegirls who jumped his sister.

"I don't know about that, Heim. Maybe we should dock it at the other spot. I don't trust your girl."

"We can't take it to the other spot. That shit has eyes on it already. We moved out the remaining shit we had there a few days ago and already set it up at the new joint."

I closed my eyes and cursed to myself. Shit was definitely getting hotter, which meant we needed to get this new shipment situated, and then shut down shop for a little bit.

"All right, man. We'll meet up in about an hour to discuss what we need to do." My line beeped. It was Sarai, but I ignored her call. "We also need to talk about this Peaches shit and find someone else to be over the storage spot."

"Yeah. Okay."

"All right. Oh, and Heim, how is Savvy?"

"Healing" was all he said before smacking his teeth and releasing the call.

"Heim still ain't fucking with you, huh?" Kiko asked, a smile on his face. "Y'all niggas act just like bitches. Mad at each other for now but will be back to being homeboys in no time. If you ask me, both of y'all—"

"Didn't nobody ask your ass shit," I cut him off, and he laughed. "Just get me to the house so I can get in and get out."

"Where do you want me to park the truck?"

"You can actually head back to the city after dropping me off. I'll just use my car since it has the hidden safe in the trunk. I load everything up in the garage and leave from there. If the feds is watching my house, I don't need them to see us carrying a few bags from my house and putting them in the back of this truck. With the garage door down, they won't be able to see shit I'm doing."

Kiko nodded his head and continued on his way to the home I shared with my wife and kids. A lot of memories had been made there that I will truly miss, but in all honesty, it was time for me to go. Sarai knew I didn't play about my kids, so I wasn't worried about her trying to keep them away from me. I just hoped the split would be amicable, and we would just go our separate ways.

When we pulled into the rounded driveway of my home, I was shocked to see one of the garage doors open and Sarai's Jaguar parked in it.

"Looks like wifey's home."

"Yeah. I wonder why," I said more to myself. "I'll see you in an hour at the club, Ki."

"All right, Lyfe. Call me if you need me, man."

I waved him off as I walked into the garage and noticed that the hood of her car was still warm, which meant she hadn't been here long. Maybe she forgot something and was hopefully on her way back out. I wanted to get my shit and leave without having a screaming match or trying to restrain Sarai from putting her hands on me. The last time I tried to talk to her in a civilized manner and let her know that she and I were done, Sarai grabbed everything she could to throw at me and was even able to get a hit or two in when I turned my back to her and tried to go up to the hospital Savannah was in.

"Sarai," I called out when I entered the kitchen from the garage door entrance, but there was no answer. "Sarai," I called again. And still no response. An eerie feeling began to creep up my body, so I opened the drawer next to the fridge and pulled out the gun I kept there for safe-keeping. After checking the clip and turning the safety off, I walked farther into the house. I searched the whole entire first and second floor, but there was still no Sarai. Her keys were in the glass bowl next to the front door, and her purse was thrown across the table, so I knew she was here.

I was almost on my way to the second den to check for her there when I noticed the sliding doors in the living unlocked. Pushing them open, I slowly stepped onto the manicured lawn and headed toward the guest house on the other side of the pool. The two garden doors were closed, but the blinds were open, which told me that someone was in there. Turning the knob, I let myself in with my gun aimed high and ready to shoot whoever wasn't supposed to be here. Two voices were talking in hushed tones as I neared the kitchen where I could hear a zipper being zipped up and a heavy bag being thrown on the floor.

I stood behind the wall and said a silent prayer, asking God to forgive me for the lives I was about to take. With one last push, I turned into the kitchen, ready to shoot, but was shocked by what was really going on.

"Sarai!" I shouted, scaring the shit out of my wife to the point that she dropped the scale.

"Ly . . . Ly . . . Lyfe. What are you doing here?" she stuttered.

I looked around the kitchen and noticed two black Prada bags. One zipped up, and the other one with a few kilos of my shit.

"I could ask you the same thing. Why the fuck are you in here with my dope? What the fuck do you think you're doing?" My voice was raised, and I could see the fear in Desiree's eyes. Sarai's too, but I could tell she was trying to save face for her girl's sake.

She shrugged her shoulders and continued to weigh the bag of pure white. "I didn't feel like going into the shop today, so I had Gina open up for me. And don't trip over this little bit of work. You told me to help myself, remember?"

I massaged my temples over this bullshit. I had the feds already digging into my background, and here she was with over 200 Gs of dope weighing it in our guest kitchen like that was the thing to be doing.

"Sarai, I gave you the green light a long fuckin' time ago. Before I bought you the salon, nail shop, and the rest of the bullshit that you own, but you didn't want it. You wanted to be the legit half of this partnership so that if anyone ever questioned our money, we would have something to show for it. Weren't those your words? You're basically stealing from me, and you know how I feel about niggas taking from me," I barked, stepping in her face and grabbing her by the throat. The chair she was sitting in crashed to the floor, and a yelp from Desiree echoed through the room.

"Lyfe—Let me fuckin' go," Sarai said in between breaths.

I pointed the gun at her head. "I oughta kill yo' muthafuckin' ass. All the shit I've done for you. How dare you take from me? You know I would give you anything."

She kicked wildly and scratched at my hands, attempting to make me loosen my grip unsuccessfully. When her eyes started closing and her skin became a little paler, I finally released my hold from around her neck and let her fall to the floor.

"That wasn't even right, Lyfe," Desiree mumbled.

"Bitch, shut your ass up before I put a bullet in your head because your dumb ass is right here with her stealing my shit." My heated gaze turned to her, and she looked at everything else *but* me to avoid any eye contact.

"For real, Lyfe," Sarai coughed, "you putting your hands on me now? I'm your fucking *wife*."

"Man, fuck you, Sarai. I grabbed your hood rat ass out of the gutter and made you a fucking queen, and you turn around and do *this* to me? Then you wonder why—"

"Wonder why what?" I could hear the hurt in her voice, but I didn't care about that shit.

"Man, get the fuck on. Pack the rest of this shit up so that I can take it somewhere else before you get us both locked up for being so damn stupid."

Sarai's eyes stayed on mine as she shook her head, a single tear falling down her face. I'd never seen Sarai cry the whole time we were together, so this little show of emotion did something to me, but not enough to make me want to take her back.

"You must really love that girl, huh?"

I blew out a frustrated breath. "What girl, Sarai?" I knew who she was talking about, but I'd play the game with her if she wanted me to.

"Savannah. You really do love her more than you love me, huh?"

"I've always loved Savannah. She's always had my heart."

"Did I ever mean anything to you, Lyfe? I gave you two kids, a home, a family. Does that not mean *anything* to you?"

"Sarai, you already know what it is. Our marriage has been over for years. We never really pushed the divorce thing, I guess, because we were both okay with doing ourselves, but now I don't wanna miss out on the love I've always wanted just to keep pretending to play house with you."

I walked over to the black Prada bag that was open and counted the kilos in it. Confused, I picked up the closed bag and counted the kilos already packed in that one.

"Lyfe, what about—"

"Where's the rest of my shit?" My voice was low, but I know Sarai and Desiree heard the coldness in it.

"Wha . . . What?"

I turned to face Sarai, the all-black outfit she had on covered with white powder. Her pupils were a little dilated from the contact high she was experiencing. Blue latex gloves covered her hand but with a rip where her wedding ring was sitting. Her black hair was in a bun at the back of her head with small strands flowing back and forth from the ceiling fan air. Sarai was indeed a beautiful woman. One of the reasons why I was attracted to her in the beginning. But now, her looks weren't enough to keep me with her thieving ass.

"Where the fuck is all of my shit? I know good and damn well that I had over 200 Gs of pure here, and now, it looks like there is only . . ." I shifted through the kilos again. "It looks like there's only about $90,000 here. Where is my shit?"

Desiree, who was near the table, was slowly inching her way toward the door, but I held my gun up to her, and she froze in place, hands shooting up to the sky. Her long bangs covered half of her face. She also had on all black like Sarai, but her outfit hung loosely in a few areas where Sarai's hugged her thick frame like a glove.

"Please don't kill me, Lyfe. All I did was take the bags to the car. I've never stolen anything from you."

"If one of y'all don't start talking now, I'm going to forget that I know y'all."

Before either of them could open their mouths, my phone rang. I knew it was Kiko from the ringtone. I tried to ignore the call, but after he called a second time, I knew something was up.

"Yeah?" I answered. Eyes still trained on Sarai and gun still aimed at Desiree.

"Yo, Lyfe, man, we just got hit," his rushed voice yelled. The way that he was breathing let me know that he was running.

"What do you mean we just got hit?"

"Two of our spots just got hit. Heim is on his way to the warehouse, and I'm on my way to the storage spot. I figured you would want to meet me there."

"Shit," I hissed, tucking my gun in the back of my jeans. "Shit. Okay, okay. I'm on my way. Shut everything down. Call a meeting and tell everyone to meet at the club. And, Kiko, you better know who was behind this shit by the time I get there," I growled into the phone before ending the call. "Shit."

"What's wrong, Lyfe?" Sarai asked, running to my side and grabbing my arm, but I shook out of her hold. "Baby, talk to me."

"Finish packing up this shit and put it in the trunk of my car in the hidden safe." I took the gun from behind my back and gave it so Sarai. "You and Desiree stay y'all's asses here until I get back and don't let no one in. Where are my kids?"

"At my mama's, why?" she rushed out. "What's going on, Lyfe?"

"Nothing. Call your mama and tell her to grab the kids and head over here. I'll have someone at her house in a few minutes to pick them up," I said over my shoulder as I walked out of the guest house and into the main house, Sarai on my heels.

"Lyfe, wait."

"Sarai, go finish packing the rest of my shit like I said. I still want answers on what happened to the rest of my dope when I get back, and you better have a good explanation as to why more than half of my product is gone." I grabbed the keys to her car out of the glass bowl.

"Lyfe—"

"Go do what the fuck I said," I yelled at the top of my lungs, my heavy baritone echoing in the empty house. The look in Sarai's eyes told me she wanted to tell me something, but at the look in mine, she relented and went back out of the sliding doors toward the guest house.

Jumping into her Jag, I started the engine and adjusted the seat and mirrors before I took off out of my driveway. Running a few lights, I made it to the interstate in no time, ready to hop on and make it to the storage facility before the police showed up. The light for me to turn was red, and as I waited, I thought about all of the bad things that have been happening to me in the last few weeks. Savannah was still mad at me, Sarai was stealing from me, and now someone hit two of my biggest spots. What else could possibly happen?

The light turned green, and I had just pressed on the gas to go but had to slam on my breaks when an unmarked car cut in front of me and stopped. Four more unmarked vehicles followed suit and had me boxed in. Two detectives walked swiftly to the driver side of my car, opening the door and roughly pulling me out. Once on the ground, a knee was lunged into my back, and handcuffs were slapped on my wrist. When I tried to speak, my body was picked up and slammed onto the hot hood of one of the unmarked cars.

"Mr. Lyfe Simmons, we have a warrant to search your cars and house." He waved a search warrant in my face. "We've been watching you for some time now and finally got enough evidence to look for those drugs you and your partner, Naheim Zaher, won't stop dealing."

"I don't know what you're talking about. And is this all necessary?" I asked, referring to the way I was being treated and all of the police now surrounding me and this whole little scene. "If all you wanted to do was search the car, you could've easily asked," I taunted, knowing Sarai wasn't dumb enough to put any of the drugs in her car.

"Oh, don't worry. Detective Morales and I intend to search every inch of this fine automobile.

How much did this thing run you? Thinking about getting one for my girl who dances down at The Crazy Horse." They laughed.

"Franks, you would buy that stripper girl a nice ride like this?" one of the other detectives asked.

"Hell yeah. I think she's worth it."

"I don't think your detective salary can afford a car like that," I said, as the officer who hand-cuffed me lifted me from the hot hood and leaned me against his squad car.

Detective Franks's smile dropped from his lips. "Let's go ahead and get this search over with so we can move to his house. I'm sure there are plenty of trinkets I can find there to use as collateral to buy my stripper girl a car like this."

His eyes stayed on me as he rounded the passenger side of the Jaguar and opened the doors. Leaning in the backseat, they searched every inch of the car from front to back and came up with nothing. The car was empty, just like I hoped it would be.

"Franks," one of the detectives called, "there's a safe under the passenger-side floor mat, but we need a pass code to get in."

All eyes turned to me. Feeling that Sarai was still smart enough to not put anything in the safe, I gave them the code.

"1-0-4-4"

"And we didn't even have to beat you up for it," Franks joked, but no one laughed but him.

He stood over the passenger door as the hidden strongbox was searched. I was expecting the detective who opened the safe to rise up with empty hands, but when he stood up from his hunched position with not one, but two guns hanging from his fingers, my heart dropped to the floor.

"Well, well, well. What do we have here?" Franks's gloved hand grabbed one of the guns and removed the clip. "Empty," he said with a smile on his face. "Which means there are some casings with this gun's name on it. Wonder how long it's going to take for us to match it to a murder."

"Those aren't mines," I said in all truth. I'd never seen those guns before in my life. So why were they in Sarai's car?

"That's what all the guilty assholes say. Take his scumbag ass in and make sure the boys show him a good time," Detective Franks laughed as he dropped each of the guns into evidence bags.

"I want my phone call," I yelled out as I was pushed into the back of a waiting car. "I want my phone call."

Franks walked over to my side of the car and leaned over. "We finally got your ass, boy. Two guns and I'm pretty sure your dumb ass slipped up and left something else at your residence." He shook his head. "Better be sure that call you make is to your old lawyer and not that hotshot mistress you've been gallivanting around town with. She fine and all with that smooth chocolate skin, but her mouth is too reckless for me. Oh, and you should've seen the look on your wife's face when we told her that you were going to have Ms. Zaher representing you." He chuckled. "Boy, I feel sorry for you. You know what they say about a woman scorned. I wonder if she will be just as accommodating as you while we search your house. Think she'll open up any of the hidden safes you have there?"

He looked at me with expectant eyes, but when I didn't respond, he shrugged his shoulders. "Oh well, even if we don't find anything at your house, I'm pretty sure we have more than enough to charge you with once the ballistics on those guns come back. Until then, you enjoy your time in federal lockup. Get him out of here."

The door slammed shut and the officer driving the car I was in pulled off. My mind kept going back to the two guns that they found.

Where the hell did they come from, and who did they belong to? Sarai didn't have a need for them, and I damn sure didn't put them there. But someone did, and I just needed to figure out who.

Coming Soon:

Love, Lies,
and
Consequences 2

See what starts to happen next . . .

Reign

"You've been a hard woman to catch up with, Ms. Reign."

I picked up my glass of wine and took a sip. My eyes focused on the beautiful purple, orange, yellow, and pink hues the sky turned into as the sun began to set. After a couple of weeks of rescheduling dates, I was finally sitting in Monroe's backyard, enjoying soft music, delicious wine, great conversation, and the tantalizing smell of the steak, salmon, and vegetables my sexy neighbor had cooking on the grill.

Pulling the gray cashmere throw that he gave me over my bare legs, I smiled as I thought about how I had ended up in his backyard over an hour ago. I was tired and had just gotten home from work. Didn't have any plans to go anywhere but in my bed, when Monroe texted me, reminding me of our date. Not up to socializing, I sent a text back asking if he could give me another rain check. I wasn't expecting him to press the issue of me declining again, so I dropped my phone on the couch, stripped out of my clothes, and was on my way to the bathroom when there was a light knock on my door. Instead of answering it stark naked, I slipped on a pair of my workout shorts and a sports bra. I wasn't expecting any guests; however, I was a little shocked when I pulled the door open and was met with Monroe's sexy smile and his lustful eyes as they roamed my body up and down.

The Baltimore Ravens T-shirt he had on clung to his muscled frame, and the dark gray sweatpants hardly left anything to the imagination when I looked down at the print between his slightly bowed legs. I bit my bottom lip to hold in the moan that tried to escape my mouth, but I knew he heard it when he let out a small chuckle. We greeted one another and gave each other longing looks before the topic of me skipping out on our date was brought up. The excuse of being tired and needing some rest fell on deaf ears and was basically a waste of my breath when I attempted to get out of our date again. Before I could even try to come up with some other plausible excuse to give to him, Monroe grabbed my hand and literally started to drag me out of my house and over to his. I had no choice but to throw on some slippers, grab a sweater to block the slight chill in the air, and lock my door. Monroe bluntly let me know that he wasn't going to go another week without seeing me. Although the act was kind of barbaric and low-key scary, it did make me feel a little special. Hiem ain't never did shit like that while we were messing around. He either just showed up to spend the night and get some ass, or he would send me a text right when I got off of work to come over to his house and chill.

After taking another sip of my wine, I turned my attention back to Monroe. "Obviously I'm not that hard to catch up with. I'm here now, right?"

His back was turned to me as he messed with some of the foil packets on the grill and flipped the steaks over. "You are. But I've been wanting to spend time with you for a few weeks now, and you've been ducking and dodging me like crazy."

"Ducking and dodging?" I asked as I sat up straighter in the lounge chair. The sizzling sound from the steak's juices hitting the charcoal sounded off as he brushed some melted garlic butter over them.

"Yes, ducking and dodging. At least that's what it's called when someone doesn't answer your calls like they used to, or send a text message instead of picking up the phone." He closed the grill and turned around, taking a seat on the chair across from me. "If that's not ducking and dodging, then what is it?"

I shrugged my shoulders, eyes still on his. "I guess I just needed some space to clear my head on a few things, and I didn't want to take shit out on you."

"Things like what? If you don't mind me asking."

"Just things."

He nodded his head at my aloof response and opened his beer. After taking a few sips, he slouched down in his seat, getting comfortable, and raised his legs onto the ottoman, crossing them at the ankle. His black and varsity purple Nike Foams matched his Ravens shirt.

"Does these *things* have anything to do with those scratches on your neck and arms?" I pulled my sweater tighter at the lapels, trying to cover up the catlike scratches Peaches' ghetto ass gave me when she and I were fighting at the club.

I shook my head. "No."

He took another sip of his beer. "You sure? Because if that nigga is hitting you, Reign—"

"No one is hitting me, Monroe." I cut him off. "I just had a little altercation a couple weeks ago when my best friend and I were out having fun."

"Was it with ol' girl you were fighting on your porch when we officially but unofficially met?"

I thought about that night Peaches came to my house looking for Hiem and I beat her ass. I don't know why she thought she had a better chance of getting at me the night at the club—maybe because she had her little posse with her. I don't know. But they didn't matter anyway, because I still beat the brakes off her ass, with them pulling on my hair and sneaking in hits from the back. Savannah, on the other hand, got her ass handed to her, which still had me hot until this day. I couldn't wait to run into those bitches again. Peaches and Sarai too. If Lyfe and Hiem didn't handle it before I did, they were going to be dealt with.

I got up from my seat and walked over to the doc station, where his iPhone was set up, and scrolled through his playlist. Once I was settled on a song, I grabbed a beer out of the ice chest and sat back down.

"So, what is it that you do for the feds?" I asked changing the subject. Monroe didn't need to know that I was out here in these streets fighting behind Hiem's ass, especially when I told him that I was officially over whatever it was Hiem and I had.

Monroe smirked, aware of my subject changing, but he didn't question it. "So, you're okay with me working for the feds now? Because last time you hightailed it out of my house after I told you that I worked for them." He sat up in his chair and set his half-empty beer bottle on the ground next to him. "Wait, so does your interest in my personal life mean that you're okay with seeing where we can go with whatever this is forming between us?"

I squirmed in my seat a little bit at his intense gaze, but never lost eye contact.

"I mean, I don't know about you, Reign, but I've been feeling you ever since I laid eyes on you."

"Um . . ."

He held his hand up. "Hesitation means there's doubt. So, if you're not as interested in getting to know me as I am you, then tell me. I'd rather you let me know where I stand now than to wait until I'm a hundred percent invested in our relationship and you don't feel the same way." He removed his legs from the ottoman and scooted up to the edge of his seat, his arms draped over his knees and his legs slightly apart. "I'm not trying to change your mind or prove to you that I'm better for you than your ex, Reign, but I do want you to give me the chance to show you that if you do give me your heart, I will protect it, cherish it, do my best to heal it, and make sure that it's never broken again. And I'm not saying that I won't make some mistakes along the way, but if you're willing to understand that some of those mistakes will never be intentional, then I hope you decide to throw anything that may hinder our journey out of the window and take this ride with me."

We sat in a comfortable silence for a few minutes, with me taking in everything Monroe had just said. I didn't think I was ready to jump into anything serious just yet, but with an offer like the one he gave me, I would be a fool not to take it.

"Okay . . ." I smiled and tried to cover up my blush by taking my beer to the head.

"Okay?"

I nodded my head. "I'ma trust that you are a man of your word and take this ride with you."

He let out a loud sigh and clapped his hands. "That's what I'm talking about, baby. Whooooo!" he hollered, and I laughed. "You don't know how nervous I was about telling you that. . . . And now that that's out of the way, let me back up for a second and answer your question." He cleared his throat. "As far as my job with the Federal Bureau of Investigations, I'm a behavioral analyst, which means I reconstruct crimes based on evidence, interview criminals and terrorists to obtain insight on their motives and actions, create profiles of perpetrators, as well as provide insight into serial criminals, which may assist in their apprehension."

"So, you're like a real-life Horatio Caine, but with the feds?"

He laughed, and I couldn't help the smile that formed on my face. "If you wanna put it that way, I guess you can say that."

"Wow."

Monroe smiled, and that flutter that I felt the first time he and I had dinner started to play around in my belly.

"Is that wow a good thing?"

"It isn't a bad thing. I just thought you were going to tell me that you were an agent or something like that." I mean, he did look the part. His build, his size, his look screamed "agent" to me, not a behind-the-scenes geek.

Monroe shook his head and picked up his beer. "I prefer more of a behind-the-scenes type of occupation. Always was fascinated with science and everything included in that, so when I went to college, it wasn't hard to figure out what I wanted to major in. I got my master of science degree in criminology from the University of

Baltimore and started working for the FBI six months after that."

I listened to Monroe tell me about his childhood and college years in Baltimore for the next hour or so, and then told him about me and my upbringing. By the time we were done learning about each other, the food was ready and we were both hungry. After setting the table and refilling my glass with wine, we were ready to sit down to a candlelit dinner on his patio to enjoy the meal that he made.

"You have three choices to choose from for tonight's movie selection," he said from behind me, cases of DVDs in his hand.

"Movies?"

"Yeah." He pointed to the projection screen slowly rolling down from the awning. "I thought we could make this a movie and chill night since I don't have Netflix hooked up to the monitor yet."

I took the three cases from his hand and looked at the titles: *The Best Man*, *Something New*, and *Life*. Although the selections were some of my favorites, I didn't feel like watching any romantic comedies.

"You don't have anything with more . . . action?"

He bit his bottom lip, and my pussy started to thump. "Not really. These are the only three movies I didn't throw away when I moved into this house. I usually watch Netflix, Hulu, or ESPN when I get the chance to watch TV. We can go in the house if you want." He picked up our plates and started for the house, but I stopped him.

"No. I wanna stay out here." I stood up from my seat. "Let me run to my house real quick to get one of my favorites, and then we can watch that. Cool?"

Placing our food back down on the table, Monroe walked over to me and pulled me in his arms, the warmth of his body covering me whole. He grabbed my ponytail and pulled it back, lifting my face to his.

"Go get the movie, but don't take too long. You know I don't have a problem with coming to get you." He smiled at his little joke, and so did I. When his face moved closer to mine, I didn't turn away. The second his soft lips pressed into mine, my body started to tingle all over. The next brush of his lips found the corner of my mouth, and I sucked in a breath as those same tingles became tiny explosions. "Now hurry up before our dinner gets cold. I would like to enjoy the rest of this date before I say fuck it all together and take you to my bedroom instead."

Swallowing the lump that I didn't even know was in my throat, I stepped out of his embrace and stumbled over to the end table and snatched my keys off of it. Turning around, I could still feel Monroe's eyes on me as I walked out of his backyard and over to my house.

The neighborhood was kind of quiet for it to be a Thursday evening. Usually there were a few kids playing football in the middle of the street and others running around playing tag until their mothers called them in, but for some reason, it was quiet. A slight chill ran down my spine as the wind began to pick up, causing me to pull my sweater a little tighter and wrap my arms around my body. I made a mental note to change into a pair of yoga pants and grab a jacket after I found my *Underworld* DVD. I hadn't watched it in a while, so I knew I would have to dig through the crate in my closet to find it.

Stepping onto my porch, I surveyed the street again, still surprised that none of the kids were outside. My phone, which I'd left on the couch, was lighting up as soon as I walked through the door. I picked it up and headed to my bedroom, unlocking the phone and scrolling through my missed calls and messages. Savannah had called me a few times, and so did my mom. Hiem had sent me a couple of text messages, and Peaches was still playing on my phone. Since we'd had that little fight, she would send these little dumb memes and videos of girls getting beat up. I didn't know what she was trying to imply, seeing as I kicked her ass both times we went at it.

Throwing my phone down on the bed, I walked into my closet and grabbed the crate that held all of my DVDs. When I pulled it down from the top shelf, a few boxes of shoes fell to the floor, but I didn't have any time to pick those up. I need to grab this movie and get my ass back over to Monroe's house before our food got cold, and to see if I could get in a few more of those kisses after we ate. Just thinking about the butterflies that were going crazy in my belly whenever he was around me had me smiling like a teenage girl in love. I even touched my lips, missing the feel of his on mine. If this was the type of feeling you were supposed to have when seeing someone, then I was missing out all of these years messing with Hiem. I mean, don't get me wrong; I loved Nahiem, and still did, but what I felt for him was didn't compare to the giddy way Monroe had me feeling in a matter of weeks.

It took me almost fifteen minutes to go through my movie collection, but I finally found the DVD I was looking for and placed it in its case. After changing into some warmer clothes, I grabbed the movie off my bed and was just about to leave my room when I stopped dead in my tracks. The hairs on the back of my neck were standing straight up, and my body started to shake as I watched a figure dressed in all black standing in my doorway. I took a few steps back, getting ready to try to grab the gun I knew Hiem always kept in my closet, when my eyes focused on the frame of the person who had now stepped into my room. His build was familiar, as well as his walk. When the smell of his cologne hit me, I instantly knew who it was.

"Nahiem, what the fuck are you doing?"

He walked farther into my room, his face now coming into focus as he stepped closer to where I was standing.

"Hiem, what the fuck? Why are you dressed in all black, lurking around in my house? And as a matter of fact, how the hell did you get in here?" I tried to remember if I'd locked the door after coming in, but I don't think I did.

"Where you going?" he asked, his voice a little above a whisper. From messing around with Hiem all these years, I'd come to know his different moods. The fact that he wasn't answering any of my question and asking his own told me that this little visit was about to be some drama.

Not wanting to fuck up the mood that Monroe and I had going on, I decided to ignore Hiem's question and go on about my business. If he was there once I came back, then maybe I would be willing to talk, but right now, I had some food, a movie, and over six feet of smooth brown sexiness waiting on me to get back to his place.

I tried to walk out of my room and pass Nahiem's crazy ass when he roughly grabbed my arm and swung me back, causing me to fall on my bed. The movie in my hand flew to the floor, and my headboard hit the wall hard.

"What the fuck, Hiem?" I screamed, jumping back up. "Are you fucking crazy?"

Before the last word left my mouth, I was being pushed back down on the bed and boxed between Nahiem's arms. He laid his body down on mine and nuzzled his face in the crook of my neck.

"You fucking that nigga, Reign?" he asked after kissing me softly behind my ear. "Are you giving that nigga my pussy?"

I placed my hands on his chest and tried to push him off of me, but I couldn't. "Hiem, get up. Please."

"Answer my question first."

I reared my head back and could feel my attitude already shifting toward bad. "Nigga, who I'm fucking shouldn't be any concern of yours, seeing as this is my first time seeing you since the bitch you fucking overstepped her boundaries again and came for me."

The fact that Nahiem was questioning me about my relationship with Monroe was bullshit. In all the years that he made it a point to remind me that we were not in an exclusive relationship and he fucked on bitch after bitch after bitch, Nahiem had never questioned me about another nigga. Maybe because, like a dummy, I was trying to show my loyalty to him in a way that only I knew how: by not fucking another nigga. My body and heart belonged to him, and instead of cherishing my gifts, his dog ass wanted to have his cake and eat it too.

Nahiem took the rubber band from around my ponytail and ran his fingers through my hair. It was something he would always do whenever we finished having sex, and he would tell me how much he loved me and would change for me one day.

"Are you fucking that nigga, Reign? I'm only going to ask you one more time."

He tried to kiss me, but I turned my head. "If I am, why do you care?"

"Because . . ."

"Because what?"

"Because regardless of what bitches I fuck, you will always belong to me, and I don't want no other nigga around you. Especially one who works for the feds."

My body froze at Hiem mentioning where Monroe worked. I tried to open my mouth to ask him how he knew that, but nothing came out. He kissed my forehead and slowly backed up off of me. When I sat up, Hiem stood motionless at the foot of my bed. His eyebrows were furrowed, and there was a look on his face that I'd never seen. One of his hands disappeared behind his back, and when it reappeared, he had a black 9 mm in it. All of his fingers wrapped around the butt of the gun except his index finger, which rested against the nozzle. My tear-filled eyes went from the gun to his.

"Why . . . why do you have that gun in your hand?"

Nahiem's eyes were just as red as mine, tears in the corner threatening to come out.

"You know I love you, right, Reign?"

"Hiem."

"Right?"

I nodded my head yes and slowly stood up from my bed, arm outstretched, trying to get him to put the gun down and understand how we came to this moment.

"I know you love me, Hiem, but I don't under-stand why you pulled a gun out on me. I'm not fucking Monroe, or anyone else for that matter. Please, if you put the gun down, we can talk."

"How much do you know about that nigga? Did you know he worked for the feds when he moved over here?"

I shook my head. "No. I wasn't even talking to him then."

He stepped closer to me. "Are you talking to him now?"

"What do you mean?"

"The feds picked up Lyfe a couple days ago, and I think they hit a few of our stash houses and the warehouse. Tore the club up from top to bottom looking for drugs, and even came to my crib. They had me for a few hours but had to let me go after they didn't have shit to charge me with."

Lyfe got picked up by the feds? That was news to me. I wondered if Savannah knew. She had to know. Maybe that's why she had called me so many times that day. I hadn't picked up earlier because I assumed she was calling to complain about the papers she got from Lyfe's wife, Sarai, like she'd been doing since the day she got them. But maybe I was wrong. I had planned on calling her back after I got out of the bathtub, but that was interrupted when

Monroe came and dragged me to his place. I left my phone here the whole while I was at his house, so I had missed the last dozen calls she made. I wanted to grab my phone now and call her back, but I didn't want Hiem to think I was calling someone else.

As if the conversation Hiem and I were having at this moment wasn't crazy enough, my phone started to ring, and Monroe's face and name flashed across the screen.

"Answer it," Hiem demanded. "And put it on speaker phone." He shoved my phone in my hand and slid the phone icon to the left.

"Hey," I answered, trying to sound as happy as I had thirty minutes ago.

"Hey, are you coming back? The food got cold, so I had to reheat it in the microwave. If you can't find the movie, we can just eat in the house and watch something in there."

"I . . . I . . . um, I found the movie. I was on my way back, but my best friend called me and we kind of got lost in the call."

"Oh, yeah?" I could tell by his tone that he didn't believe me. "If she isn't doing anything, she can join us if you want her to. I know you said she was feeling kinda down lately with some of the things that was going on around her."

"Yeah . . ."

We sat in silence for a minute. Hiem's eyes were on me, and mine were on the phone.

"Reign, are you okay? You don't need me to come over, do you?"

I started to say no, but Hiem shook his head and mouthed for me to say yes.

"Uh, If you could. Can you? I need to talk to you about something important."

There was a long stretch of silence before Monroe spoke again. "Okay, I'm on my way. Do you want me to bring the food so we can just eat while we discuss whatever it is you want to talk about?"

My stomach growled, and I couldn't deny the fact that I was hungry. "Yes, please."

"All right, see you in a few," he said before releasing the call.

"When that nigga gets here, you let me do all of the talking."

"Can you at least put the gun away? I already told you I haven't told him anything about you for him to report back to anyone. He's not even an agent with the bureau. He does that crime scene analysis stuff."

"Like Horatio Caine?"

I tried to stop the laugh from coming out, but it did. "Yeah, Hiem, like Horatio Caine."

"Hmmm," he said, walking over to my bed and taking a seat. "Well, for your sake and his, neither one of y'all better be talking."

"Are you really going to sit here and threaten to kill me, Nahiem? Do you really think I would tell on you and Lyfe? We've all been friends for years. Shit, your sister is my best friend. I would never do that to her or you, even though you've fucked me over all of these years. I've been nothing but loyal to you, Hiem, not fucking no other niggas, or entertaining them for that matter, while you run around doing whatever the fuck you want to do, and the minute I stop fucking with your ass and put my interest in someone else, you wanna question my loyalty and accuse me of dropping dimes on you and some of the people I consider family?"

The doorbell rang at the same time as Hiem's phone did. While he answered it, I went to let Monroe in.

"Hey," I said, grabbing the food from his hands and taking it to the kitchen. The food was kind of warm, but not warm enough, so I took the perfectly cooked steaks off of the plate and reheated the salmon and veggies.

"What movie did you end up picking out?" he asked.

"Oh, I wanted to watch *Underworld*, but if you don't want to, we can pick something else."

When I came out of the kitchen, Monroe had closed the door and was sitting on the couch, thumbing through one of the magazines on the coffee table. I looked toward my bedroom, expecting Hiem to come out at any moment, but he never came.

"I'll be right back," I said, excusing myself, wondering what Hiem was up to. When I got to my room, he was nowhere to be found: not in my bathroom, not under the bed, nor in my closet. I picked up my phone to see where the hell he could've gone when I noticed my bedroom window open and a note on my nightstand.

Reign,

My bad for pulling out on you, but I had to make sure you weren't the one snitching. Finding out that you were dating someone a part of the same organization trying to put me and Lyfe away forever did have me questioning your loyalty for a second. I was wrong for thinking you would ever turn on me, Savvy, or our family, and for that I apologize. Something came up, so I had to go. As of now, your boy is in the clear and you don't have to worry about me fucking with him. Have fun while it lasts, though, because I'm coming back for what's mine. No games, no other bitches, just me and you.

Loving You Always,
Hiem

Had this been a few months ago, I probably would've believed everything Hiem wrote in this note. Even after he pulled the gun out on me, I probably would've still took his ass back, hoping and waiting on the day for him to finally love me and only me. But after everything that had gone down, I was done with Nahiem and everything associated with him. Because he was my best friend's brother, he would still have my loyalty, but as far as my heart and body, that shit was a complete wrap.

Kwan

"Welcome home, Kwan."

"Welcome home, nigga."

"My boy is back in town."

I gave a half hug and fist pound to every one of my family members and friends I passed as I walked into the crowded living room of my mother's house. Although I told her that I didn't want to have a welcome home party, she gave me one anyway and invited some of the niggas from my crew, as well as a few of the people I grew up with around the neighborhood of Ashley Park. Some faces were familiar to me, while others I couldn't quite remember. A few of the niggas in attendance were friends of my brother and wanted to pay their respects since I wasn't around for the funeral.

"Hey, nephew," My Aunt Cora slurred as she wrapped her arms around my neck and pulled me down for a hug. "Look at my handsome Kwany. Boy, those six years did you good. I know you gotta be fighting all of these thirsty-ass little girls around here off of you with a stick."

"Cora, leave my baby alone and let him through," my mother yelled. She was in the kitchen mixing something together in her favorite red bowl, auburn hair pulled back in a French roll as always. Her rich caramel skin was glowing as bright as the smile on her face. Red fingernails matched the red dress she wore. Furry house slippers on her feet dragged across the broken-tiled floor as she moved her little frame to the beat of the song playing. After mixing whatever was in the bowl, she pulled her wooden spoon out and licked the back of it.

"Hmmm. I think I need a little more salt. What do you think?" She turned her spoon toward me and put it up to my mouth.

"What is it?"

"Boy, I know it ain't been that long since you had some mashed potatoes. Now taste this and tell me if it needs some salt."

"It taste good to me," I honestly told her.

"Anything would taste good to you after six years of eating slop, bread, and water." She smiled and hit me with the towel that was over her shoulder. "Now where's my kiss?"

I returned her smile and pressed my lips to her cheek. "You know you're my favorite girl, right?"

"Am I? Hmph. Could've fooled me, the way you came in and greeted your Auntie before me."

"Mama, you know it wasn't even like that. Aunt Cora grabbed me before I could make it to you."

"Well, don't let it happen again. Now get your ass out of here and enjoy your welcome home party. I know you didn't really want one, but you know ever since Ke—" Just at the mere mention of my brother's name, my mother teared up. "Keon passed. I promised to make it a point to celebrate my babies. Wrong or right, in jail or not, I gave birth to you, and I'm going to make as many memories as I can before you leave this earth and the opportunity is gone."

I pulled my mother into my arms and held her as she cried for my younger brother. Kissing her forehead, I pulled her from my chest and wiped some of her tears away.

"I promise on my life that I'm going to get the niggas back who took Quick away from us. Have their families feeling the same pain that we feeling right now."

My mother placed her small hand on my cheek and shook her head. "Let it go, Kwan. Let whatever it is and whoever it is go. I already lost one son to some bullshit. I don't wanna lose another one."

"But Mama . . ."

"But Mama nothing. Promise me you won't do anything to get you sent back to prison."

"Mama, I can't—"

"Promise me." She grabbed my chin and made me look in her face.

I flexed my jaw and shook my head. "I promise."

"That's my boy. Now go on out there and enjoy your party. Sam and Rell are back there already, as well as a few of your other friends. Make sure you speak to your granny and say something to your other aunts and uncles."

I nodded my head and turned toward the back sliding doors, walking right through the thin screen that looked like it had been cut in half. The smell of barbecue swirled through the air as my uncle flipped a few burgers and ribs on the grill on the outside patio. The Gap Band's song "Outstanding" was blaring loudly through the speakers as a few of my aunts and other family members two-stepped on the extended wooden porch. An assortment of alcohol was on top of the cooler, halfway gone or waiting to be opened. Pans of hot dogs, chicken, hot links, potato salad, beans, and a peach cobbler were sitting in some of those cheap aluminum chafing dishes I'm sure my mother has had for some years now. Walking over to the ice chest, I grabbed myself two beers, walked over to the domino table, and sat down.

"What's good, Kwan?" my boy Rell asked, pulling me into a half hug. "I know your ass glad to be back on the streets, boy."

"Yeah, I am."

"What you been up to since you touched down?"

I took a swig of my beer. "Shit, you already know. Money is the motive and move for me, so anything that has to do with money has my undivided attention right now."

He slammed a domino down and shook the table, causing the pieces to clink loudly. "Twenty, muthafucka! And your bitch better write down my points."

"Bitch?" some little light-skinned chick sitting behind my other boy Sam squealed. "Babe, you gon' let him disrespect me like that?"

Sam played his turn and drank whatever he had in his red Solo cup. "I mean, you have been fucking up while keeping score. The man wants his points."

Everyone around the table laughed, and her face turned red from embarrassment.

"Fuck you, Sam," high yellow called out, throwing the writing pad on the table, messing up the domino pieces. "I knew I should've hung out at my cousin's house today. At least the niggas over there know how to talk to a lady."

"Then take your ass over there. Ain't nobody beg you to be here. You the one that wanted to tag along."

"Whatever. Fuck you and your friends," she screamed as she headed toward the side of my mother's house, pulling the short dress she had on down with every step. Her stilettos heels sinking in the grass caused her to stumble a bit.

"And that's why I will always call you a bitch," Rell called to her retreating back. "Nigga, why you bring her anyway?" he asked Sam. "You should've brought that other girl you fuck with, the one who used to work at that Popeye's down there on Wilkinson. At least the bitch would've had some biscuits and chicken on deck."

"Nigga, fuck you. And why you worried about who I bring anyway? Aren't we supposed to be here celebrating our boy being free?" Sam returned, looking at me and smiling.

Rell, Sam, and I had been friends and the niggas to see back before I got this little six-year bid. We had majority of Charlotte on lock, and we were serving any and everything the streets wanted. But when I got caught up with that little case behind Shawna and her baby daddy disappearing, shit basically went to hell, giving Lyfe and Nahiem the opportunity to take over our spots and push our little crew out. Rell and Sam still had money coming in with some of the legit businesses they had under their names, but as far as me, all my money came from the drugs we were distributing. Once that dried up, so did my pockets. Had it not been for the small stash I left at my mom's house and the money Sam, Rell, and Peaches were sending me while locked up, I didn't know where I would have been right now. A nine-to-five was never in the cards for me, and I wasn't one of those niggas who preferred to live off of a female either. I had to get it by any means necessary, and if that meant I had to kill Lyfe and Nahiem to get back what was rightfully mine, then that's what I was going to do.

"Aye, yo, when's the last time you talked to Peaches?" Rell asked as he shuffled the dominos. I had pulled my chair up to the spot light-bright had vacated, and I was ready to play a few games.

"A few days ago. She dropped by the house to get some of this dick and give me some information." Sam smirked, and Rell smiled.

Since the night I showed up at her house, Peaches and I had been rekindling the relationship we had. The love I had for her wasn't as strong as it used to be, but it was still there. One of the reasons why was I knew she was still dealing with Nahiem and maybe even fucking his ass, but as long as she was able to keep giving me some intel on their stash spots and what they had going on, then I was okay with it. Money outweighed love in my book any day, and loving Peaches wasn't gonna make me a paid nigga again.

"Was any of the information she gave you useful?" Sam asked, his eyebrow raised. "Because that last spot you had them young niggas hit wasn't the jackpot, but we did get enough shit to put us back on the map, you know what I'm saying?"

I nodded. "I already know."

"So, what did she tell you? And give me ten before you start talking." Rell placed his domino down on the table and took a bite of his burger.

"Nothing really. Just that the feds had questioned Lyfe's bitch and was probably gonna come down on him and Hiem pretty soon."

"The feds? Aww, shit. I'm pretty sure they've been watching those niggas and their spots for a minute. You sure you wanna still fuck with them like that, or should we let some of the heat die down before we hit them again?"

"Give me ten. And no, I think we should do this last hit and then go from there."

Peaches had told me about the storage facility Nahiem had let her run for a few weeks before Lyfe told him to cut her out. According to Peaches, the storage spot was where the majority of their money and drugs were. I thought the feds would have gotten ahold of that, but with the property, licenses, and business in someone else's name, there was nothing associating it with Lyfe or Nahiem. Peaches did make a copy of the office key, but wasn't no telling if Lyfe had the locks changed. Besides that, there was a state of the art security system in place, which would be super hard to bypass without passwords, fingerprints, and shit like that. We needed someone on the inside who had access to all of that, and we needed them much sooner than later.

"Hey, Kwan. Welcome home," a few girls said as they giggled and walked by. A couple of them I recognized from hanging around my brother, and the others were all new faces.

"What's up, Mika and Pumpkin? How y'all been?"

"Not as fine as you," one of their friends replied.

"Girl, you better get on away from over here before you get hit with some of this grown-man dick and lose your fucking mind." Rell laughed while playing his hand and eating more of his burger.

"Shut your big black ass up, Rell. Ain't nobody talking to your Green Mile–looking ass."

"Aye, you say that as a diss, and I take it as a compliment. You know how much pussy I get because you bitches tend to mistake me for Michael Clarke Duncan? Shiiiiiiidd. More than you can ever imagine. So, I'll take that diss."

The girl who he was talking to rolled her eyes and walked off. Mika and Pumpkin, however, came closer to the table.

"Where your plate at, Kwan?"

I looked at the dominos in my hand and studied the board. "I haven't eaten anything yet, Mika. I wasn't hungry."

"Well, are you hungry now? I can go fix you a plate."

I looked up at her and watched as she licked her lips and placed the sweating bottle of beer to her mouth, taking a sip, but not before sticking her tongue out and licking around the rim.

I chuckled, honestly flattered by her flirting with me, but she was off limits. Quick already told me that he had hit her a few times while I was in jail, which meant that me having sex with her was a no go, even though he was dead. My brother and I never shared females when he was here, and we wouldn't start sharing them now that he was gone.

"You know what? Yeah, I could use something to eat. Get me a little of everything, and make sure you put some of my mama's peach cobbler on a different plate."

The smile on her face was so big. "Okay. I will be right back."

When she and Pumpkin turned around, all eyes at the table went to their backsides and watched as their asses jiggled away and onto the porch.

"Gawd damn, these females are getting younger and younger with bodies like full-grown strippers. You better watch out for that one, though. She'll have you caught up and getting your ass kicked by Peaches."

I grinned without a response and continued on with our game until Mika brought my plate back and I dug down on that. While Sam and I ate a second round and Rell his third, we talked about shit we had to handle, as well as who we could try to get in Lyfe's and Nahiem's crew to turn and help us get to the storage spot. My mama pulled me to the dance floor for a few of her songs, and I danced with her until the old cat she was fucking with took over after "I Call Your Name" by Switch came on.

While my family and friends continued to enjoy the party, Rell, Sam, and I passed a blunt around and chopped it up some more. Peaches had texted me and told me that she couldn't make it. Something came up that she just couldn't get out of. When I asked her if she was coming over to my house later that night, she responded with that shoulder shrug emoji.

I'd just finished smoking my second blunt and was about to roll another one when a nigga

I hadn't seen in a while walked into the back-yard. He kissed my mama on the cheek and then walked over to my uncle, who was still on the grill, and said something to him. When he walked past Mika and her little crew, one of the girls grabbed his arm, and he stopped to talk to them.

"What the fuck is that nigga doing here?" I asked as my eyes stayed focused on him.

"Who?"

I chucked my chin up. "Hash. Since when does he come around?"

Rell waved me off. "Nigga, his ass been com-ing around for a few years now. Him and Quick started kicking it real tight after you got locked up."

"Is that right?" My eyes squinted when the fading sun shone bright for the last time and disappeared. "He was hanging with my little brother?"

"Yeah. They were always together. I think for Quick, Hash's ass was filling the void you left after you got sentenced, and for Hash—" Sam shrugged his shoulders. "I don't know why he started hanging around Quick. Ain't that nigga like the same age as us?"

I nodded my head, my eyes still on Hash's ass. When he looked over to where we were standing, he raised his head as if to say "What's up?" and started walking over to us. Rell, Sam, and I all were quiet and in our own thoughts as to what this nigga wanted when he rolled up.

"What up, Kwan man? Welcome home." He put his hand out for a shake, and I blew smoke on it.

"What you want?" I got straight to the point. My voice was much lower than what it just was, and my mind was already going over ways I could kill this nigga if he jumped out of line.

"Damn, man. That's the kind of greeting I get after looking after Quick while you were gone?"

"Looking after Quick?" I walked into his personal space, attitude already on ten from what he just said. "Nigga, how the fuck was you looking out for my brother while I was gone and he dead?"

He raised his hands in surrender. "Look, man, I ain't have shit to do with that. That was all Lyfe and Nahiem."

What he said wasn't anything new that I heard or was told. The fact that he knew who killed my brother and hadn't done anything yet wasn't a good look to me. I never trusted this nigga when I met him some years ago, and I didn't trust this nigga now. Something about him was off, and I had a feeling that he was the reason why Quick was dead.

"Why you come over here, Hash?" Sam interrupted our stare-down. "You already know we don't fuck with you like that."

"I know, but I just got some information that may be beneficial to you." He reached in his pocket and pulled out his phone. "Some real good information."

He fumbled with his phone some and finally pulled up a video that he had saved to some file in a folder. At first, I didn't know what was going on because whoever was filming was kind of far away, but once the camera zoomed in and focused, I was able to recognize Lyfe's bitch ass being handcuffed and placed in the back of a law enforcement car I know all too well.

"Aye, yo, is that Lyfe? Being arrested by the feds?" Rell asked, snatching the phone out of Hash's hand and playing the video over. "Yo, where the hell did you get this from?"

"Yeah. Where you get it from?" I repeated. Although the video was from another cell phone, it was kind of funny how it was now in Hash's possession.

"I know somebody that knows somebody," was all that he said.

"Is everything okay?" my mother asked from my side as she wrapped her hand around my waist and pulled me in for a hug. "Y'all look like y'all were about to fight a second ago."

I took a swig of my beer. "We good, Mama."

Her brown eyes looked into mine. The freckles on her nose were more noticeable now that the makeup on her face was almost sweated off. "You sure? Because you already know what we talked about earlier."

"I know, Mama. We just talking and catching up. Nothing else."

She looked at me, to Hash, and then back to me again. "All right. I made you a pound cake to take home with you. Don't forget it whenever you get ready to leave, okay?"

I kissed her on the forehead and nodded. When she was back on the patio with my aunts, uncles, and everyone else who was still at the party, I turned my attention back to Hash.

"So, what does you showing us this video mean? I'm sure Lyfe's ass done bailed out already and is back at home chilling and fucking on his fine-ass wife."

I didn't know Sarai like that, but I knew that she ran with Peaches and Desiree from time to time. She and I met a few times whenever Peaches would bring her around, but other than that, she stayed under Lyfe and having that nigga's babies.

Hash smirked. "He's not out yet. The judge denied his bail after they found those two guns in the car."

"Two guns?"

"Look, that's neither here nor there. Now, I know it's you, Kwan, who's been hitting up his stash houses and taking all of his shit. I also know that your next target is more than likely that storage spot he keeps all of his money and drugs at. I might have someone who can get y'all in and pass all that security bullshit. Once you take that man's livelihood and everything he owns, you can finally kill that muthafucka and make us both happy."

"Why would you be happy?" Rell asked, handing Hash back his phone. His curiosity was piqued just like mine.

He stepped back with a silly grin on his face. "Let's just say there's a certain woman I've been interested in for some time now, and with him out of the way, she can finally get with a nigga who knows how to treat her right and make her happy."

"So, all this payback for you is behind a bitch and not my brother?"

"Wait, what—"

"Word on the street is you were kicking it real tough with Quick while I was gone. Wouldn't you want get rid of the niggas who killed him for that reason and not some bitch?"

"Kwan!" Mama called, but I ignored her and walked up on Hash.

"Man—what? Yeah, of course I want revenge for Quick. That was my nigga. What do you mean? But I also want Savannah Zaher, and I will stop at nothing to get her, even if that means I gotta give someone else the opportunity to take Lyfe out so that I could have her."

"Do you hear this pussy-whipped nigga?" Sam laughed. "Her shit must be made out of gold if you wanna kill her nigga and keep her for yourself."

"Dog. You always got bitches around you. What makes this one so special?" Rell asked and looked over at Mika and her crew, who were looking at us.

"Let's just say I was invested in something that could've been, but had to take a seat when this nigga Lyfe popped his ass back up in the picture."

"We'll get at you."

Hash looked at all three of us and then nodded his head. "Well, let me know so that I can get my guy on that security issue. It really was good seeing you, Kwan, and I'm glad that you're home. I'm sure Quick is smiling down on us from heaven right now."

I balled my fist up, ready to sock this nigga for mentioning my brother when his ass wasn't even worried about seeking revenge for him. The only thing that stopped me from breaking his jaw was my mama, who was watching my every move.

Hash turned his ass around after not getting any response from me, Rell, or Sam. He flirted with Mika for a second before walking over to my mother and giving her a hug. He turned around one last time and nodded his head at me before he disappeared behind the side of the house.

"So, what's the move, man? Even though the nigga wants Lyfe gone for some pussy reason, if he has someone who can help us get into this storage place, I think we should do it," Rell said.

"Me too," Sam added. "The nigga ain't no real street nigga like us, but if he has resources that we don't, I think we should fuck with him to see what's up."

I sat down at the table and rolled another blunt, a million thoughts running through my mind. So far, I was able to get into Lyfe and Nahiem's shit with the help of Peaches and a few lucky chances. I didn't know if I really trusted this nigga Hash. Something about him didn't sit right with me, and my gut was telling me to check out some shit first before we got in bed with this nigga.

"How much do y'all really know about him? Like, what's his background?"

"Shit." Rell sat next to me and took the blunt that I had already lit. "I don't know. The dude making money, though. I heard he sold pills or some shit like that to a high-end clientele. I think we should fuck with him. Do this one last hit and get back on top."

"Do he got family or people around here?"

Sam took the blunt. "I don't know. Never really been on our radar. The only person who could probably really answer any of those questions, though, is gone."

My eyes connected to Sam's, and we shared a look. "Are you thinking what I'm thinking?"

He nodded his head. "Yep, and I'm already ahead of you," he said as he pulled out his phone and sent a text.

"Do y'all know anything about this Savannah Zaher chick Hash talking about?"

"You need to ask Peaches' ass." Rell laughed. "Seeing as she's fucking with her brother."

"Brother? Savannah is Nahiem's sister?"

He nodded his head. "Yep. Moved back out here some months ago. Got a law office downtown somewhere and got Lyfe's nose wide open. So much to the point that the nigga had her in his club all hugged up and kissing on her for the world to see. Of course you know Sarai came up there and acted a fool. Peaches and her crew of hood rats was with her too. They beat the brakes off of that Savannah chick. Li'l mama didn't have a chance to swing or anything. They packed her out and tried to go help Peaches when that li'l bitch Hiem fucks with, Reign, was beating her ass, but by then, the fight got broken up and everybody started running out of the club."

I remembered Peaches telling me that the reason for the bruises on her face and body a few weeks ago was from her beating someone up, but she never told me it was behind Hiem's other woman. I felt some type of way about her lying to me, but she would never know that. If Peaches was out here fighting the next woman over a nigga, that meant that her feelings for him were deeper than I thought. And if her feelings were that deep, when it came to offing that nigga, would she pull the trigger, or would she betray me and give him a heads up? I had a lot of things to think on and figure out before I made my next move. I'd be damned if I lost it all again behind a bitch who didn't know where her loyalties lie, or a nigga who was sprung over some pussy that would never be his.